SAFEGUARD

A Sean Coleman Thriller

JOHN A. DALY

Virginia

Safeguard: Book Four in the Sean Coleman Thriller series
© 2019 John A. Daly. All rights reserved.

This is a work of fiction. All of the characters, names, incidents, organizations, and dialogue in this novel are either the products of the author's imagination or are used fictitiously. Any resemblance to actual persons, living or dead, or actual events is purely coincidental.

Published in the United States by BQB Publishing
(an imprint of Boutique of Quality Books Publishing, Inc.)
www.bqbpublishing.com

978-1-945448-51-5 (p)
978-1-945448-52-2 (e)

Library of Congress Control Number: 2019940434

Book design by Robin Krauss, www.bookformatters.com
Cover design by Ellis Dixon, www.ellisdixon.com
Front cover photo by Erin Timm
First editor: Olivia Swenson
Second editor: Caleb Guard

Praise for John A. Daly and the Sean Coleman series.

Praise for *Safeguard*

Safeguard is a fast, fun page-turner whose twists and turns kept me reading well into the night. John Daly delivers his mix of wry humor with pulse pounding action that keeps you guessing til the very end. An entertaining, engaging read.

**— Megyn Kelly,
journalist and #1 New York Times bestselling author**

Praise for *From a Dead Sleep*

Some writers are thoughtful. Some have style. John Daly has both. When I read his work, it's time well spent.

**— Bernard Goldberg,
New York Times bestselling author of *Bias***

An epic thriller with a memorable, unorthodox main character . . . a riveting read . . .

— *Colorado Country Life Magazine*

A fast-reading suspense book that surprised me so much, I had to finish it in one sitting.

**— Alice de Sturler
of the American Investigative Society of Cold Cases**

A thriller that packs a punch! This was a very exciting debut novel from John A. Daly. This novel packs a lot of jaw-dropping action into its well-structured narrative—a narrative that gives life to the myriad of characters that inhabit its pages and provides plenty of plot twists and turns to keep you glued to the pages.

— **Reading, Writing, and Riesling book blog**

I loved this book. The suspense had me sitting on the edge of my seat . . . The author did a fabulous job with the setting details—I could picture every touch, smell, sight that the characters went through . . .

— **Yawatta Hosby, author of the novel** *One by One*

From a Dead Sleep is a page-turner, an exciting, well-written thriller with a solid back story and more than enough plot twists to keep you guessing.

— **Marilyn Armstrong, Serendipity book blog**

Praise for *Blood Trade*

"This book has so many twists, turns, mis-directions and layers of plot that I even forgot to eat where I was so involved. The characters are larger than life and when you think you know them there is another surprise just around the corner."

— **Best Selling Crime Thrillers**

5 stars. "Blood Trade is an awesome read that keeps you on your toes. You never know what is going to happen next and each new piece of the puzzle that is revealed is something you'd never expect. This is not one of those "guess who did it" thrillers. You honestly can't do that. You'll have the ah-ha moments when your realize who did something, but you'd never guess it was that person before-hand.

John A. Daly is masterful at writing a good thriller and I can't wait to read more thriller novels from him."

— **The Goth Girl Reads**

"This is the first book I've read from John Daly, it is not the first in the series but I was not confused. This book could be read as a stand alone. The main character Sean Coleman is not your typical Hot guy that can't do anything wrong. He has an alcoholic past, and the town where he lives doesn't take him serious, and is just a joke to them. Thus making a Believable character with flaws, that is more real."

— Vanessa Visagie, Vanessa Reviews

"The second in a series that will certainly continue, this book is a darned good read. The status of hero is shared by a super cop now living in a small community and his hapless (formerly) alcoholic brother-in-law. The main characters are well developed and the storyline good. This reader was torn between who to cheer for (the 'goodies' or the 'baddies') on several occasions and in many respects, the plot is quite unique.

An enjoyable read with characters that wouldn't fit in with either the 'gung ho' or the 'splendidly rich and beautiful' crowd that usually populate American action stories and all the better for it!

This is a stand alone book despite being the second in the series. My enjoyment wasn't marred by not having read the first and I will certainly go back and read the predecessor."

— Mary Edgley, Goodreads

Praise for Broken Slate

*(finalist in the 2018 Colorado Book Awards and
2018 CIPA EVVY Awards - Thriller Category)*

"John Daly has a magical writing style, and his books keep you up late at night turning pages. Sean, the protagonist, helps you see the world through his eyes in a total escape from daily life. You won't want to put it down."

— Dana Perino, Former White House Press Secretary

"Crackling with gunfire and suspense, the opening pages of *Broken Slate* make clear that John A. Daly writes with assurance and style —and without fear or political correctness. This third installment in the Sean Coleman series brings us an engrossing thriller, centered around a deeply flawed but compelling character: an antihero for the post-9/11 age."

— James Rosen, Fox News chief Washington correspondent and author of *The Strong Man* and *Cheney One On One*

"What a great f***ing book. Seriously . . . Sean Coleman is the kind of character that pisses you off---he's emotionally broken, often thoughtless, and sometimes a jerk. He's also loyal, honorable, and anything but a super hero. In short, John Daly's Sean Coleman is a lot like you and me."

— Terry Schappert, U.S. Army Special Forces, and host of *Warriors*, *Shark Attack Survival Guide*, *Dude You're Screwed!*, and *Hollywood Weapons: Fact or Fiction?*

"High-octane indeed! A nonstop riproarer of a thriller with plenty of mystery, family drama, dysfunction, betrayal, and psychological issues to boot, *Broken Slate* is #3 in John A. Daly's Sean Coleman Thriller series, a not-to-be-missed series that will really wake up a reader. So much adrenaline! Such convoluted past histories! So much to devour!"

— Mallory A. Haws, The Haunted Reading Room

To my wife, Sarah, whose love and support I am
eternally grateful for.

To my children, Chase and Olivia, who are almost old enough
to start reading my books.

To Ken Robinson, the late caretaker of Missile Site Park,
who helped inspire a novel.

Chapter 1

It had been overcast for most of the morning, but the swift arrival of a brown haze and low churning clouds had been tugging at Chuck Notestine's gut for the past ten minutes. The sky didn't look right. It didn't *feel* right. A sinister chill filled the air, bringing with it an anxious silence that suggested something other than a common afternoon storm in Greeley, Colorado.

Rain began to spit from above, quickly evolving into dense drops that pelted Notestine's face like a schoolyard bully looking to cause a scene. A sudden burst of wind screamed into him, knocking him back on his heels, and sending his clipboard to the ground. He lumbered off balance across dirt and grass, swearing. He found his footing just as a pair of tumbleweeds bounced off his body. He rose his arm up to protect his eyes when more began whisking their way past him.

Inside his trailer, just a few yards away, his radio let out a screeching, familiar howl that tightened his stomach. He swung his head toward the camper's open door. It flapped wildly from the continuing gust.

"The National Weather Service in Denver, Colorado, has issued a tornado warning for the following counties," came a monotone, automated voice through the speakers.

The rest of the message was lost on Notestine as he lifted his gaze over the roof of the trailer and the chain-link fence that wobbled behind it. Through tears drawn from the wind, he gasped at the sight of a hulking stretch of darkness that filled the southern sky. It began along the prairie horizon and stretched and widened its way up to the heavens. It hadn't been there a minute earlier.

"Shit," he growled.

His heart pounded while his head swiveled like a weathervane back and forth across the acreage. He glared past cement blocks and ventilation pipes that pointed up from the ground. The pine trees just inside of the west fence were now arched like bows, their tips penetrating the barbed wire up top. The tall grass to the north danced like waves in an ocean, obscuring his view of the back part of the property. He wished he had mowed it all down with the tractor a day earlier, as he had planned.

"Avalanche!" he cried out, freckled hand cupped to his mouth. His eyes scanned the area. "Here boy! Avalanche!" He let out a loud whistle that was barely audible over the elements.

The wind strengthened, shoving him a few steps to his side as the steel lid of his barbeque pit toppled past him. The rain came harder and faster, and within seconds, small pellets of hail began bouncing off the ground. He couldn't believe how quickly the situation was going to hell.

When a chunk of ice caught him square on the forehead, he let out a grunt and turned back toward his trailer. The colorful awning in front of it had collapsed and was now wrapped around the picnic table where he normally enjoyed his morning coffee. The door pounded the trailer's sidewall as items crashed to the floor inside. Notestine was tempted to rush in and grab some cash and keepsakes before it was too late, but his seventy-one-year-old legs and the approaching blackening void convinced him otherwise.

The widower had survived Vietnam, two heart attacks, and a head-on collision in '89 that should have killed him. He sure as hell wasn't going to cash in his chips for Mother Nature—not with one of the safest strongholds in the state buried just a couple hundred yards away.

"Avalanche!" he wailed as he made his way onto an old cement walkway riddled with cracks.

With his arms folded over his head to protect himself from the increasing hail, he brushed past a return-air box and some ducts. He slid his way around the corner of an enormous horizontal steel door raised a couple of feet off the concrete. It stretched out for a hundred feet, and by the time Notestine had reached the opposite corner, he found himself hunched over and desperately out of breath.

"Avalanche!" he called out again, his voice waning.

Through the maddening shrieks of the wind, he thought he heard a distant bark. When he faced to the northeast, he caught a glimpse of something white and stout barreling through long grass and shrubs. Notestine's eyes swelled and his lips formed a desperate grin.

"Here boy! Come here, boy!" he yelled, waving his arms frantically.

His loyal companion of the past two years emerged from the grass, continuing his sprint toward his master. Blowing debris and hail peppered the pit bull's body as it galloped across the sidewalk. When Avalanche reached Notestine, the dog went to its hind legs and placed its front paws on the man's sternum. His long tongue jetted out between pink jowls, aiming for his master's face. Notestine spun away, letting the dog drop to all fours. He turned his focus to the top railing of an outside metal staircase a few yards away. It led down a steep, concealed hill.

"Come on!" he yelled to the dog.

The sound of marble-sized hail striking the metal door rang out like a carnival shooting gallery as the two left the cement. Avalanche jogged alongside Notestine until they reached the top step. The man's hands went to the rails, but when he turned his head to take another look at the twister, his eye caught the top of a light-colored, hardtop camper on the other side of the west fence.

"Oh God," he gasped.

He had seen the camper hauled in by an early '70s Chevy pickup that morning, while he was replacing trash bags in the campground—one of his duties as the site caretaker. But with the rest of the park empty, he had forgotten about it.

Notestine prayed that the truck's driver had left, and that only a vacant camper remained, but with wavering tree limbs hindering his view, he couldn't know for sure. He was about to take his first step down the stairs when his conscience began pounding him as hard as the hail.

"Dammit!" he snarled, turning back toward the camper. He placed both hands to his mouth and yelled, "Tornado! A tornado is coming!" He could barely hear his own voice. He knew anyone inside the camper wouldn't be able to.

He blew air through his nose before nodding his head and squaring his jaw. "You stupid son of a bitch," he muttered. He then made his way through the wind and hail toward the fence.

When he reached the fence, he peered through an opening between some swaying pines on the other side. With a better view of the campground, Notestine spotted the pickup parked right in front of the trailer. The driver hadn't left.

Avalanche let out a loud yelp, and Notestine spun his head toward him. The dog's head was lowered and his tail was wedged between his legs. The hail was bouncing off his body, but the dog refused to leave its master.

"Avalanche, go to the tunnel!" Notestine commanded. "The tunnel!"

In a flash, the dog turned and bolted toward the stairs. He flew down them effortlessly, quickly leaving Notestine's sight. A memory of Avalanche as a puppy comically falling down those same stairs flashed through his mind. The incident was how the dog had earned his name.

Notestine swallowed and rifled through his jeans pocket as he let the wind shove him into the fence. He pulled out a ring of keys. His hands shook as he sorted through them. When he found a small copper key, he placed it in his mouth and held it in his teeth. The rest of the keys dangled in front of his chin.

Covering his head with one arm, he used the other to grab a handful of fence. He pulled himself along it as the sky darkened and the wind roared like a train engine. Notestine refused to look to the south again. He feared what he would see.

When he reached a padlocked gate, he pried a family of tumbleweeds from it and stripped the key from his mouth. He poked it into the lock. With a quick twist and the lift of the latch, the gate swung open and slammed wickedly against the other side of the fence, knocking from it a sign reading, "No Trespassing. Government Property."

The wind ushered Notestine past an overturned bench and the tall, steel flag pole that he attended to every morning and evening. The American and Colorado flags hoisted high above were ripping free of their hooks. Wooden planks that made up the walls of a small outhouse to his right moaned from strain. Loose shingles from the building's roof were ripped free and carried high into the air.

Notestine kept his legs moving to prevent himself from falling. He crossed a dirt road, where airborne gravel assaulted his backside. When he reached a picnic shelter at the edge of the campground, he threw his arms around one of its metal pillars. The shelter was cemented into the ground, making it a useful crutch for Notestine to steady his body against. The wobbly roof above gave him some relief from the hail.

Breathing hard and tasting blood in his mouth, Notestine angled his eyes toward the camper. As he had noticed that morning, the twenty-foot travel trailer had an unusual look to it. There was a customized extra axle and dual wheels at its rear, as if to haul extra weight—something he had never seen before on a camper.

Through flying trash and dirt, he spotted a male figure in a hooded sweatshirt hunched on his knees between the back of the truck and the trailer. The man was small in size—his arms and legs so short that he almost looked like a kid. A glimpse of a mustache from between the edges of his hood, however, proved otherwise.

At first, Notestine believed the man was clinging to the truck's trailer hitch for dear life. The man's moving arms revealed that he was working hard to attach the hitch to the trailer. Exhaust was pumping from the truck's tailpipe before disappearing in the wind. He was trying to outrun the tornado . . . with trailer in tow.

"No!" Notestine yelled, waving one arm as best he could in the wind, while holding on to the pillar with the other. "It won't work! Come inside!"

Whether it was Notestine's subdued voice or the movement of his arm that caught the man's attention, the hooded stranger was now staring back at him. The man pulled himself to his feet by the rim of the truck's tailgate and waved Notestine off with his arm. A torn-off tree branch bounced its way across the ground and struck the man in the shoulder, knocking him down.

"Dammit," Notestine growled. He let go of the pillar and lumbered his way toward the man, the wind and the debris it carried trying their best to veer him off course.

There was so much hail on the ground that it felt as if he were crossing over snow. Its descent from the sky had begun to let up, but with the wind only worsening, Notestine knew the situation couldn't be more dire.

By the time Notestine reached the man, the stranger had pulled himself back up to his feet and was desperately hugging the sidewall of his truck. Notestine joined him. The wind had knocked off the stranger's hood, revealing the round face of an Asian man with dark eyes, angled eyebrows, and long salt-and-pepper hair.

"You can't outrun it!" Notestine yelled at him, spray flying out of his mouth. "If we don't get inside the silo right now, we're both dead!"

"No!" the man yelled back. "I need my trailer!"

"You'll die!" Notestine screamed. "The tornado will crush your truck and trailer like a beer can!"

"I can't leave it!

"Forget it! It's not worth dying for!"

At that moment, something about the stranger's face rang familiar to Notestine, as if the two had met before. The thought quickly fled with the sick, deafening howl that blasted through air above. Both men's heads spun to witness a horrific sight to the south: long steel arms from a heavy-duty farm irrigation system tumbling toward them across the prairieland.

Notestine grabbed the man by his sweatshirt. "Inside! Now!"

In one fluent move, the man snapped his arms upwards, freeing himself from Notestine's grip. Before Notestine could process what had happened, he found a pistol pointed directly at his face. Behind it were the man's narrow, unflinching eyes.

"What are you doing?" Notestine cried. He staggered back a few steps along the side of the truck, eyes wide and mouth open.

"I'm leaving." He spoke with an eerie directness and calmness that seemed miles apart from the current situation. "Because this trailer *is* worth dying for."

With that, he turned and pried open his truck door. When it swung open, he leaped inside.

"Fuck!" Notestine shouted, backing away from the truck.

The stranger put the Chevy in gear just as a large object struck Notestine from behind. Notestine felt as if he were floating outside of his body for a moment. His teeth rattled in his mouth as he dropped to his knees. More objects rained down on his body, and he covered his head with his arms as golf-ball-sized hail began to bounce off the ground beside him like rubber balls.

A new explosion of wind shoved him forward to his stomach. He raised his face from the blanket of ice beneath him, watching the taillights of the stranger's trailer leave the dirt road loop that hugged the campground. The camper bobbled though long grass and scrub, and just as the truck pulled it down into the gully below, he watched the back of its shell drop open like a drawbridge whose chains had snapped, exposing some type of construction equipment. Both the truck and trailer were gone from view a second later.

The earth below Notestine trembled, and a relentless, ear-splitting whistle echoed off the insides of his head. He felt himself being dragged along the ground, and he fought to grab onto anything he could. His shoes were pulled from his feet, and his fingers raked through soil, grass, and ice until they found the metal base of a mounted charcoal grill whose top had snapped off. It only stuck out about six inches from the ground.

It was too late to run. Too late to take shelter. The only chance he had was staying flat and saying the quick prayer that flowed from between his lips. His hands clutched the grill's pole as his shirt was ripped from his body and his flesh stretched from his bones. When the wind twisted him onto his side, he angled his eyes up at the sky. It was nearly black, full of nebulous clutter that expanded with each passing moment.

A long plank of wood crashed to the ground beside him before being carried off again. Mangled water pipes cartwheeled past his head. A rush of air slid under his body and flipped him onto his back, stripping one of his hands loose from the pole. He forced his eyes open against the wind and watched as objects fell back to earth. The last thing he saw was a sink basin from the outhouse, half a second before it crushed his skull.

Chapter 2

With a flashlight clenched in his trembling hand, a stalky eight-year-old boy with short, dark hair and rosy cheeks stood in front of his uncle's Ford pickup. Its thirty-year-old engine ticked in the cold night air. The boy placed his free hand over one of the truck's large, round headlights. It was lit, but he couldn't feel its warmth. His eyes slid over to the tall, thick pine trees a couple dozen yards away. His spread fingers cast distorted, sinister shadows across their branches.

A gun shot rang out, and the boy's head whipped toward a familiar wooden home to his left. The echo of the blast rattled through his head as breath visibly poured from his mouth. He clicked his flashlight on and heard his own heartbeat as he raced to the front steps of the building. When he reached them, he saw that the front door was half open. He aimed his flashlight through the doorway, revealing the details of a shag rug on a wood floor. At the far corner of the rug was a dark red stain that glistened under his beam.

The boy swallowed. "Uncle? Are you okay?" he shouted though the door, his voice cracking. "What happened?"

When he received no answer, he bit his lip and slowly began climbing the stairs. The planks beneath his feet groaned from his weight, and though there were only three steps, his legs were heavy as if he were climbing a fire tower. He reached the top and pushed the door wide. Its hinges cried.

A gurgling sound rose from the floor a few feet away, and when the boy guided his flashlight toward it, he saw the wavering soles of a pair of cowboy boots staring back at him. The boy gasped. He jogged forward, his legs pumping but his body making little progress. He felt as though his feet were being swallowed by quicksand. He finally snarled and lunged forward. He fell to the floor in a heap, his flashlight exploding into pieces beside him.

Though the beam was gone, the room was now brightly lit. The man on the floor just inches away wore jeans, a flannel shirt, and a belt buckle the size of a boxing champ's prize. A tall straw cowboy hat sat on the floor, blocking the man's face from the boy's view.

As the gurgling noise continued, the boy's hand went to the hat. His fingers formed around its crown, and the boy pulled it toward his own body, exposing an elderly man's face. It was Uncle Zed.

The man's desperate eyes glared at the boy. He wore a beard of blood that began at the bottom of one of his long, silver sideburns, and disappeared behind the other side of his chin. A hole was at the center of his neck, and his mouth hung open. The gurgling emitted from somewhere in between.

The boy's eyes welled up with tears.

"Shhhh," Zed managed to say before the word he was trying to utter came out. "Sean."

The boy rose to his knees, and he leaned forward above the man's face. Their eyes held firm, exchanging a lifetime of loss and regret.

"Dad?" Sean answered.

The violent blare of a car horn suddenly pulled Sean's attention toward the front door. The doorway was no longer there, nor was his old home.

When he pulled himself upright in his bed, naked under sweat-soaked sheets, the bright sun poured in through a dirty window above a small sink. It burned his eyes, and he lifted his large forearm to block it. A wave of pain throbbed through his skull while a dog barked continuously outside.

He twisted his head toward the opposite half of the sagging

mattress. A pair of brown eyes, narrow in concern, glared back. They belonged to a woman, probably in her mid-thirties. She had dark skin and long, disheveled hair. Her thin eyebrows curved inward above her purple eyelids and round face.

"I'm not your dad," she said matter-of-factly.

Sean nodded, eyes adjusting. "Yeah. I noticed." His voice was dry and coarse, and he let out a cough.

When the horn outside screamed again, he realized that the clamor hadn't been part of his dream. The barks of the dog persisted.

"Jesus," Sean grunted, rubbing his face with the palms of his hands. He glanced around the small musty room, fighting for his bearings and searching for his alarm clock. It wasn't on the nightstand next to him, where it usually sat. Instead, there were three empty beer bottles.

"They've been yelling and honking for the past five minutes," said the woman, her Spanish accent stronger in her irritation. She lay under the covers, bare shoulders and arms exposed.

Sean smelled beer on her breath. Or maybe it was *his* breath. "Why the hell didn't you wake me up?" he asked.

"I tried!" she snapped, her face leaping into a scowl. She sat up with one of her arms pinning the sheets against her chest, seeming to take Sean's statement as an accusation rather than a question. "You were out cold. Hell, I thought you might have even been dead. Your eyes were half open and shit. It was fucking creepy. Do you always sleep like that?"

"I don't know. It's hard to get a good look at myself when I'm asleep."

She rolled her eyes and plopped back to the bed.

"Sean Coleman!" The man's agitated voice sounded somewhere well beyond the narrow walls of the trailer. "Cub Scout Pack 202! Our tour was supposed to start at nine!"

"Ah, shit!" Sean moaned.

He clenched his teeth and crawled out from under the muddled sheets. The bed groaned. A spell of lightheadedness forced him to ease back down for a moment, his hand clenching his forehead. The horn wailed again.

"Keep your shirt on!" Sean yelled so loudly that the woman next to him jumped. "I'll be there in a second!" The dog continued to bark. "Shut up, Avalanche!"

Sean lowered himself to the linoleum floor, sifting through a pile of unwashed clothes at the base of his bed. He grabbed a pair of underwear briefs and some jeans with a foreign stain along the back thigh. He shook the jeans until he heard the jingle of metal from inside one of the pockets, and then laid them on the bed. He hastily slid on the briefs, hopping up and down before grabbing the corner of his kitchen stove for balance. The jeans went on next; they felt tighter around his waist than he expected.

"That's pretty nasty," said the woman.

Sean rose his head to her.

"That big scar on your stomach," she said, pointing with her chin. "Is that from a knife? Shit, there's one on your shoulder too. I didn't notice those last night, what with all the . . ." She waved a vague hand. "What happened to you?"

"I'm clumsy," he answered, in no mood to share stories from his past.

He pulled a black short-sleeve collared shirt from a hanger on the handle of a tiny closet. The emblem on its chest pocket read "Weld County." He slipped the shirt over his head and pulled it down over his bloated stomach.

He quickly checked himself in a mirror beside the closet, cursing under his breath as he combed his hair with his fingers. It was a matted mess, longer than the crew cut he used to keep. It was grayer too, but with enough dark remaining to keep most people from mistaking his forty years of life for fifty. The three-day stubble on his chin and neck would have gotten him in trouble with his boss if he were there, but this morning he only had to cater to kids.

In the corner of the mirror, he watched the woman lower her arm to the floor to pick up a lace bra. Her black wavy hair dangled over the edge of the bed.

"I'm gonna need a ride home," she said, nursing a yawn.

"I can't do it right now." He leaned forward and pulled a pair of beige work boots over his bare feet. "This will take about an hour."

The woman quickly sat up. "I don't *have* no hour." She placed her arms through the bra and secured it in the back. "I need to be at work by 10:30. That means taking a shower, clean clothes, and makeup first."

"I said I can't right now, Maria," he growled, twisting his head back toward her. "I've got *my* job to do."

"Who's Maria?"

Sean's shoulders lowered. "Sorry . . . Anna."

"Try again, asshole."

"Goddammit, we just met last night," Sean said. "Cut me a fucking break, all right?"

The woman tightened her jaw and shook her head, taking her eyes off Sean to lift up the blanket. She searched under the sheets for the rest of her clothes. She seemed to find them, her body soon shuffling and contorting under the covers.

"Listen," Sean said with a tilted head. "There's a phone on the dresser. If you can't wait for me, call a friend to pick you up. But if you do that, you're going to have to wait for them on the other side of the gate."

The woman's head popped out from under the covers. Strands of hair hung in front of her face, but the anger in her eyes couldn't be hidden. "What?" she barked.

"I'm the only one who opens that gate. Facility rules. Government rules. And if I'm down below when your friend shows up, I won't be around to do it." He reached for a bottle of aspirin on a countertop next to him.

"So you're kicking me out? Right now?" Her voice rose so loudly that Sean worried the people outside would hear it.

Sean tossed a couple of aspirins in his mouth and swallowed them without water. "No. In five minutes. Make the call if you're going to make it."

Before the woman could respond, Sean turned and unlatched the trailer door, pushing it open and closing his eyes when his face again met the wicked glare of the sun. He lowered his head and stepped outside, skipping a steel step. His scalp, at the top of his six-foot-five, 245-pound body, clipped the top of the doorframe, drawing a grunt from his mouth.

The dog had started barking again, and Sean yelled, "Quiet!"

He used his hand as a sun visor until he could better focus on the world, trudging across dirt and grass to a narrow paved road. The road led about thirty yards to the south, up to a tall chain-link gate with large metal signs mounted on the other side. The gate connected with a stretch of fence that enclosed roughly four acres of the thirteen-acre property. Barbed-wire angled outward from the fence's top bars.

On the other side of the gate were a couple of parked cars. Next to them were two men and seven or eight boys of different shapes, sizes, and ethnicities. The boys wore blue uniformed shirts and yellow neckerchiefs. None of them could have been older than ten. They wrestled and chased each other between the cars as the two men—one of average build, and the other obese—glared at Sean through stone faces.

"This is gonna suck," Sean muttered, reaching back and scratching a recurring itch at the base of his skull. He didn't like it when kids came to the facility. They were distracting, and they tended to touch things they shouldn't.

As Sean approached, a white pit bull with a pink snout and red collar trotted up to him from the gate. Its tail wagged and its tongue dangled from its mouth. Sean had inherited the dog from the previous caretaker—an old man who'd been killed in the adjoining campground back in late August when a freak EF3 tornado passed through.

He was the only fatality that day, despite a lot of building damage and some overturned train cars in Windsor, a small town a ways to the northwest. First responders found the dog sitting next to its owner's body. They'd identified him as "Avalanche" by a silver tag on his collar.

Sean admired loyalty, and after some dark family revelations from the year before had prompted him to leave his mountain home of Winston, he was ready for some of it in his life. Having heard the story of Avalanche from the county supervisor who'd hired him, Sean agreed to keep the dog rather than let it be taken to the pound. Considering the breed's rap for being unpredictable and aggressive, the dog may have been euthanized.

As it turned out, Avalanche wasn't the least bit contentious—an animal so friendly around people that he only barked when he wanted attention. He wasn't a great watchdog but tossing him a tennis ball or a Frisbee from time to time helped drive away some boredom. Avalanche was low maintenance, and Sean liked that.

When the dog reached Sean, it did a one-eighty and began walking beside him in the same direction. The canine's eyes bounced back and forth from Sean to the scout pack.

Sean nodded to the men as he approached the gate. They didn't return the gesture. He pried a ring of keys from the front pocket of his jeans and stuck one of them into a padlock that hung between the gates. As he released the lock and pulled up on a throw cane bolt, he heard one of the boys reading the largest sign secured to the mesh.

"This area is a former Atlas E . . . inter-continental . . . ballistic

. . . missile silo." The boy annunciated slowly and carefully. "The area—"

Another scout, apparently too impatient to cater to the first one's heavy delivery, took over the narration. "The area is open to the public on a contacted tour basis. Arrangements for tours can be made by contacting the Weld County Buildings & Grounds Department."

"Which is *exactly* what we did," added the man of average build, who was still glaring at Sean. "For nine o'clock this morning." The man wore glasses with thin frames, and a red Budweiser baseball cap.

Sean glared back as he swung the gate open inward. "I'm letting you in, aren't I? Let's not get hysterical."

"Hysterical?" the man said, jerking his head back. With an inflating chest, he opened his mouth to add more, but a scout with large freckles and raspberry blond hair interrupted him.

"Does your dog bite, mister?"

Sean lowered his head to the boy. "Only if you touch things you're not supposed to." His face was deadpan.

A couple of the other scouts laughed. The adults didn't.

"Seriously though," said the obese man. He wore a long Colorado Rockies baseball shirt and a dark goatee. "Is the dog safe? He looks like a pit."

"That would be because he *is* a pit."

The man's face stiffened.

"The kids will be fine," Sean added. "As long as they keep their hands off the equipment."

The truth was that Avalanche couldn't have cared less what anyone touched, but Sean had used the warning on a number of occasions to keep order and save himself some stress throughout the tour.

Sean opened the gate. Its hinges creaked as he stepped backward and pulled it open wider. He guided the group in with his hand.

"And if everyone does as they're told on the tour, you'll all get a souvenir at the end."

Several of the boys cheered. A couple dropped down to their knees in front of Avalanche, who proceeded to lick one of their faces. It prompted some laughs.

"Real killer," said the large man in the Rockies shirt. A smirk had loosened up his face.

The other man wasn't amused by the display, his face turning sourer. He'd likely caught a whiff of the alcohol on Sean's breath.

Sean reached into his pocket and pulled out a nearly expended roll of white mints. He twisted the top one free of its foil and popped it into his mouth. "What are your names?" he asked, his eyes shifting back and forth between the men. "I left the paperwork inside."

"Mike," said the larger man, extending his hand. Sean shook it.

"I'm Mike too," said the other, crossing his arms in front of his chest.

"All right," Sean said, nodding. "Big Mike and Budweiser Mike. Got it."

The loud slap of a door swinging shut drew all eyes to the front of the trailer. Sean's overnight guest had emerged. She walked toward the group with tense purpose in each step. Her hair shone from wetness, and she wore a red sleeveless top, leather miniskirt, and high-heeled shoes. A black purse dangled over her shoulder. Both scout fathers turned to Sean, their faces tense.

Sean met their glares. "A different tour . . . from last night," he muttered.

The woman made her way toward the gate, whisking past the group without making eye contact with anyone. She had just about reached the entrance when she stopped and spun around to face Sean. Her nostrils flared as she bit her lip.

"Sofia!" she stated loudly, placing her hands on her hips.

"What?" Sean asked.

"My name. It's Sofía."

Sean cocked his head and let out a sigh. He then turned to the spectators. "Boys, this is Sofía. Sofia, this is Cub Scout Pack . . ."

"Two-oh-two!" one of the boys responded with pride.

"Hi Sofía," a few of them greeted in unison, their wide eyes scrutinizing her appearance. Some of the boys giggled.

Sofia rolled her eyes and shook her head. She turned and made her way through the open gate. Once out, she spun around to deliver a closing remark, but Sean was already latching and padlocking the gate behind her.

She gasped and threw her arms up in the air. "Well, I guess it's goodbye then!"

"Guess so. Goodbye."

Sean turned his back to her and rejoined the group. Her huffs and puffs could barely be heard by the time Sean had begun his official introduction.

"I'm Sean Coleman, everyone," he announced unenthusiastically. "I am the sole caretaker here at Missile Site Park. That means I manage this facility from top to bottom. I keep the grounds, which includes the camping area you can see over on the other side of the fence," he pointed to the west, "and I run and watch over this *historic facility*, which is a retired Atlas E missile silo. It was owned and operated by the US government during the Cold War, and—"

"The what?" asked one of the scouts, raising his hand. His face was scrunched.

Sean grunted and lowered his head in annoyance. He didn't like being interrupted mid-sentence. "Which part didn't you understand?"

"The cold what?"

"The Cold War. As in the United States versus the Soviets." Sean fought back a scowl when his words were met with mostly blank stares. "Nuclear weapons aimed at each other. Any of that ring a bell?"

The boy who'd asked the question twisted his head from side to side, gauging the sentiments of his peers. Most of the others scouts looked equally perplexed. Only a couple nodded.

Big Mike offered an apologetic shrug. "I guess they haven't gotten to that in history class yet."

"Great," Sean muttered, turning back to the boy. He scratched the back of his head. "Just ask your parents to rent *Rocky IV* for you. That'll straighten you out. Maybe *Red Dawn* too. Let's just get started. Come with me."

Sean led the group onto a concrete platform just north of his trailer. Though level, the cement was marred with long, deep cracks that had formed over time. A row of thick vertical piping, teal in color and shaped like candy canes, stuck out of the mortar. Beside it was a large air vent, concrete at its base. A metal trapezoid made up its roof.

"This single-use missile site was active from 1961 to 1965," Sean said, walking backward so the children could hear him clearly. He didn't want to have to repeat himself. "It housed exactly one Atlas rocket and one warhead. Five-man crews worked here over twenty-four-hour shifts. During that time, they were in charge of monitoring the missile's status, and if called upon, were prepared to initiate the entire launch sequence." Sean had recited those lines so many times, he could do it in his sleep.

He guided the group past some more pipes and vents to an enormous steel platform raised a couple of feet off of the cement. It was dark in color and approximately a hundred-by-twenty feet in size. Avalanche jumped on top of it.

"Who thinks they know what this is?" Sean asked the group. Before anyone could answer, he continued. "This is an eighteen-inch-thick door. In the event of a launch, it would be slid back, and the missile below it would be raised vertically into position. It would then be fueled and launched into the air. The entire launch sequence would be completed in under fifteen minutes."

"What kind of fuel?" asked a boy near the back.

"Rocket fuel."

"Can you explain to the boys what rocket fuel is?" asked Budweiser Mike. His demeanor was still cold.

Sean glared at him for a moment. "It's a very powerful fuel," he said, unfamiliar with the specifics.

Budweiser Mike scoffed and turned to the kids. "It's a high-oxygen fuel. Its combustion takes place in a controlled manner, and it produces a huge volume of gas and a chemical reaction."

The boys looked at each other in bewilderment until the slow, deliberate clapping of Sean's hands drew their attention back to him. He had Budweiser Mike's attention too.

"Now *that* was an excellent answer," Sean said, his tone oozing with sarcasm. "I might just give you *two* free souvenirs at the end of the tour. Well done."

Budweiser Mike's eyes narrowed. Big Mike turned his head away, smirking.

"Who's ready to head underground?" Sean asked with some canned flare in his voice. The boys cheered, several raising their arms.

He led them north, off the concrete and through an area of overgrown grass to a metal grated staircase. Its steps wound down a steep hill to a paved, angled drive that came in through a back gate on the east side of the property. The drive disappeared behind a concrete barrier, descending into the base of the hill.

The group trotted down the stairs, stepping around patches of long grass that had sprouted up through the grating. As they descended, Sean pointed out more ventilation ducts and an old blacktop area on the other side of the fence. Weathered, rimless basketball backboards stood at each end of the rectangular court.

"That's where the guys manning this place used to shoot hoops when they weren't working," Sean said.

When they reached the bottom, and the boys began spilling out onto the pavement, the *oohs* and *ahhs* that Sean had grown accustomed to at that point in the tour made themselves heard.

A couple dozen yards down the drive stood an imposing twenty-four-by-twenty-feet steel blast door. It looked like something out a movie where armed military police would be stationed in front of it to protect top-secret government experimentation. Its vitality, however, had long since left.

As with the piping above, the door was teal in color, though deterioration from sections of rust gave it some character. About two thirds of the way up the door was a long, horizontal dent. Sean had been told that it was caused by a large military truck accidentally backing into it years ago. Rust was heavy around the blemish.

The door was surrounded by concrete: two diagonal sidewalls that kept the earth from the hollowed hill at bay, and a walkway above with a steel railing. Each wall displayed painted murals with different symbolic meanings. At the bottom of the wall on the right was a standard-sized metal door, teal and similarly corroded, with a large lever for a handle.

While the scouts and the grown-ups were still exchanging chatter, Sean cleared his throat and began to speak. "The blast door down there is eighteen inches thick, and back when this facility was active, it would be opened manually—by hand—to let a military transport trailer back a missile down this driveway and inside." He began walking backward again, leading them down the drive.

"Does it still open by hand?" asked Budweiser Mike. "The blast door?"

Sean shook his head. "It was replaced with an automated mechanism a few years back, which isn't working right now. Some guys from County were supposed to come out a few days ago to fix it, and haven't." He stopped walking when he was just a few feet from the door. "So we're not going to be able to open it today."

"Aw," echoed some of the boys.

Budweiser Mike just nodded, while Big Mike turned to the boys and shrugged his shoulders to lighten the mood.

"What do those pictures mean?" one of the scouts asked, his finger swinging from one painted sidewall to the other.

"Yeah," another one said. "Is that a polar bear?" He pointed to an image of a white cartoonish animal with a long thin snout. It carried a missile in its arms and wore spectacles and a red hardhat. The picture was painted from the waist up with an acronym and some numbers stenciled below.

"A polar bear?" Sean asked, his face tight. "Do you not know what a polar bear looks like?"

Some of the boys laughed. Budweiser Mike squared his jaw and narrowed his yes.

"That's a mole," Sean continued. His words mostly fell on blank glares. "You know, one of those furry, rat-looking things that live underground."

"Because *this site* is underground!" another scout shouted.

"Bingo. We got a smart one!" Sean stated, pointing him out. He then turned back to the mural. "The mole's lifting the missile out of the ground, just like this silo was designed to do. The '566' and the 'SMS' below him stand for the 566th Strategic Missile Squadron. That's what this site was part of. It was out of the Francis E. Warren Air Force Base in Wyoming."

"What about the others?" asked the scout who'd made the polar bear guess. "Like the squirrel with the cowboy hat, and the shield and fist?" His finger traced the wall.

Sean scratched his beard. "You know what? Why don't we just go inside? There are cooler things to see there." And the sun was still hurting his eyes.

The group concurred, and one of the boys in the back reached for the handle of the door along the wall. With a grunt, he pulled on the door with his entire body.

"I'll need to unlock that first," Sean interjected. "It's always kept locked when no one's . . . inside." His words dwindled as he watched the boy slowly open the door, hinges screeching.

Big Mike snickered, glancing at Sean.

"Ah shit," Sean muttered under his breath. He'd forgotten to lock the door after taking Sofia through it the night before. Details of the hazy stint began coming back to him. "Wait, wait, wait!" he shouted.

When the scout stepped through the doorway, the boy inadvertently kicked over a couple of empty beer bottles that were parked just inside. One shattered. Sean winced and quickly negotiated himself around the cluster of children until he had one hand on the door and the other serving as a gate in front of the child. The others boys leaned forward, eager to catch a glimpse of what had just happened.

"Those idiots!" Sean lamented aloud, his mind racing to formulate a scapegoat. "The County sends their maintenance guys down here to deal with leaky ceilings, and they end up leaving their lunch trash behind. They think I'm here to clean up after them."

Sean pushed the debris aside with his foot and glanced over his shoulder at his audience, trying to determine if they'd bought his story. The boys' eyes were on the glass. The Mikes' eyes were on each other. Both shook their heads.

"This bomb shelter has leaky ceilings?" asked one of the boys. A few chuckled.

"Yeah," Sean answered, propping open the door with a brick. "Back when it was in use, this place was as solid as a rock. Enough to withstand an atomic-bomb blast. With the amount of cement used in this place's foundation, you could build a sidewalk from here to Salt Lake City."

"Whoa," said the same kid. "My grandma lives in Salt Lake City."

Sean ignored him. "But things break down over time if you don't keep up on them."

His words lingered in his own mind for a moment, as his gaze lifted up to the sky. A brown hawk hovered above before disappearing over the adjacent wall.

Sean's attention lowered back to the kids. "These days, some water gets in through the cracks when it rains. Even a few small animals manage to find their way into the bunker, one way or another."

"Moles?" a boy asked.

"No. A snake once."

Sean stepped to the side of the doorway, exposing a circular pedestrian tunnel about eight feet in diameter. Along its ceiling were some bright caged bulbs, which Sean had neglected to turn off the night before. They lit up about thirty-five feet of ribbed metal walls and a paved walkway. At the end of the tunnel was a concrete wall where a poster with a blue emblem and a burgundy background hung.

The scouts chattered with wide eyes. Big Mike wore a grin as he peered inside. Even Budweiser Mike stood with both eyebrows raised. Sean was used to the reaction from new visitors. The tunnel held an ambiance of intrigue and importance that made one feel as if they were entering a portal into a covert world that few had laid eyes on. That was certainly how Sean had felt the first time he'd entered the compound in the midst of his job interview.

In a way, the gateway reminded him of an old television show he used to watch back in the '80s called *The Equalizer*. It starred actor Edward Woodward as a former US covert operations officer. The title character lived in a shoddy apartment building in a bad area of New York City, but once the door to his apartment was opened, the living quarters were revealed to be lavishly decorated with expensive art and contemporary furniture. No one would ever confuse the missile silo for a swank pad, but the reception was similar.

Sean led them all inside, his voice echoing off the walls as he explained how the facility's crew would enter and leave through that very tunnel. When they reached its end, the group stood in front of the poster. The emblem at its center matched one of the murals painted beside the blast door outside: a steel fist clenching three lightning bolts and an olive branch, in front of a pair of clouds. Below the shield, fancy lettering spelled out "Strategic Air Command."

Sean tried to explain the symbolism, but the boys were much more interested in an adjacent tunnel to the right. It was similar in style to the first one, but it was three or four times longer and protected by a padlocked chain-link gate. At its far end was a bright wall with another large picture.

"We're at a junction point right now," said Sean. "Down there is what we call the Command Wing. It's where the control room and the old living quarters are. We keep a lot of old county archives down there these days."

A couple of boys noticed the darkened doorway over Sean's shoulder, which led into the missile room.

"On the other side," Sean continued, pointing to his right, "is the Launch Wing."

Most of the kids were still fixated on the tunnel, some even pressing their faces up against the gate's mesh to steal a closer look.

"Let's go on down there," said Sean, nodding at the tunnel and pulling his keys from his pocket. As far as he was concerned, the more quickly the tour moved, the sooner it would be over. He waded through the kids and opened the lock.

The group followed him into the tunnel, Avalanche taking the lead. It was better lit than the first one. One of the boys whistled as they traveled down it, creating an eerie, wandering echo soon drowned out by adolescent chatter. When they reached the end and spread out along a steel platform, Sean pointed out the poster on the wall.

It was an enlarged black-and-white photo showing what that same tunnel had looked like in the 1960s when the site was operational. Pipes, air ducts, and some kind of conveyer system had lined the walls back then, making the walkway considerably narrower. The image was just one of many historical photos that decorated the facility.

"What's this handle for?" one of the boys asked, lowering himself to a knee and pointing to the platform they stood on. "Is this a trap door?"

Everyone, including Avalanche, followed the boy's aim to a flush ring pull handle embedded in the metal. The others laughed when Avalanche licked the boy's finger.

"Not a trap door," said Sean. "Just a hatch. There's a little storage area under the floor. I'm not sure what it was used for back then."

Sean led the group down three steps and around a corner. They walked down a short ramp where Sean drew them through a doorway labeled "Control Room." The mostly bare room with a linoleum floor wasn't particular impressive, but as more photos on the walls revealed, the twenty-by-twenty space was once overflowing with television monitors, large control panels, tall computers, and wall clocks reflecting international time zones. Shelves had been filled with binders, and grease boards had been marked up with writings like "Status" and "Emergency Checklist."

"Are these the guys who worked here?" asked a scout as he stared at the only color poster in the room. It hung on the wall opposite Sean.

It was a crew photo of five men who once operated the site. They were posed in front of the control room's vertical computers.

"Yeah," said Sean.

Four of the men were white and one of them was black. All wore tight haircuts and white jumpsuits over black turtlenecks. Sean didn't know most of their names, though that information was assuredly packed away somewhere in the archives.

"They seem nice," added the scout. "Well, except the guy in the back."

The other boys chuckled.

The scout's observation was the same one Sean had made on his first day of training inside the silo as an interim caretaker showed him the ropes. While four of the operators in the picture displayed gleaming smiles that exuded American optimism, the tallest of them wore sunken eyes and a straight mouth that hinted at bitterness, perhaps even despair. Sean found out why after making a joke about the outlier. The man, Collins, had lost his wife and children to a car accident weeks earlier. A month after the picture was taken, Collins took his own life—inside the missile silo.

It had happened in the living quarters, so Sean had been told. His colleagues found him hanging from the ceiling. Collins was a former astronaut who'd left the space program after a severe knee injury during a training exercise grounded him. The trainer told Sean that past caretakers had talked about hearing odd noises in the silo, especially at night. They'd find old tools or other Cold War relics mysteriously knocked to the floor or moved to a different table. They attributed it to "Collins's ghost." Sean wasn't sure if the trainer was pulling his leg, but in the nine months that Sean had worked at the facility, he hadn't heard or seen anything out of the ordinary.

Regardless, Sean felt it best not to share the death tale with the scouts. He didn't want to give Budweiser Mike a heart attack.

Though Collins had seemed out of place when Sean first saw the picture, now it was the other four men in the picture who seemed suspicious. He couldn't fathom how *anyone* who worked in the silo could have mustered up such smiles. Sean felt that if he were ever sitting on 4.4 megatons of nuclear explosives, his stomach would be twisted in too many knots to even manage a smirk.

Sean brought the group into the living quarters, which were now used almost exclusively for storing old county records. The public wasn't allowed inside for legal reasons, but Sean let everyone take a peek through the doorway to check out the eighteen-foot walls and the large, binder-filled book shelves that nearly touched the ceiling.

"And this isn't even where we keep most of the archives," said Sean.

He led them past the old kitchen, a small room that was fenced off and filled with large cardboard boxes. When they reached a dark, imposing steel door, Sean stopped and the kids gathered around him. The door read "Weld County Historical Archives - 1975" in a stenciled font near the top and hung open about a foot.

"Is that a safe?" asked a scout. Everyone else's attention turned to the door's lever-style handle and the silver combination lock embedded beside it.

"That was its intended purpose at some point, after the silo had been deactivated," Sean answered, leaning forward and pulling the heavy door wide open. "But I'm betting none of you have ever seen a safe this big."

The boys' eyes enlarged at the unexpectedly large room that appeared beyond the door. It went back a good sixty feet and appeared to be just as wide. Inside were towering rows of wooden shelving that dwarfed what they'd seen in the previous room. The shelves were filled with stacked boxes of different sizes, and the aisles between each row were about eight feet wide. The ceiling was so high that it couldn't be seen from outside of the room.

"It's like Home Depot," said one of the boys. His friends laughed.

"Or Lowe's," added Budweiser Mike, his mouth curled in a self-satisfied grin. When he received no reaction, he said, "You know, the other home improvement store. It's like Home Depot."

Sean sighed, continuing on. "This used to be the generator room. The stuff stored in here isn't quite as sensitive. It's become kind of a catchall. Along with county records, you'll find equipment, office furniture, and old leftover items from the sixties. You can all go on in. Just don't touch anything."

"It's a successful store chain," Sean heard Budweiser Mike say to Big Mike as the boys walked inside with Avalanche leading the way.

"I know," replied Big Mike, placing a conciliatory hand on Budweiser Mike's shoulder.

The adults joined the boys inside, and Sean let the scouts roam the walkways for a few minutes as he explained that the ceilings were made of two-foot-thick concrete, and that the bricked-up portions of the wall were where ventilation fans used to be. When he overheard two boys daring a third to climb up the steps of one of the mobile staircases, Sean decided it was time to move on.

· "Okay guys," he said with a raised voice, commanding the group's attention. "Who's ready to see the cool *rocket* stuff?"

As one, the boys turned to him with excited faces and arms raised high.

Chapter 3

The scouts were still buzzing as they ascended the outside staircase they'd come down earlier, Avalanche again in front. Some talked about the missile bay and the flame pit they'd explored, musing over what could happen to a human body trapped inside it at launch time. Others seemed more interested in the museum artifacts that had been on display in the bay, including an old metal dentist's chair that looked more like a medieval torture device than a medical tool. A few examined the "I had a BLAST at Missile Site Park" pins that Sean had given them.

One of the boys amused himself by repeating the phrase "sluge tank" over and over again, referring to a large sludge tank in the liquid-oxygen room that had been mislabeled years earlier. The repetition wore on Sean, but the scout's buddies found it hilarious.

Once up top, Sean fielded a few more questions as he ushered the group toward the front gate. But in the short amount of time it had taken them to reach the entrance, the boys' attention spans had dwindled. They talked among themselves about video games, superheroes, and sports. A couple of them brushed their hands along Avalanche's short fur whenever the dog trotted past them.

Big Mike brought up the rear, still huffing and puffing from his grueling trip up the staircase. He wiped his forehead with the back of his arm. The other Mike was closer to the front of the pack. He seemed eager to leave.

Once the group made their way around the side of the trailer, Sean spotted something through the fence that tightened his gut: a brown Jeep Cherokee parked on the other side of the fence, behind one of the men's cars. A yellow star emblem decorated its passenger-side door.

"You've got to be shitting me," Sean muttered, his words drawing a glance from one of the scouts.

He kept his eyes on the jeep as he continued forward, tilting his head against the glare of the sun to try and see through its window. When he finally got a good look, he found that the cab was empty. His eyes shifted along the fence-line, searching for the driver. That's when he detected a unique, murky whiff in the breeze that hadn't caught his nose in almost nine months.

Sean scowled. "And he brought reinforcements."

The scout beside Sean turned toward him. "Are you talking to me?"

"No. Mind your own business."

When the group reached the gate, Big Mike hustled up to Sean and extended his hand. "Thanks . . . for the tour," he wheezed.

"Sure thing," Sean answered, meeting his gaze.

The other Mike simply nodded.

Sean nodded back, unlocked the gate, and pulled it open. "Stay," he told Avalanche, who rested his butt on the ground.

"What does everyone say to Mr. Coleman?" Big Mike called out.

"Thank you, Mr. Coleman!" the chorus rang.

"And Avalanche?" Big Mike added.

"Thank you, Avalanche!"

Sean fought back a smirk. "Enjoy your summer, guys."

He let the group funnel out through the gate, then followed them.

"Keep staying," Sean told Avalanche. He turned and scanned the area again, this time spotting two male figures standing by the entrance sign next to the road, about 150 feet away.

One of the men was short and slender. His dark hair was thinning so badly that it looked nearly transparent under the sun's glare. He wore khaki pants and a neatly pressed long-sleeve shirt with a collar. A Glock pistol hung in a leather holster at his side.

The other man was larger and taller, with a dark complexion and long salt-and-pepper hair wrapped in a ponytail. Puffing on a dark cigarette, he was clad in a denim jacket, jeans, and tall moccasin boots.

The men's eyes were glued to Sean as they subtly exchanged words. The short man soon raised his hand in a greeting to Sean, an artificial grin stretched across his face.

Sean stood there, expressionless, while car doors slammed and engines cranked. The scout leaders' vehicles carefully made their way over to the road and past the men. Their tires kicked dirt into the air and formed a dust cloud that lingered as they disappeared down the road.

Sean finally shook his head, raised his chin, and shouted, "What's going on, Gary?"

The two men again exchanged words, the one with the cigarette nodding. He stayed put as the shorter man began walking toward Sean.

The smoker was Ron Oldhorse, a Native American survivalist who lived in the mountains outside of Winston. Sean hadn't seen him since early September. The man approaching him was Gary Lumbergh, Winston's chief of police. He was also Sean's brother-in-law. Their last meeting had been around Christmas, and it hadn't ended well.

Lumbergh's jaw churned as he worked a stick of gum in his mouth; it was an idiosyncrasy Sean used to tease him over. The police chief's eyes raised and lowered in scrutiny of Sean's disheveled appearance, but just as Lumbergh opened his mouth to speak, his head shot to his right, his eyes bulging. Avalanche was barreling right toward him.

The dog galloped across the dirt drive and lunged upright, planting his large paws on Lumbergh's chest. The chief stopped in his tracks and stumbled backward on loose footing. He instinctively placed one hand between him and the dog's slobbering jowls, while the other hand went toward the grip of his pistol.

"Oh please," Sean said, rolling his eyes. He crossed his arms in front of his chest.

Avalanche bounced along on his hind legs, moving in conjunction with Lumbergh. Deeming the dog not to be a threat, the chief moved both of his hands to its chest, trying to avoid contact with its long, protruding tongue. He finally twisted his body, forcing Avalanche to all fours.

"Dammit," Lumbergh muttered, lowering his head and raising his arms to take stock of his shirt.

A loud, short whistle let out behind Lumbergh, and Avalanche instantly took off in pursuit. The dog sprinted to Oldhorse, who was lowering himself to one knee. A rare grin dawned Oldhorse's chiseled face as the dog vigorously bathed it. Its front paws sat on Oldhorse's shoulders for support.

"Avalanche!" Sean yelled sternly "Get back here!"

The dog ignored his master and began wrestling around on the ground with Oldhorse. Avalanche's tail swung back and forth like wiper blades on high.

"Oh, come on," bemoaned Sean.

Lumbergh tugged at his shirt to straighten it, and then used the back of his hand to brush off some dirt and grass. "You know Oldhorse," he said, shaking off his annoyance. "He has a way with animals."

"Yeah, a modern-day Anthony Perkins."

Lumbergh's eyes narrowed. "Norman Bates?"

"No. Dammit." Sean let out a deep sigh. "I meant *Marlin* Perkins. Now what are you doing here?"

Lumbergh slid his hands into his pockets. He took in a breath and let his eyes peer past Sean. In the distance, beyond a lone telephone pole, a long mountain range emerged from a thin haze.

It extended across the entire western horizon. The land the men stood on was adjacent to a small, treeless campground, and stood on higher ground than that of the surrounding area. Between them and the mountains were cornfields, prairie, and a two-lane highway that divided the picture. The landscape stretched out for a good twenty miles.

"We just wanted to check on you," Lumbergh finally said, training his eyes back on Sean.

Sean scoffed. "You and Oldhorse?"

"No. Me and Diana. We haven't heard from you in months. You don't return calls. You don't come visit your niece—who's growing up quickly. And Toby . . . My God, he asks about you almost every day."

"Tell him I'm fine."

"I'm not going to lie to him, Sean," Lumbergh shot back. "I don't think you're fine. You look like shit. You smell like booze. You're living out here in *pastureland*, all by yourself in a trailer."

"I've always been a loner, Gary. Whether it be here or back in Winston. That hasn't changed."

"It's different now, and you know it." Lumbergh lifted his hands from his pockets and crossed his arms in front of his chest. "Back in Winston, you had a life. You had your own business. You were sober. And you had *us—family*."

A chuckle quickly dropped from Sean's mouth. It evolved into a deep laugh that burned with cynicism. "*Family* . . . that's rich," he sneered. "One hell of a pedigree there."

"Sean . . ."

"Gary," Sean snapped, drawing Oldhorse's attention. "I grew up thinking my dad had abandoned me. For thirty goddamn years, my mother let me believe that he had gotten fed up with us and left, and that it was somehow *my* fault. Then, lo and behold, it turns out the asshole wasn't even my dad. My father had been living in the same town as me for *all of those years*, and neither he nor I knew it! And why? Because she was too embarrassed over having an affair. Because she was bitter that the affair was why her husband left."

"Listen, Sean—"

"No, *you* listen! My dad died from a bullet in his fucking throat, not ever knowing he even had a son."

"The two of you at least had a relationship, Sean," said Lumbergh, patting the air in front of him as a call for peace. "Be thankful for that. You loved each other. You got to spend time with each other—"

"It's not the same!" Sean roared, forming fists. "There's a hell of a lot of difference between having a *fun uncle* to hang out with from time to time and being tortured every single day for thirty years over your dad having deserted you!"

Lumbergh nodded. His eyes softened with empathy, the sight of which compelled Sean to take a moment before continuing. He looked away, squaring his jaw.

"Everything you're saying is true," said Lumbergh. "Your sister and I will never make excuses for what your mother did—for keeping that secret from you and from her for all of those years."

"*Half*-sister," Sean interjected, glaring at Lumbergh.

"That doesn't matter. I'm just saying that I agree that what your mother did was wrong. But she's gone now. She's been dead for four months, and there's no reason to let your anger with her keep you from being the person that you can be—the man you *were* a year ago."

Sean shook his head and cleared his throat. He raised his hand to his hips. "Why are *you* still in Winston, Gary?"

Lumbergh's face tightened. "What do you mean?"

"What I mean is that you gave up a great job in Chicago as a police lieutenant to come out here and take care of my mother with Diana because no one trusted *me* to do it. Now that Mom's gone—now that she's buried six feet under—why the hell are you still keeping the peace in a small-pond mountain town like Winston, Colorado?"

Lumbergh shook his head and sighed. "Well," he said, taking a couple of seconds before continuing. He finally offered a smirk. "It's grown on me. Diana's always liked Winston. It took me a couple of years to get used to it, but I like it too. I like the job, I like the fresh air. And I like the people." He held Sean's gaze.

Sean shook his head and turned his back to Lumbergh. His eyes traced the outline of the mountains. They felt even farther away than they had his first day on the job. His chest moved in and out as he formulated his words.

"You don't want me back, Gary."

"Yes we do."

"No. You don't. You were right when you said I'm not the man I was a year ago. That man's gone."

Lumbergh let some air escape his lungs. "He doesn't have to be."

"For now, he does. And you know that. There's a reason you didn't show up here with Diana and little Ashley. There's a reason you didn't bring Toby along. You didn't want them to see me like this, not after what happened at Christmas. I scared the hell out of everyone."

"It was the booze talking. We can get you into a program."

"It was more than that, and you were right not to bring them here." Sean faced Lumbergh. "What I don't get is why you brought Oldhorse." His eyes shifted to the Native American. "I hope you two weren't planning on a kidnapping, because I'll send you both home on stretchers."

Lumbergh fought back a grin. "No. I have another reason for being here." His lips straightened. "Oldhorse's father is sick. Lung cancer. The old man lives at a place over in Kersey now." He shook his head. "The poor bastard never smoked a cigarette in his life, and he comes down with lung cancer. Late stage. You never know how life's going to turn out. Oldhorse hasn't seen him in a while, so I told him I'd give him a ride."

Sean nodded, his eyes wandering over to Oldhorse, who was

still on the ground with Avalanche. "That's good. Good that they're talking. Good that they'll get to say their goodbyes." He turned his gaze back to Lumbergh. "Oldhorse doesn't have a driver's license, does he?"

"Or a car."

"Is that because of that federal warrant for him for the thing up in South Dakota?"

Lumbergh gasped. His mouth dropped open. "How in the hell do you know about that? No one knows about that."

"Relax, Gary," Sean scoffed. "The secret's safe with me. Toby spilled the beans on it a while back. He overheard his mother and Oldhorse talking about it one night. I told him not to tell anyone else."

Lumbergh let a deep breath escape his mouth. "Because it's important that that doesn't get out. They'll toss him in prison."

"I know. Don't sweat it." The men held each other's stare for a moment. "Really," Sean assured him.

———

Having repeatedly heard his name, Oldhorse had turned his attention to the two men down the drive. Their animated conversation was their own business, but the breeze had carried over a few stray words, and Oldhorse wondered if Lumbergh was having any luck convincing his brother-in-law to return to Winston.

From a personal standpoint, Oldhorse couldn't have cared less. He'd long viewed Coleman as a bad seed—a man angry at the world, who never minced words or insults. But as he knelt in the dirt rubbing the back of the dog's ears, he thought about the one person who needed Coleman back more than anyone else. And it wasn't Lumbergh or his wife. For that individual's benefit alone, Oldhorse hoped the police chief's efforts were successful.

———

"Listen, Sean," said Lumbergh. "I'm not going to take up any more of your time. I've said my piece. You know how the family feels about you—that we want you back. Just think about it, and if you could pick up the phone every once in a while, I know your sister would appreciate it."

"Half-sister."

Lumbergh sighed. He opened his mouth to say something but decided instead to silently cede the point. "It was good to see you, Sean," he finally said. "Take care of yourself."

"You guys heading back up to Winston tonight, after Oldhorse talks to his father? That's a lot of driving for one day."

Lumbergh shook his head. "No, Oldhorse is going to stay in Kersey a few nights. I'll come back for him."

Sean nodded.

Lumbergh pursed his lips and returned the nod, raising his hand in departure. He turned and began his way toward the jeep. Over by the road, Oldhorse had climbed back to his feet. Avalanche stood obediently beside him, his tail wagging and his eyes trained on Oldhorse's face.

Sean lifted his chin to acknowledge Oldhorse. Oldhorse returned the gesture.

"Come on, Avalanche!" Sean called out with his hand raised to his mouth.

The dog stayed put, switching his attention back and forth between the two men. His tail moved even faster.

"Avalanche!" he yelled again.

Oldhorse smirked and lowered his head to the dog. He said something to the animal, and a second later, Avalanche was racing back to Sean.

"Son of a bitch," Sean muttered.

Moments later, Oldhorse and Lumbergh were back in the jeep. Lumbergh waved goodbye as they turned and drove out to the road. They disappeared down it with a cloud of dust, just as the scouts had.

That morning was the most company Sean had had in months, yet as he stood in the empty drive with only the sound of a breeze catching his ear, he had never felt so alone.

Chapter 4

Tiny flakes of white paint swirled in the air on their gentle descent to the ground. They disappeared into a patch of long grass and weeds at the edge of the blacktop. The metal pole, rusted and slightly tilted, hummed from the punishment of its warped, wooden backboard.

Each smack of the basketball against the board sent a crunch echoing across the land, unheard by anyone but Sean. The campground was empty, which had made the day's trash collection and restroom cleaning a cinch. The last camper—a college-aged kid with long hair—had left late Sunday afternoon. With no one around but Avalanche, who sat at half-court beside some grass poking up from a crack in the pavement, Sean didn't mind looking like a crazy man.

He dribbled the ball with authority, his jaw square, his nostrils wide, and his eyes burning a hole through the backboard. When he spotted an unblemished spot of paint just below its upper left corner, he gripped the ball in his right hand, and twisted his body to the side. He thought about his father, and then his mother.

She had died four months ago. A second stroke had finished her off. It had happened just a few weeks after the Christmas debacle. He had never gotten to make amends for the things he had said to her that night—for what he had said to everyone, and the frightening physicality of his rage. The scene often replayed itself in his mind.

"You're dead to me!" he had yelled, stumbling around in the

kitchen with deranged eyes—effects of the multiple boilermakers he had downed at a local pub before arriving. "You're all dead to me." But it took a broken chair, shattered window, and the wails of his crying niece before things got bad enough for Lumbergh to pull his gun on Sean and demand that he leave.

Standing there on the court, Sean snarled and launched the basketball like a rocket from a bazooka, using all of his body. The ball collided with the backboard so hard that its corner snapped off. Sean clenched his fists and yelled at the sky as if delivering a war cry. Avalanche jumped to his feet.

Sean's chest throbbed. His teeth clenched, and the corners of his mouth slowly curled into a demented grin. He had spent many hours on the beat-up old court, and he had told himself dozens of times that he should buy a rim for the backboard; he could work on his shooting and set some goals. But Sean had no one left in his life to impress, least of all himself. And sometimes it felt better to destroy than to achieve.

His breathing eased, and the grin soon left. He scratched the itch at the back of his head and meandered his way to the edge of the court. There he collected his ball from the scrub. Behind the pole was an open beer bottle. He grabbed it by its neck and held the rim to his mouth. The brew was warm and dry going down his throat, but he didn't care.

His eyes spread past picnic shelters, a couple of trees, and a telephone pole to the mountain range in the distance. Some dark clouds hovered above them—rain due to come in that evening. He had one more tour to give at five o'clock. A church group from Berthoud. He didn't usually start tours that late, but the group had requested it, and someone at County put it on the schedule.

Sean never wore a watch, but he figured from the sun that it had to be at least three. He wiped some sweat from his forehead and trudged through some overgrowth to the campground, where he tossed the empty bottle into a trash barrel. A glance to the south reminded him that he hadn't hoisted the flags that morning.

The national and state symbols were supposed to be up by eight and down around sunset. His boss was a stickler about it, and Sean never knew when Lawrence Mahan, Weld County's Director of Buildings & Grounds Department, would make a surprise visit.

Mahan was a micromanager by nature, but his wide range of responsibilities and the site's remote location and limited facilities largely kept him out of Sean's hair. Still, when he'd show up unannounced to scrutinize the grounds, he had a knack for making Sean feel as though he were under investigation. Mahan would check every underground room for burnt-out lightbulbs and secured doors. He'd peruse the campground for everything from excess grease build-up on the grills to the minimum number of toilet paper rolls in the restroom cabinets: six. The last time he'd come by, Mahan had decided Sean needed to move a bunch of old military rations from the floor of one room to the top of the shelves in that room— probably for no other reason than to wield his authority and put some extra work on Sean's plate. He even carried a tape measure in his pleated pants pocket, for which to assess the length of the prairie grass both inside and outside the gate.

The practice reeked of condescension, but Sean would bite his tongue and bear it for the sake of the job. Mahan was an unhappy man. Single and living alone. No relationship. No kids. Exercising some authority here and there was probably what gave him a sense of purpose in his life. He'd usually leave the site after forty-five minutes, and it would be a couple of weeks before Sean would see him again. He was about due.

Sean made his way to the restrooms, which were a few yards from the flagpole. Avalanche followed him, tail wagging. Sean unlocked a metal box mounted to the back of the building. He opened it and pulled out a pair of carefully folded flags before heading over to the pole. He clipped Old Glory to the rope, and then the state flag below it. He pulled them full-mast, the metal clips clanging against the pole as they went up. He watched them flutter in a breeze he couldn't feel.

In the distance, the faint sound of thunder echoed. His eye caught a quick flash of lightning above the mountains. He hoped the church group would arrive before the weather reached him, otherwise he'd have muddy footprints in the tunnels to clean up the next morning.

Chapter 5

Sean grabbed a gray rain poncho from a hook on the wall beside his closet. He slipped it over his head and squeezed out a grunt as he pulled the tight neckline over his face. Through the blinds above his kitchen sink, he stole a glance at the vehicle whose engine was so loud he had heard it over the pouring rain. It was an old full-sized school bus, painted white with red trim along its luggage compartments. Its brakes screeched as it came to a stop at the front gate.

Avalanche sat stoutly at the door, tail wagging. He twisted his head to Sean for just a second, before his eyes went forward again.

"I don't know, boy," said Sean, shaking his head. He watched rain bounce off the top of the bus. Its windshield was steamed over, its wipers at full speed. "Not sure I feel like cleaning up after an Avalanche mudslide tonight. Probably best to leave you in here where it's dry."

When the dog's ears lowered, Sean chuckled.

"How about some *Magnum P.I.*? That show's got dogs."

Sean pried a video cassette from its jacket and popped it into his VCR. He pushed play and adjusted the volume. Avalanche leapt onto the bed and lay down. Sean lowered his hand, rubbing the dog's scruff before making his way to the door. He closed it after exiting the trailer into the rain, pulling his hood over his head.

People of various heights were already piling out of the bus as Sean approached. They wore matching raingear—long white jackets with oversized hoods drawn forward. Sean raised his hand in greeting, but no one seemed to take notice of the gesture. The engine puttered as it came to a halt.

"First Presbyterian?" Sean called before sidestepping a puddle and working the lock.

As more individuals exited the bus, a short figure among them turned his head toward Sean and nodded. Little more than a forked beard could be seen of the man's face, drooping hood concealing eyes and nose.

Sean opened the gate and pulled it wide. He glanced at the side of the bus, where remnants of old lettering made for unintelligible verbiage. The vehicle looked in decent enough shape for its age, though the tires were nearly bald. The four windows at the rear were blocked with makeshift curtains, but the dome lights toward the front let Sean see the last two occupants preparing to exit.

The driver of the bus was very tall and thin. He had a high forehead and long blond hair—a hippy-looking type. He drew his hood over his head before Sean could see much of his face. There looked to be just under a dozen congregation members in all.

At the wail of a baby, Sean's head spun to two individuals huddled against the bus toward the back of the group. One of them was a petite woman with long dark hair that dangled from under her hood. She cradled an infant in her arms, though all Sean could see of the child was the blanket that covered it. The man next to the woman shifted his body between her and Sean.

"Need an umbrella?" Sean offered. Rarely had he seen people bring infants on the tour.

The man shook his head and raised his hand as if to forestall Sean from coming closer, but said nothing.

"It's okay," replied the presumed mother in a dainty voice.

Every other head in the group turned to her. Sean narrowed his eyes at the reaction, and he noticed that several in the group wore backpacks over their shoulders. The packs were roughly the same color as the raincoats, so they hadn't immediately stuck out.

"We'll be in the silo soon, won't we?" continued the woman. "It's dry in there."

The short man with the forked beard moved behind her. He placed his hand over her shoulder. Her body jolted from his touch, not expecting it.

"Yeah," Sean said. "It is." He watched the group's heads slowly turn back to him.

The baby cried out again, the fuss louder and longer this time. The mother shushed the child and swayed her arms.

When the fussing began to taper off, Sean spoke again. "We can do the silo part of the tour first, get you all out of the rain. The weather might let up by the time we're done, and then I can go over the outside stuff. Everyone okay with that?"

Every member of the group nodded, nearly in unison.

"Chatty bunch, aren't you?" Sean added.

No one laughed.

Sean squinted at the awkwardness of the scene, shaking his head. "All right then, let's head on in."

He motioned them through the gateway as the driver closed the bus's doors. Some of the congregation whispered among themselves, but most were silent. As one of the men passed, his shoulder bumped solidly against Sean's, almost as if the man had done it on purpose.

"Excuse me," Sean said, his tone laced with a hint of sarcasm. The man said nothing in return. Sean kept his eyes on him as he passed, spotting a toothpick sticking out of his mouth.

As Sean waited for the driver, he noticed that the bus bore a Texas license plate, which he found curious since the group was from in state. The driver made his way through the gate, carrying a duffle bag in his hand. It was bulky and appeared to have some weight to it.

"Did you guys pack a lunch or something?" Sean joked before closing and locking the gate behind him. When the driver ignored his question, Sean shouted out, "Hey!"

The man stopped and turned around. His height let Sean see more of his face than the others. He was clean-shaven with a chiseled chin and high cheekbones. His blue, sunken eyes glared through Sean with an eerie intensity.

"You guys aren't bringing in any fancy camera equipment, are you?" asked Sean, nodding at the driver's bag. The others slowed to a stop and turned to watch the exchange. "Normal snapshots are okay, but you need special approval from the county for anything more than that."

It was a rule Sean had never understood. Still, he wasn't going to lose his job over not enforcing it. If Director Mahan showed up and found tripods and long lenses inside the silo, there'd be hell to pay.

The driver's jaw quivered for a moment. He opened his mouth to speak but no words came. The short man with the forked beard suddenly reappeared behind him, placing his hand on the driver's back. The driver's eyes fell to the ground.

The short man raised his hand and slid back his hood, exposing dark, narrow eyes. He had a round face and was of Asian descent. A soft smile formed on his thin lips below a mustache that began at the corners of his mouth.

"We have no cameras, my good man," he said, his voice upbeat. "There is no problem." He pressed the palms of his hands together in front of him as if he were saying a prayer, looking directly at Sean. His smile grew wider. "My name is Hiroto Kishiyama. It was I who set up the tour through the county. We very much appreciate you taking the time to educate us on this facility."

Sean squinted, shoving his hand into his pocket for a piece of paper that wasn't there. "I have someone else's name on the reservation. A Mitchell something . . ."

"Ah yes," said the man. "Our driver, Mitchell Myers." He glanced over at the front of the bus. "I had forgotten it was under his name."

"No big deal," Sean said.

Inside the trailer, Avalanche began barking wildly. His front paws smacked against the window in the door as he jumped up and down. It wasn't the dog's typical request for attention. The animal was acting more aggressively, with some growling pouring out between barks.

"Quiet!" Sean snarled, cupping his mouth with his hand.

"Oh, he looks like a nice doggie," said Kishiyama. "How old is he?"

"Hell if I know," Sean said. He quickly remembered the type of group he was addressing. "Sorry, *heck* if I know. I inherited him last year. He usually isn't this mouthy."

"Probably the rain."

"Maybe." Sean turned back to Kishiyama. "What's with all the packs your group brought? You look like you're on a hiking trip."

Kishiyama chuckled, his nose scrunching. "No, no hiking trip. The door on the bus doesn't lock. I suggested everyone bring their belongings in with them."

Sean nodded. "Well, being that there's no one around for miles but you all and me, I'm thinking their stuff would have been pretty safe on the bus."

"So noted," said Kishiyama, nodding and pulling his hood back over his head. "Shall we continue on?"

"Yes, we *shall*," replied Sean, emulating Kishiyama's dialect with his tongue planted firmly in his cheek.

The rest of the group had proceeded forward to the cement platform, leaving Sean and Kishiyama at the back of line.

"I've been through Berthoud a couple of times," Sean said to Kishiyama. "I don't remember seeing a First Presbyterian down there."

Kishiyama smiled. "Our church is off the beaten path. A bit to the west, up in the mountains." A pause, then, "Tell me, Mr. Coleman, are you a man of faith?"

A half smirk formed on Sean's face. "In God? Yeah, I am, though we don't speak often. In people? Not so much."

The moment the words left Sean's mouth, he thought about how strange they must have sounded to the man—a complete stranger. Sean silently scolded himself for even throwing them out there. It wasn't like him to offer up something so personal. He blamed the long afternoon and dreary weather, and quickly changed the subject.

"Has your congregation been here before—to this site?" asked Sean, turning to Kishiyama as they walked.

A few moments of silence crawled by before Kishiyama answered. "No. Why do you ask?"

"Well, your friends are all heading in the right direction without me pointing the way. Most people that come out here haven't got a clue where to go. It's not like there are any signs once you're through the gate."

"A perceptive bunch, I suppose," answered Kishiyama, raising his small hand to his mouth. "Wait for our tour guide, please!" he called.

The group halted. Heads twisted back toward the two men.

"They were fine," Sean said, waving off the concern.

"Is that your car?" Kishiyama asked. His arm stretched to point a finger to an open area behind the trailer. A pale-blue '78 Chevy Nova was parked there beside a wild bush.

"Yeah," Sean answered. "I've had it for a while."

Kishiyama smiled brightly. "They don't make them like they used to, do they?"

Sean shrugged. "I suppose not. It breaks down from time to time though."

Kishiyama continued smiling, saying nothing.

"Excuse me," said Sean. He picked up his pace, negotiating his way around the group and taking the lead. He guided them across the cement platform.

"We'll come back to all of this later," he shouted over the rain, pointing to the piping, vents, and large steel door. "There are some stairs up ahead. Make sure you use the railing because they get slippery." He turned to the couple with the baby. "Especially you."

The woman nodded her head.

When they reached the metal staircase, Sean stepped aside and motioned them down it, one by one. "Watch your step," he warned as their shoes clanged on the grating.

When the bus driver skirted past, eyes forward and head lowered, his bag bumped against Sean's leg. What sounded like metal objects struck together inside. Sean watched the driver tense up and raise the bag under his shoulder as he continued down, not acknowledging the contact he'd made. When Kishiyama slid by, he nodded at Sean. Sean moved in behind him and followed him down.

"You sure your driver's not carrying cameras in his bag?" Sean asked, sliding his hand along the wet railing and staring at the back of Kishiyama's head.

"No sir," Kishiyama answered. He glanced over his shoulder at Sean.

"His bag seems a little . . ."

"Mitchell tinkers with radio parts," Kishiyama cut him off. "A passionate hobby of his."

"Radio parts, huh? Do you mind if I take a look at them before we go inside?"

"Not at all," Kishiyama replied. "Might I ask what the concern is over camera equipment on this tour? Surely there aren't any government secrets left in a Cold War facility that was retired decades ago."

"You're right. It's stupid. Between you and me, I think it's some ego trip with the county. Self-important crap. The directors probably don't want anything inside turning up in a magazine without them receiving the proper credit."

Kishiyama chuckled.

The group spread out along the driveway once they left the

stairs, nearly all of them looking at the large blast door a few dozen feet away. Some whispered to each other. The father of the baby placed his arm around his wife, taking in the sight.

"Mitchell," Kishiyama called. "Mr. Coleman needs to take a quick look through your bag. There are county rules that we must abide by."

The driver's depressed eyes shifted between Sean and Kishiyama before he stepped forward and laid the bag on the pavement.

"It's no big deal," said Sean. "Just covering my bases. I'll make this quick so we can all go inside." He learned forward and dropped to a knee.

Sean unzipped the bag as others gathered around. Sean glanced up at them, curious by the attention he was receiving. He nudged his head at the door down the drive.

"Why don't you all wait over there?" Sean said. "This will only take a few seconds. The overhang above the door might give you a little cover from the rain."

"Yes, let's give our host some room, everyone," added Kishiyama, pointing at the door. "There are much more impressive things around us to look at. Take your time, Mr. Coleman."

Kishiyama shepherded the group down the drive, engaging in some light conversation with a couple of them. Mitchell remained behind with Sean.

"Come here, Stretch," Sean said to Mitchell, directing the driver forward with a finger. "Lean over your bag so no rain gets on your equipment. I don't want to damage any of it."

Mitchell complied, his lanky torso providing adequate cover. Sean spread open the bag. Inside was a hodgepodge of mostly vintage radio parts: dials, knobs, speakers, power supplies, spindled wiring, and tubes—some still in their original boxes. There were also a couple of CB receivers, a guitar amplifier, and an old white kitchen radio that looked mostly intact. It may have been from the '50s or

'60s, its tuner shaped like the sun in mid-rise with stations ranging from 55 to 160.

"Quite a hobby you've got here," said Sean, gazing over the large collection. His lips curled into a bit of a grin. "My uncle . . . I mean, my father used to be into HAM radios quite a bit when I was a kid."

Mitchell nodded, his eyes meeting Sean's and finally showing a hint of warmth. "Me too," he muttered, his voice coarse.

"What?"

"Me too. I'm . . . into HAM radios."

Sean zipped the bag back up, nodding. "What's your handle?" he asked.

Mitchell glared back for a moment before answering. "Remnant."

"Remnant, huh?" he said. "Not bad. My father's was Ring of Fire. He was a Johnny Cash man."

Mitchell nodded. A nervous grin revealed crooked yellow teeth, including a big gap on the upper-right side of his mouth where two were missing.

"Well, you've got no cameras or video equipment of any kind, so we're good to go." Sean lifted himself to his feet, his knee popping as he handed the bag back to Mitchell. "Let's go on down and get out of the rain."

The men rejoined the rest of the group.

"I'll explain the meaning of some of these murals on our way out," Sean told the group, raising his head up at the cement walls.

As Sean dug through his pockets for his keys, he watched Kishiyama standing away from the others, his back to them. His hands were on his hips and his head was tilted upward, transfixed on the large dent at the top of the blast door. He wore a subtle grin. When he noticed Sean watching him, his head turned toward the image on the wall of the mole holding a missile in its paws. Sean pried out his key ring and unlocked the door. He pulled it wide.

The group tightened up, with people positioning their heads to get a look inside. When Sean entered, something crackled under his shoe—a small shard of glass from the broken beer bottle earlier. He pushed it off to the side with his foot.

"Come on in," Sean said, leaning against the tunnel wall and motioning the group forward. They stayed put, however, shifting their attention back and forth between the tunnel and Kishiyama, who was still examining the mural.

"Hello?" Sean said, his face tightening.

Kishiyama twisted his head toward them. "Oh, I'm sorry," he said with a grin. "I was just admiring the artwork. Yes, I would like to know more about these symbols later."

The group parted like the Red Sea, making room for Kishiyama, who walked to the front of the line. He nodded at Sean.

"All right then," Sean began, raising his voice. "This is the main entrance, where the five-man crew that manned this facility would enter and leave in twenty-four-hour shifts." He turned and made his way down the tunnel, followed by the echoes of a barrage of footsteps. "This single-use missile site was active from 1961 to 1965. It housed exactly one Atlas rocket and one warhead. The crew was in charge of monitoring the missile's status, and if called upon, they were prepared to initiate the entire . . ."

When the door slammed shut behind them, Sean sighed. He turned as he said, "No. Let's just leave that door open until we're—"

His eyes widened at the sight of a pistol pointed directly at his face. He gasped, his hands out in front of him and his heart pounding. "What the hell?"

The revolver, which looked to Sean like a Dan Wesson Supermag, was held by a member of the group standing directly behind Kishiyama. His hood no longer covered his head, revealing a bleach-blond crew cut and a toothpick sticking out of his mouth. The man's piercing hazel eyes didn't flinch as he held the gun steadily in both hands with his arms stretched over Kishiyama's shoulder.

"Just take it easy, Mr. Coleman," said Kishiyama, his voice cold and his face rigid. "There's no reason anyone needs to get hurt. In fact, we just saved your life."

Chapter 6

There was a flurry of movement behind the man with the gun. Raincoats were pulled from bodies and dropped to the floor in wet piles. Arms worked and sounded like gears in a large machine as metal components were snapped into place. When Sean saw a woman checking the action of a black revolver, his eyes went back to Kishiyama and the gunman.

"You all better put that shit away and leave before you get yourselves hurt," he warned, his nostrils flaring and his fists clenched.

Some within the group slowed their motions and turned their attention to Sean, their eyes marveling at his boldness.

"What kind of fucked up church is First Presbyterian anyway?" Sean added.

A smirk slowly developed on Kishiyama's face. "That's very amusing, Mr. Coleman. I must tell you that this wasn't the reaction I was expecting from you, given the circumstances. Where on earth does the county keep finding such fearless men?"

Sean glared back, unsure of his meaning.

"As I said," Kishiyama continued. "No one needs to get hurt. Not us. Not you. And if you do exactly as you're told, I promise the outcome will be quite preferable to the alternative."

"What the hell are you talking about?" Sean growled. "Why did you assholes come here? To steal something? There's nothing in this place worth stealing. It's an underground ghost town."

Even as the words left his mouth, Sean knew that burglary was unlikely the answer. What he was witnessing was a coordinated operation. Most of the group were now armed with handguns, glaring back at him in matching black t-shirts and black-and-gray camouflaged cargo pants. A couple of them held short semi-automatic rifles that they had somehow managed to conceal under their raincoats. Due to the narrowness of the tunnel and people lined up behind each other, Sean couldn't see everyone. Mitchell, however, was tall enough to stick out toward the back. He was standing by the door—likely the person who'd closed it. He was in the middle of tying a strip of black cloth around his head—a makeshift headband, possibly to keep his hair out of his eyes.

"There'll be plenty of time later to explain everything," said Kishiyama. "Right now, all I need from you are the keys in your pocket." He held out his hand as the man behind him leaned in closer, his gun bearing down on Sean.

Sean's own gun was back in his trailer. He never brought it along on the tour, per county rules. It crossed his mind for a moment to try and grab the pistol in his face, but he quickly dismissed the idea. Even if he could gain control of the firearm, someone else in the group could put him down with a single shot before he could use it. They couldn't miss at such close range. There wasn't a backdoor out of the complex, so no escape that way. Fighting back didn't make sense—not at this point anyway.

Sean scoffed and reached into his pocket.

"Slowly," Kishiyama warned.

Sean cautioned his movements as he dug for his key ring. The keys accessed just about every room and closet throughout the complex. Up top, they went to the front gate, the tractor, and a couple of maintenance sheds. How the group intended on using them, he didn't know.

When he held out the keys, Kishiyama reached for them, but Sean let them fall from his hand to the ground. He'd always wanted to do that—homage to a host of detective shows and action movies from the '80s.

"Fucking son of a bitch," the bleach-blond man with the gun muttered, his jaw squaring. Without a raincoat, his athletic build was now apparent. He gripped his weapon tightly as his eyes burned a hole through Sean.

"You kiss your mom with that mouth, church boy?" Sean quipped.

"Let's not even mess with this guy," the man told Kishiyama, shifting the toothpick to the opposite side of his mouth. "He'll be more trouble than he's worth."

Kishiyama lifted his hand, calling for restraint. "If it gets to that point, Gregory, we'll deal with it." He lowered to a knee to retrieve the keys. When he rose with them, he added, "Until that happens, remember why we're here."

"Which is why, exactly?" Sean asked.

"In good time, Mr. Coleman." Kishiyama stepped to the side and let the man he'd called Gregory slip in front of him. He began sorting through the keys in his hand. "Which ones go with the outside gates?"

Sean said nothing.

"Ah," said Kishiyama. "These two are labeled *gate*." He slid the keys off the ring and handed them to the woman behind him. She passed them down the line.

"Drive it around to the east entrance, Mitchell," ordered Kishiyama. "Make sure you lock up after yourself."

Mitchell nodded and opened the door. Light shone through the entrance for just a moment before he stepped outside and shut the door behind him.

"Turn around," Gregory told Sean.

"Why?"

"I'm going to frisk you."

"You wish," said Sean, snorting.

"Don't test me, asshole," said Gregory, his eyes serious. "Turn around and let's get this over with."

"Don't make this more difficult than it needs to be, Mr. Coleman," added Kishiyama. "It's not in your best interest."

Sean bit his lip and slowly turned around, placing the palms of his hands on the steel of the tunnel wall. He lowered his head and spread his legs. He felt one of Gregory's hands slide up and down the inside and outside of his thighs and then his ankles. Next came the underarms and rib cage.

"Getting off on this?" Sean said.

"Shut up," Gregory replied. He finished up. "Now take off your rain poncho."

Sean did, yanking it over his head and dropping it to the floor. Someone kicked it into the pile of raincoats the group had removed.

"Now go."

"Where?" asked Sean, lowering his hands.

"Down the tunnel. Toward the living quarters. And no sudden movements."

Sean offered Gregory a fleeting glare before biting his lip and heading deeper into the tunnel. Footsteps, adding to his own, followed him. No one spoke, other than the baby, who fussed a little and was shushed by its mother. The noise, echoing through the tunnel, was eerie in the midst of what was happening.

"What kind of assholes bring a baby into this?" Sean asked, raising his voice loud enough that the entire group could hear him. "You couldn't find a sitter before heading out to the fields to wave guns in someone's face?"

No one answered. When they reached the tunnel junction, the group filled the area. Two armed men blocked the opening they had just emerged from. Sean noticed that they were twins—identical. Both were of average build and height with their dark hair parted in the middle. They had their eyes on Sean, and so did Gregory, who stood just a few feet away, blocking the doorway to the shop area and missile bay. His gun was still out in front of him.

"Which one opens this up?" asked Kishiyama, pointing to the gate in front of the second tunnel. The keys were in his other hand.

"The short gold one," Sean answered.

As Kishiyama shuffled though the key ring, Sean shifted his eyes along the group, silently counting heads. There were nine people, not including the baby. Mitchell outside made ten. Six men and four women. The women were all thin brunettes, close in height, with long, unkempt hair. None wore makeup. Kishiyama was the oldest of everyone. The others looked like they were in their twenties. Early thirties, tops.

The light clanging of metal drew Sean's attention back to the gate.

"It doesn't fit," said Kishiyama, turning toward Sean.

"Oops," said Sean with a smirk, the false direction having given him enough time to better assess his captors as they stood in one spot.

"You smug son of a bitch," Gregory muttered.

Kishiyama rolled his eyes and tried a couple others until he found the right one. The lock released and the gate was pulled open. In calculated order, the women began holstering their weapons, and every man but the apparent father of the baby began handing their bags and backpacks over to every woman but the mother. Some of the women struggled under the weight of the additional straps over their shoulders, their torsos hanging at an angle.

Kishiyama raised his left arm and began pushing buttons on the side of a black digital watch on his wrist. It chirped with each command. "Find the rooms," he directed. "It's currently 5:14. Start to get things situated. You'll most certainly have to move some items around."

Confused by the implication, Sean watched silently as two of the women strained and shuffled their way past him, walking toward the doorway that led to the Launch Wing. The mother with her baby followed after them. The remaining woman walked, with similar difficulty, into the north tunnel that Kishiyama had just opened, toward the Command Wing.

Kishiyama turned to the twins. "Wait here. Open the blast door when Mitchell gets back. Not before. Guide him in."

"Good luck with that," said Sean, drawing all eyes to him.

"What do you mean?" Kishiyama said, irritation oozing from his voice.

"The blast door's busted. It won't open for you."

Kishiyama's face stiffened. His mouth slid open and his eyes met with Gregory's.

"You're lying," said Gregory, turning to Sean.

"Like hell I am. Try it for yourself. But when the motor starts shrieking, and it sends a chill up your spine like ten sets of fingernails on a chalkboard, don't say I didn't warn you. I hope getting that bus inside here isn't part of your master plan, because it ain't happening."

Kishiyama's nostrils flared as his eyes fell wayside. The group's purpose for being there seemed contingent on the blast door operating properly.

"Check the door," Kishiyama told the twins. "See if he's telling the truth." He turned to Sean. "This way." Kishiyama entered the north tunnel, not looking back.

"Move," ordered Gregory, shoving the barrel of his gun into Sean's back, directing him to follow.

Sean complied with Gregory following closely behind.

"Gregory," said Sean.

"What?"

"Nothing. I was just thinking about your name. Sounds snooty, like something some rich asshole parents would name their spoiled trust-fund kid who couldn't wipe his ass without their help."

A few seconds floated by before Gregory answered. "Just keep testing me, asshole."

Ahead of them, Kishiyama shook his head. His hand slid along the wall of the tunnel, as if he were admiring the hood of a classic car. His gaze lifted upward, following the row of lights along the ceiling. The three men crossed over a metal grate, spray-painted yellow. At the end of the tunnel, Kishiyama stood on the hollow platform and stared at the poster that hung on the wall beneath a half dozen rust-stained water pipes that split in different directions.

He nodded at the image of the tunnel's opening in its 1960s form, and then, without hesitation, crossed under the pipes, walked down the three steps, and went across the ramp toward the control room. The room was lit up as they strolled past it. Sean saw the woman inside. She was on her knees and digging through a backpack. They stepped onto the linoleum floor just outside of the kitchen area, which was now used as a storage room.

Kishiyama stopped and stood there for a moment with his back to Sean, his hands resting on his hips. His head glided back and forth from the archives room further down the hall to another blown-up picture on the wall. The large photograph was from many years ago—an image of the old kitchen when it was still in use. At its center were a trash can and water fountain, where a couple of file cabinets now stood. A couple stacks of cardboard boxes now sat where the image showed a refrigerator, an oven, and some pots and pans.

When Kishiyama turned, there was a grin on his face and a twinkle in his eye. Both quickly disappeared upon Sean's inquisitive gaze.

"You've been here before, haven't you," Sean said, more in the form of a statement than a question.

"Only in my imagination" said Kishiyama. "These days, you can get blueprints for the Atlas E right off the Internet. I must say, it's much different in person. The character. The nostalgic sense of patriotism. It's really quite impressive."

"Yeah, it's a real kick in the ass," Sean quipped. "But you didn't come here locked and loaded to reminisce about the '60s. And since there's little left in here militarily and technologically that you can't get off eBay, I'm assuming this has to be about the archives."

Kishiyama's eyes narrowed.

"Tell me," Sean continued. "Which county records are so important to you people that they're worth all of the laws you've broken today? Property deeds? Bank statements? What are you planning on leaving with?"

Gregory scoffed, shaking his head. "Can we at least muzzle this asshole?" he said to Kishiyama.

Kishiyama ignored the question, addressing Sean instead. "Why do you assume our plan is to steal something, Mr. Coleman?"

"Oh, I don't know. Maybe because people who break into places and wave guns around don't normally do it simply out of boredom. And since I don't have any rich parents like *Gregory* probably does, I'm guessing that kidnapping me and holding me for ransom isn't the plan either."

Kishiyama shook his head and took a breath. "We're not going to steal anything, and we're not looking for any form of compensation."

"Then what is it?"

Quick footsteps echoed through the tunnel, and one of the twins emerged from around the corner, out of breath. "He wasn't lying," he said, swallowing. He leaned forward and put a hand on his knee. "The blast door won't budge. We can't pull the bus inside. We're going to have to bring the food and everything else through the tunnel."

The food?

The woman in the control room poked her head through the doorway, homing in on the conversation. In her hands she held a rolled-up sleeping bag. It began to unravel after she pulled at the elastic strap around it. The opposite end of it spilled to the floor.

Sean's head spun to Kishiyama. "Oh, you've got to be shitting me."

Chapter 7

"This isn't the fucking YMCA, you idiots!" Sean roared, his head snapping from person to person. "If you were looking for somewhere to stay the night, there's a goddamn campsite right up top. You don't even have to pay to use it, and you sure as hell don't need guns!"

Kishiyama placed his hand to his face.

"How much more of his bullshit are we going to take?" Gregory said, head tilted to meet Kishiyama's line of sight.

The woman in the doorway, having dropped her sleeping bag to the floor, took a few steps forward. She brushed dark bangs from her brown eyes and raised her hand timidly, like a student vying for her teacher's attention.

The twin noticed her and cleared his throat to grab Kishiyama's attention. When Kishiyama turned, he looked the woman up and down before speaking. "Go ahead, Tammy."

"Maybe we should . . . bring him in. You know, into the circle." There was hesitation in her voice, and her head lowered in reverence once the words left her mouth. She had a hint of a Southern accent. "You always say that assimilation leads to innovation."

The twin subtly nodded, seemingly in agreement. His eyes were on Kishiyama.

Assimilation? Sean thought to himself.

Tammy continued. "He's a unique individual. I think we can already see that. He may have some talents that—"

Kishiyama quickly commanded her silence by raising his finger in the air. Sean couldn't see the expression on the leader's face with his back to him. Kishiyama crossed his arms behind his back, clasping one of his hands around the opposite one like a butler awaiting orders. He then nodded at Gregory, whose gun was still on Sean, and walked toward the woman. Just as she lifted her head to meet his eyes, his right arm swung forward. His open hand connected with her face, snapping her head to the side and sending a wicked echo through the corridor.

The twin's eyes shot wide. So did Sean's. Incensed, Sean clenched his teeth, formed fists, and made a beeline straight for Kishiyama. Gregory yelled for him to stop, but Sean pushed forward. He whisked past Gregory and heard Kishiyama shout "no" just before something heavy cracked against Sean's skull—the butt of Gregory's weapon. Sean stumbled down to a knee, pain rushing across his temple. He grabbed onto Gregory's forearm and yanked the gunman toward him.

"Fuck!" Gregory shouted, the toothpick falling from his mouth as he fought for control of his pistol. A second later, a different gun was leveled at Sean's face, and then another.

"Stop this now or they *will* shoot you!" Kishiyama shouted.

The sound of a pistol being cocked from just a few inches away drew Sean back into the scope of the situation. He cursed and unhooked his hands from Gregory, letting him pull his arm away.

"Real tough guy, hitting a woman," Sean grunted, his chest heaving in and out as he lifted his head.

One of the pistols aimed at him was held by the twin, whose wide eyes revealed only a hint of conflict. The sight of Tammy's face behind the other gun stole Sean's breath. Her hair was disheveled, her cheek was red, and her eyes burned though Sean with an intensity that resembled hatred more than gratitude. A stream of blood trickled from her nose to her upper lip.

Sean held her stare, searching for a sign of sentience behind it. He found none. He shook his head in disgust and slowly climbed back to his feet. Over her shoulder, he saw Kishiyama's face contort into a smirk.

"What are you guys? A fucking cult?"

"Not a cult, Mr. Coleman." Kishiyama answered as if he had been prepared for the question. "A tribe. A family. People brought together to serve a higher purpose."

"Like I said," answered Sean, wincing from his aching skull. "A cult." He twisted his head toward Gregory. Gregory glared back, his eyes narrow and his gun unwavering. "If you touch me again, you're not going to like what happens."

Gregory said nothing, but the hint of a grin washed over his face.

"Do you know the combination?" Kishiyama asked.

Sean's gaze shifted toward the ringleader. "What?"

"The vault door behind you. It looks operational. Do you know its combination?"

Kishiyama was referring to the entrance of the old generator room.

"We don't lock it. We don't even close it. The stuff the county keeps in there isn't any more important than the stuff in the other rooms. Less important, even."

"I don't care about that," replied Kishiyama. "What I care about is whether or not you know the combination."

"Answer him!" shouted Gregory.

Sean dismissed the henchman with an eye roll. "Yeah, I know the combination. Why should I give it to you?"

A grin returned to Kishiyama's face. "You don't need to give it to me. Not yet." He turned to the twin, whose eyes switched back and forth between the two. "Take over for Mitchell. Tell him to come back here, and to bring his tools."

The twin nodded, lowered his gun to his side, and disappeared down the tunnel. The remaining adherents kept their focus and weapons on Sean. Sean stared into the eyes of the woman, trying to imagine what could be going through her head as a minute or two of tense silence passed.

The returning echo of footsteps announced the emergence of Mitchell from the tunnel. He held a red metal toolbox in his hand and his eyes bounced around the room, taking inventory. His face tightened when he noticed the tender skin on Tammy's face. She paid him no mind.

"The fire alarms and phone line have been disabled, I assume," said Kishiyama.

Mitchell nodded. "His car too."

"You touched my car?" Sean said with arched eyebrows.

"Good," said Kishiyama. "Go inside the vault. See if there's anything else in there we need to be concerned about. If so, take care of it."

Mitchell nodded and complied. Once beyond the vault door, he took a quick turn to the right and disappeared out of sight.

"What's your monkey boy doing in there?" Sean asked, his arms now crossed in front of his chest. "Setting up a picnic table to serve your Kool-Aid on? Maybe you can find a pitcher in the old kitchen."

"This isn't about death, Mr. Coleman," said Kishiyama. "It's about life." The moment the words left his mouth, both Gregory and the woman slid their eyes to their leader. They subtly nodded.

Sean glanced back and forth at the two of them. "Well, that's creepy as hell," he muttered, turning his attention back to the vault door.

Mitchell soon re-emerged, standing just inside the doorway. His eyes met Sean's for a brief moment before they went to Kishiyama. "Nothin' to worry about," he said.

"Good."

Kishiyama turned to the woman and whispered something in her ear. She nodded and jogged into the command station. She returned seconds later with her fingers wrapped around the handle of a plastic gallon milk jug. It was full of clear liquid, its weight angling her shoulder. Kishiyama took it from her and tossed it through the air to Sean, who reflexively caught it.

"What's this?"

"I assure you it isn't Kool-Aid," Kishiyama answered. "Just water. Compliments of the house."

"I'm not thirsty."

"You will be. Now turn around and step inside the vault."

Sean scoffed. "What are you talking about?"

"It's going to be your home for the next few hours while we continue doing what we need to do. As interesting of a fellow as you've revealed yourself to be, we can't afford to waste any more time on your antics."

"Antics," Sean said, shaking his head. He scoffed and let the jug fall from his hand to the floor. "I'm not going in there."

Kishiyama shook his head in annoyance. "I would think you would be grateful, Mr. Coleman. It's one of the largest rooms in the facility. Plenty of air. Privacy. Lots of books to choose from, if you get bored. Granted, legally binding contracts aren't a particularly exciting genre. We'd move you to different quarters, but something tells me that a room with a regular office door wouldn't hold you for very long, and we really are quite busy."

"Sorry. Not happening."

Kishiyama nodded. "I know what you're thinking. 'What guarantee do I have that they'll let me out later?' Well, you don't have a guarantee. Just my word."

"Your word," Sean sneered. "Fifteen minutes ago you were a church congregation that wanted to tour a missile silo. Now you're armed squatters threatening to shoot me if I don't comply with your bullshit."

"If our preference were to kill you, you'd already be dead. Think about that."

Sean said nothing, letting Kishiyama's words trickle through his mind.

"The room isn't soundproof, correct?" Kishiyama continued. "We'll be able to hear you from inside if you yell, including when we later ask you for the door combination. It will be entirely up to you whether or not we let you out of there. So those are your choices: a temporary coffin or a permanent one."

His arms still crossed in front of his chest, Sean scanned the room. His eyes landed for a moment on each of its occupants. He read the seriousness in their faces. He twisted his head toward Mitchell, who was still standing in the vault doorway. The tall man nodded, using whatever brief rapport he believed he'd built with Sean earlier to urge him to comply. Sean took in a deep breath and turned to Kishiyama.

"You *are* going to let me out, right? I have your word?"

"Of course," Kishiyama answered. "We're not sadists."

Sean squared his jaw and nodded, unfolding his arms. "Fine."

The moment Sean felt some tension in the small room ease, his eyes narrowed and he subtly shifted his weight to his left foot. In a heartbeat, he twisted his body and launched his nearly 250-pound frame straight toward the vault door. He targeted Mitchell like he did a quarterback as a defensive tackle back in high school.

Mitchell's eyes shot wide with shock and then horror, unable to process what was happening before Sean's open hand slammed into his chest like a battering ram. Mitchell toppled backward to the floor. Panicked orders flew from Kishiyama's mouth as Sean hooked the edge of the doorway with his hand. He flew inside the archives room, yanking the heavy door and slamming it shut behind him.

The momentum sent him toppling to the floor beside Mitchell, just as pops of gunfire sounded from the other side of the door.

Chapter 8

Bullets had peppered the other side of the door, but not so much as a dent could be seen from Sean's side. He scrambled to his knees and verified that it had indeed locked as designed.

"You stupid son of a bitch!" Gregory snarled from the other side. His voice was barely audible, as was the pounding of his fist on the door.

Sean quickly moved over to Mitchell, who was in a daze, having hit the back of his head against the floor. The tall man tried to pull himself upright, but Sean shoved him back down and straddled him. Grabbing him by the shirt collar, he pulled Mitchell up a few inches before landing a wicked punch to the side of his head. And then another. Mitchell went limp in his grip, and Sean let his head fall back to the floor. He ran his hands up and down the man's legs, then under his arms and along his sides. All he found were some keys and assorted junk in his pockets. No weapons.

"Shit," Sean said, sucking wind and wincing from his racing heart.

He pulled himself to his feet, nearly tripping over Mitchell's toolbox as he lumbered back to the door. He wiped beaded sweat from his hairline. "Sorry assholes!" he shouted with his face twisted in a vengeful smile. His hands went flat against the door. "Your word ain't worth dick!"

Mitchell was an important man in Kishiyama's outfit. Of that, Sean was sure. He was their technical guy. Whatever the group was planning, he was a key part of it.

"That was a stupid, stupid thing to do!" came Kishiyama's muffled voice. "Give me the combination right now, or . . ."

"Or what?" Sean roared back. "You'll piss and moan some more about it? Don't worry, I'll keep your boy good company. He won't be bored in here. Maybe I'll even get a few answers out of him!"

There was silence for a moment.

"Mitchell!" Gregory shouted. "Are you okay?"

"He'll be fine," Sean answered. "He's just catching up on a little beauty sleep."

"Don't hurt him, do you hear me? Mitchell, if you can hear me, don't tell him anything!"

The distress in Kishiyama's voice brought a smirk to Sean's face. He liked hearing the previously confident leader out of sorts.

"Don't you worry," Sean shouted. "I'll take real good care of him. I'll let you know when I'm ready to come out."

Something slammed against the door, probably someone's foot in frustration.

Sean dropped to a knee and unfastened the clips on Mitchell's toolbox. He opened the lid. It was full of screwdrivers, pliers, wrenches, wire cutters, and what he'd hoped to find: a roll of duct tape. He removed the tape, and his heart skipped a beat when he saw the small device that had been under it. Mounted to small, thin circuit board was the face of a digital wristwatch and a nine-volt battery. Three wires stemmed from the board. Two belonged to the battery connector. The third, green in color, twisted around to the back of the device. It appeared to be a detonator.

Sean cautioned his movements, swallowing some bile and twisting his head at an angle. He lowered himself closer to the floor, and followed the green wire with his eyes. He breathed a sigh of relief when he saw that the other end wasn't connected to anything. There were, however, two other similar devices underneath it—one with another wristwatch and one with a small, retractable antenna. He closed the box and turned his attention back to Mitchell.

Sean dragged the henchman's lanky body along the floor by the ankles, between the towering storage shelves that reached almost to the ceiling. Mitchell's headband slid off his skull as Sean brought him to the back of the room. There, he wouldn't be able to hear the yells of his people, and they wouldn't hear his. Sean pulled him up to a sitting position against a corner post at the end of the last row of shelves. He wrapped his wrists together with duct tape on the opposite side of the post. He strapped his ankles together and used more tape to secure his torso to the post. Mitchell wasn't going anywhere.

"Hey!" Sean barked, squatting and using the back of his knuckles to slap the side of Mitchell's face. "Wake up!"

It took almost a minute of the treatment before Mitchell's swollen eyelids finally started to flutter. When they opened a bit, he glared blankly at Sean through long threads of blonde hair.

"Morning, sunshine," Sean greeted.

"It's mornin'?" Mitchell muttered, wincing in confusion.

"No, it's just a figure of . . ." Sean stopped himself and shook his head. "Listen. I want answers and I want them right now. What are you people doing here? What are you all hoping to gain?"

Mitchell blinked. His glazed eyes—the skin above them discolored from Sean's fists—floated over Sean's shoulder. He was still adjusting to his new surroundings, but Sean was running out of patience. He grabbed a handful of his captive's hair and pulled back on it, lifting his chin and forcing their eyes to meet.

"Mitchell!" Sean yelled, leaning forward. He enunciated each word slowly. "Why . . . are . . . you . . . here?"

Mitchell's nostrils flared. He twisted his shoulders, quickly realizing how immobile he was. He shook his head. "You wouldn't . . . You wouldn't get it," he groaned. "You *couldn't* get it."

"Try me."

"Not your fault. You . . . you don't know of the prophecy. What we're doing . . . What we're doing will help you."

Sean's eyes narrowed. He let go of Mitchell's hair. "What prophecy? What kind of bullshit has Kishiyama filled your head with?" He flicked his finger against Mitchell's forehead for good measure.

"Not bullshit. And not by Kishiyama," said Mitchell before letting out a cough. Some bloodied spit spilled from his mouth. "He's a messenger. An organizer." His face tightened. "What did you do to him—to the others?"

"I didn't do dick to them. Your buddies in the Ya-Ya Brotherhood are on the other side of the door, probably getting ready to sacrifice a goat or something. It's just you and me until you start making some sense."

Mitchell's head lowered to the floor. His chest heaved in and out. "It won't keep 'em out. They need me. I need to be with 'em when it's time." The words stumbled out with his breath.

Sean growled and grabbed Mitchell by his shirt collar again. Mitchell's head shot upward, his eyes wide in fear and his mouth dangling open.

"When it's time for *what?*" Sean demanded. He could feel Mitchell's body trembling in his grip.

Mitchell spread his lips, as if he were about to say something, but no words came out. Instead, he turned his head to the side and squared his jaw, breathing through his nose as his chest throbbed in and out.

When Sean cocked his arm and closed his fingers into a fist, Mitchell shut his eyes, seemingly prepared to take whatever beating Sean was prepared to dish out.

Mitchell began muttering something in a whisper—a sentence. "What I do, I do for humanity." He repeated it over and over, his eyes still closed.

Sean's fist shook as he glared at Mitchell. He had never had any qualms in the past with knocking people around to get what he wanted, but with Mitchell it felt wrong, even with the seriousness of the situation. Mitchell was like a child—a person of weak mind who'd been brainwashed into some kind of doctrine. Whatever cause was at play, Mitchell assuredly believed to his core that it was of great, perhaps even noble, importance. When Sean noticed a tear beginning to form at the corner of Mitchell's eye, his desire to pummel him continued to dwindle.

"Shit!" Sean snarled, releasing Mitchell and pulling himself up to his feet. He took a few steps back and stared at his captive.

Mitchell's eyes opened, blinking in disbelief as he lifted his head toward Sean. Air poured in and out of his mouth as he assessed Sean's change in demeanor.

"Whatever voodoo bullshit you believe in, Mitchell," Sean began, pacing back and forth, "you're all going to go down hard for this. That man who orders you around—Kishiyama—he's a bad guy. He hit one of your women out there just for having the nerve to question him."

Mitchell's face tightened. His eyes lowered.

Sean took a deep breath, letting the air settle in his chest before releasing it. In formulating his next move, his mind flipped like a photobook through various detective television shows until it landed on *NYPD Blue*. Having abandoned the Andy Sipowicz strong-arm method, it was time for the cerebral collectiveness of Detective John Kelly.

"Your future is going to be behind bars for many years if this doesn't end right now," he said calmly, tilting his head. "Two of your friends out there have a little baby. That baby's going to grow up without them. Is that what you want?"

Mitchell shook his head. "That ain't gonna happen."

Sean continued. "So far you people have only broken into a county facility, but whatever you're planning on doing with all these weapons is going to take this situation to a whole different level. Understand?"

"You ain't gettin' it," groaned Mitchell. "None of that's gonna matter. Everything's gonna change." His voice grew higher.

Sean's eyes narrowed. He let Mitchell's words bounce around in his head for a few seconds. "A minute ago, you were saying that you're doing this for humanity. What does humanity get out of a bunch of people setting up camp inside an old missile silo?"

Mitchell lifted his head. His eyes held Sean's. Seconds that felt like minutes floated by. "A do-over."

Sean placed his hands on his hips and stuck out his chest. "A do-over?" he said, shaking his head in confusion. "Because humanity somehow got it wrong the first time around?"

After a moment, Mitchell answered. "Maybe." His face went deadpan. "But that doesn't matter none either."

Sean sighed and turned his attention to a row of large boxes against the wall behind him. They were set up in stacks of two—each box a three-foot cube. He grunted and pushed off a top box. It fell to its side in a heap, large binders filled with paper spilling out along the floor. He then dragged the bottom box over to Mitchell and took a seat on top of it. He folded his arms, scowling down at the man.

He took another deep breath. As he weighed everything he'd seen over the past thirty minutes, a broader picture began to emerge in Sean's mind. He leaned forward, spreading his legs a little and resting his elbows on his knees. His face softened.

"I'm from a little mountain town about two and a half hours from here," Sean said, drawing furrowed eyebrows from Mitchell. "Winston. I know you haven't heard of it. Not many have. The few people that live there are pretty isolated from the rest of the world, not just by the mountains, but also by the culture. Nobody has a cell phone. Only a handful of television channels come in, and you need an antenna to get those. The fashion scene is whatever you can find at the general store."

Mitchell listened intently.

"Things move slowly in Winston," Sean continued. "The simple life. No real crime. No one's worried about some Al-Qaeda asshole running into one of the shops and blowing himself up. It's its own little community, protected from the dangers and ugliness of the outside world."

Mitchell subtly nodded.

"Is that why you're all here? To seek refuge? To start your own little community? Maybe those guns are a big 'keep out' sign to the rest of the world. If that's the case, I can totally understand that." Sean bit the inside of his cheek to keep his face serious. His John Kelly—complete with lowered head and raised eyes—would have impressed even David Caruso.

Mitchell swallowed. "That's . . . part of it."

Sean unclenched his jaw and let the grin flow through. "Okay then. I get that. I can respect that."

The corners of Mitchell's lips curled slightly. He nodded.

"And I'm starting to believe that we have more in common that I first thought," said Sean, letting his eyes slide off of Mitchell. "Listen, I didn't take this job for the money, you know. It doesn't pay shit. I stay in that little trailer, but I spend a lot of time down here in the barracks, away from people. Honestly, people have been pissing me off for a long time."

An unexpected chuckle escaped Mitchell's mouth. He pressed his lips together, muffling it.

Sean grinned and added a wink. "It's quiet here—peaceful."

"Does it get lonely?" Mitchell asked.

The question surprised Sean, but he welcomed it, seeing it as a sign that his captive was opening up. "Sometimes. That dog up top keeps me company. Dogs are loyal. Loyal people are harder to find, but you strike me as someone who values loyalty."

Mitchell's face turned sober. "We'll wanna get your dog and bring 'im down here. It's safe down here. He'll need to stay with me. I'll keep 'im safe."

Sean's eyes narrowed. "Okay. I appreciate that. We'll do that."

Mitchell nodded.

Sean had learned long ago that the most convincing cons were those laced with reality, and for that reason, he had opened up a bit about his own life. With the empathy play seemingly taking hold, he decided to delve deeper.

"So like I said, I think I see where you and your friends are coming from, but there's a part of it that I'm having trouble with."

"Which part?" asked Mitchell.

Sean proceeded carefully. "Well, I happened to look through your toolbox, and I found what appear to be detonators."

Mitchell gulped and looked away.

Sean continued. "I'm trying to think of why you and your friends would need those. You keep saying that you're here for humanity, and I'm trying to understand that argument, but I don't get how explosives fit in."

Mitchell kept his eyes off Sean. "Who said we have explosives?"

"Oh, come on now, Mitchell," Sean said, keeping his tone friendly. "What's the point of having detonators if you don't have explosives? Are they still out in the bus?"

Mitchell said nothing.

Sean unfolded his arms and leaned forward. "Listen. As Kishiyama himself has said a few times now, you're not here to hurt people. You're here to *help*. So who is helped by blowing something up?"

Mitchell didn't budge.

"Come on, Mitchell. Help me understand. We don't have to be on opposite sides of this. As Kishiyama says, assimilation leads to innovation."

Mitchell's attention turned back to Sean, his eyebrows arched. "Kishiyama told you that?"

Sean nodded, remembering all too well that it was actually Tammy who'd let the leader's motto slip when Mitchell was outside, and she had paid for that mistake with a bloody nose.

"Talking to you right now," Sean said, "you don't strike me as a guy who wants anyone to get hurt."

"That's right, I don't," Mitchell answered defensively, his shoulders raising as he tried to sit up a bit.

"Then all I'm asking is that you explain it to me. Why the explosives? Make me understand. If this is all in my best interest, let me in on it. I can help you people if you just . . ."

"To dig ourselves out after the earth changes!" Mitchell sputtered. The second the words left his mouth, his eyes closed and he lowered his head in apparent shame.

Sean's mouth was left dangling open. His chest tensed and his arms fell to his sides. A dozen new questions entered his mind. "Mitchell, I—"

An intensely loud crash belted out from the other corner of the room, shaking the floor and bringing Sean to his feet. The sound was hollow and hummed for a moment like an aftershock of metal colliding with metal. As a loose piece of paper floated down from one of the shelves high above, Mitchell lifted his head to meet Sean's glare.

"I told you they needed me," he said.

Chapter 9

Sean raced down the aisle toward the east wall. When he rounded the corner, he gasped at the sight of the lower portion of the vault door bent a few inches inward, near its hinges. Before Sean could better assess the damage, the metal buckled again, a loud clang echoing off the walls. The steel door was being taken down like a castle gate with a battering ram. A muffled back-up beeper meant that the intruders had found the forklift.

It was a gas-powered model. A Cat. Sean had parked it in one of the other storage rooms a few days earlier, after using it to make room on an upper shelf for some old voting machines the county didn't want to throw away. The vehicle wasn't built to take down barriers, but it was doing enough damage to the door that Sean knew it would only be a matter of time before Kishiyama and his people could squeeze through the opening or break away the hinges and gain entry. And there was nothing he could do to stop them.

"They're comin' in, Sean," shouted Mitchell from down the hallway, "whether you like it or not. It's best to just wait here with me, and not fight 'em!"

Sean paid Mitchell's warning little attention, but his captive's prior statements were still fresh in his mind. *After the earth changes.* Before that, he'd spoken of prophecies and a *do-over* for humanity. Sean had gathered that Mitchell's group was trying to isolate itself from society, but it was more than that—much more. They were preparing to ride out the *end* of society.

"Trapped in here with a bunch of goddamned doomsdayers," Sean muttered.

The people coming in through the vault door were mentally deranged—it was the only explanation Sean could come up with. They somehow believed the end of the world was upon them, and that they'd be spared by living underground.

The forklift slammed into the door again, and a chunk of the cement frame above it crumbled. Sean didn't have any weapons to fight back against guns, but he might have some leverage—or so he hoped.

He clenched his jaw and ran toward the door, stopping just short of it where Mitchell's toolbox still lay on the floor. He flipped it open and took the three detonators from its hull. He scanned the large room, his eyes shifting to some tall file cabinets along the east wall.

"First place they'd look," he muttered. He'd need to hide them somewhere that wasn't obvious—somewhere obscure.

His eyes slid across rows of stacked boxes until he noticed one of the eight-foot-high mobile staircases parked halfway down the aisle. It was two aisles over from where Mitchell was bound. Sean raced toward it, the detonators clasped in his hand. From where he was, Mitchell couldn't see him. Neither could anyone who managed to squeeze their head through the door's twisted metal.

The staircase was typically used for reaching mid-level records, but Sean had a different purpose in mind. He hooked his arm around its side railing and towed the contraption behind him as he moved farther down the hallway. The wheels made some clamor, but the noise from the forklift provided some cover. He pushed it against the shelving to his left, locked its brakes with his foot, and hustled up its steps.

"Sean?" Mitchell cried. "Whatever you're doing, don't fight 'em!"

Sean reached the top of the stairs and stood on his tiptoes. He set the detonators down on the third rack of shelves between two clusters of boxes. Using the staircase's handrail as an additional step, he stood on it with both feet before pulling himself up onto the rack with a grunt.

The shelves were thick and strong, capable of supporting a great deal of weight—including Sean's. Still, the wood creaked and groaned as he slid along his chest. He pulled himself up to his hands and knees and grabbed the detonators. He glanced down at the floor about fifteen feet below before scrambling behind a stack of beat-up boxes. Each of the boxes was about three feet wide by a foot and a half tall, stamped with the words, "Survival Supplies Furnished by the Office of Civil Defense."

He'd relocated the boxes during Mahan's last visit, so he knew what was in them: old fallout-shelter food canisters. Moving quickly, Sean lifted the flaps of one of the boxes, revealing two eighteen-pound tins, side by side. Both were still factory-sealed.

"Shit," Sean grunted, pushing the box aside and grabbing the next one.

Another two canisters, marked "Carbohydrate Supplement," sat inside. One had been pried open with a crowbar. Sean had done it himself out of curiosity during the move.

He peeled the lid back some more, revealing hard, round candy about half an inch in diameter and red and yellow in color filling about three fourths of the container. It had been filled higher a few weeks earlier, before Sean had done some sampling. The candy was surprisingly tasty for being as old as the man who was now using his hands to dig a hole through them in order to make room for the detonators. He shoved the detonators to the bottom and let the sweets fall back in around them, but not before reflexively popping three pieces into his mouth. He moved the lid back in place as he crunched the candy with his teeth.

There was another wicked shot from the forklift as Sean moved the box to the bottom of the stack. His chest tightened when he heard a loud voice that wasn't Mitchell's.

He didn't know if the others were prepared to enter, or if they had already gotten inside. Either way, he was out of time. He climbed to his feet, squared his jaw, and leapt from the rack to the staircase's platform below. His momentum nearly took him over the side of the railing, but he held onto it and regained his balance.

"Crawl over me and get in there!" he heard a man instruct. The voice sounded like Kishiyama's.

Sean scrambled down the stairs, skipping most of the steps. When he yanked on the railing, its wheels dug into the floor.

"Brakes!" he gasped before releasing them.

He shoved the staircase to the opposite side of the aisle, just as he heard rapid footsteps clapping along the floor. Sean ran away from them, toward the west wall. He slid around the aisle and crossed another one to where Mitchell was.

Mitchell flinched when Sean appeared on the side opposite of where he'd left. He wondered if Mitchell's scrutinizing eyes noticed his out-of-breath state.

Sean raised his hands in the air as if he'd just been called on to do so by a police officer. He gazed down the aisle, waiting. Gregory soon appeared.

"Freeze, asshole!" he yelled, his gun aimed at Sean. One of his eyes was clasped shut as he held his target in his sights.

"Frozen," Sean sarcastically confirmed. He did his best to tamp down his breathing.

Behind Gregory came the twin, and then Tammy, all three sucking wind as they pointed their weapons forward. They began carefully edging their way toward him, intermittently glancing along the aisle as they did, perhaps suspicious that Sean had set some kind of trap.

Kishiyama soon appeared behind them, brushing dust from his shirt before his tense face lifted to meet Sean's. He raised his arm and glanced at his wristwatch, his face tightening.

"He didn't hurt me," Mitchell bellowed out, prompting a surprised glance from Sean. "I'm okay."

"No one asked," grunted Gregory, keeping his focus on Sean. Mitchell's head lowered.

Each step the group took was deliberate. They eased to a stop when they got within a few feet of Sean.

"Mr. Coleman," Kishiyama began. "Place your hands behind your head and interlace your fingers."

Sean glared back, taking a moment before complying.

Gregory moved forward, nostrils flaring.

"Gregory?" Kishiyama said, stopping him in his tracks.

"What?" he growled.

"Don't hurt him. Just secure him. Hand me your gun."

Gregory clenched his teeth and seemed to weigh the order for a moment before nodding and returning to Kishiyama. He handed him the gun, which Kishiyama immediately trained on Sean. Gregory moved in behind Sean and proceeded with the same pat down as before, but with sharper, rougher movements.

"He doesn't have a weapon," Mitchell said.

"Shut up, Mitchell," said Gregory.

Once finished, Gregory took a step back and planted a hard stomp from the sole of his shoe just above Sean's right calve. Sean's right leg buckled and he fell to a knee.

"Asshole," Sean grunted as he moved his other knee to the floor.

A loud tear of duct tape was followed by Sean's arms being pulled down behind him and held together. Gregory held the roll Sean had used to secure Mitchell, wrapping the tape tightly, multiple times, around his wrists. When he was finished, Kishiyama turned to Tammy and the twin.

"You two get back to work. We have this."

Tammy nodded and lowered her weapon. The twin was more uncertain and looked with hesitation at the leader. When Kishiyama pointed his chin toward the exit, the twin nodded and lowered his gun. He and Tammy jogged back down the aisle and disappeared around the corner. Kishiyama waited for a few moments, seemingly assuring they had left the room, before turning to Mitchell with his hands on his hips.

Mitchell twisted his body to the side as best he could, trying to give his rescuers better access to the tape that bound him. Neither moved to help.

"What did you tell him?" asked Kishiyama, his face expressionless.

Mitchell's face shifted nervously from Kishiyama to Gregory, and then to Sean.

Kishiyama repeated the question, adding emphasis to each word. *"What did you tell him?"*

"Nothing," Sean interrupted, drawing all eyes to him. "The idiot hit his head when I tackled him. He went face-first to the concrete and knocked himself out cold. He woke up just as you guys were coming through the door."

Expressionless, Kishiyama's gaze floated back to Mitchell. He examined Mitchell's beaten face. "Is that true?"

Mitchell lowered his face like a frightened child being interrogated by his father over a broken window. "No," he finally said.

"You little . . ." Sean said in disgust, shaking his head.

Mitchell kept his head down as he spoke. "He knows we're usin' this place as a . . . as a shelter—for the long haul."

Kishiyama's jaw clenched. He closed his eyes and twisted his neck a little until there was a subtle pop. "And the prophecy? Does he know about the prophecy?"

Mitchell looked up in alarm. "No!" Then he swallowed. "But he knows about the explosives, and why we brought 'em."

"Jesus Fucking Christ!" Gregory sneered. "You weren't even in here that long with him! How in the hell . . ."

He stopped when Kishiyama raised his hand. "So he knows what we're doing but not why?"

"Yes," Mitchell said nervously, nodding his head. "Maybe we should tell him—tell 'im the prophecy."

"Careful, Mitchell," Sean broke in. "Talk like that will get you smacked around. That is, unless Kishiyama only hits girls."

"Shut up," said Gregory, bouncing the back of his hand off Sean's head.

"*You* shut up," Sean responded.

"Everyone shut up!" Kishiyama screamed with clenched fists, commanding the room's attention "You all sound like children!" His voice echoed off the walls as the other three stared at him, taken back by the sudden burst of emotion. Mitchell cringed.

Kishiyama puffed out his chest and took a deep breath. When he spoke again, his voice was level. "Mitchell, if he doesn't know about the prophecy, how does he know about the explosives?"

"I found your detonators," Sean answered before Mitchell had a chance to.

Kishiyama and Gregory both swung their heads to Sean, and then to each other.

"They were in Mitchell's toolbox," Sean added. "Now, tell me about this prophecy . . ."

Kishiyama ignored the request. "What do you mean they *were* in Mitchell's box?" Sean could almost see tension spilling from the man's pores.

Sean's lips curled. "Oh, I don't know. What *do* I mean?" He displayed a half grin, having successfully emulated a wisecrack he'd seen Bruce Boxleitner use on an old episode of *Scarecrow and Mrs. King*.

The leader's right eyelid twitched. "Gregory, go check. The box was on the floor near where we came in."

As Gregory sprinted down the aisle, Kishiyama asked Mitchell if he had indeed kept the detonators in his toolbox. Mitchell reluctantly nodded. Gregory soon returned.

"The detonators aren't in there!" he shouted from the end of the corridor. "Just tools!"

Kishiyama snarled and stepped forward, planting the barrel of his gun against Sean's head. "This isn't a game," he threatened. "No more bullshit. Tell me where they are or I *will* shoot you."

"If you kill me, you're not going to find them," said Sean, showing his teeth.

"It's just one room," Kishiyama answered, seething. "There's a lot of space and clutter in here, but it's just one fucking room. It may take us some time, but we *will* find them, with or without you."

"Then what are you waiting for, dickhead?" Sean taunted, pressing his forehead deeper into the barrel and glaring at his captor.

Kishiyama's eyes widened. "I thought you were brave before, Mr. Coleman. Maybe you're just crazy."

"Yeah, maybe," answered Sean, his eyes still ablaze. "But I'm not the guy who broke into an old missile silo because he thinks the world's going to—"

"What's that?" Kishiyama interrupted, his eyes blinking with uncertainty. He spread his nostrils and leaned toward Sean, taking in air through his nose.

"What's what?" Sean asked sharply.

"That smell . . ."

Before he could continue, a loud voice echoed from the opposite corner of the room, close to the vault entrance. "There's someone outside! Snooping around!"

Chapter 10

She held her delicate hands tightly to her ears on the bay floor as the others tried again to get the blast door working. The cry of grinding metal echoed off tall, dreary cement walls that were discolored with age and moisture. The only movement came from a long rattling chain that spanned the door's width, about five feet off the ground. The door would not budge.

When the twins finally gave up—one of them throwing his hands in the air—she sighed and turned her back to the door, facing the large, eerie bay. She rubbed her tired eyes with her palms and made her way toward the exhaust area. Kishiyama had explained time after time that the crater in the floor ahead was the deepest, best protected chamber in the entire facility. Accessible only by a steel ladder bolted into the concrete, it was where fire and fury would have thrust downward from the site's missile had the United States ever gone to nuclear war with the commies.

She wasn't old enough to appreciate the seriousness of the Cold War—not the way her parents' generation did. But even with the benefit of history, the era struck her as a simpler time. At least people back then understood the threat they were facing. It was taught to children in schools and broadcast on television and radio. Some families even built underground bunkers in their backyards, as depicted in one of the drawings pinned to the walls. It showed a mother and father sorting through canned goods on shelves as their children slept in bunkbeds. The drawing hung slightly crooked, flanked by large maps, diagrams, and other photos of the earlier time.

A nuclear fallout would have been a horror, but the preparation would have at least given them a fighting chance. That wouldn't be the case this time. Only those who'd heard and believed in the prophecy would be ready—people like her and those she'd arrived with. They were taking action. The rest of the world didn't even know the name of their ultimate enemy, let alone its capabilities—an enemy far more destructive than the Soviets could have ever hoped to be.

Nibiru.

Above her, spanning most of the bay's ceiling, was an enormous steel cradle that once held the site's missile and its warhead. The cradle, secured by industrial arms and hinges painted bright yellow, was branded with a US Air Force star and a designation of "34E."

She strolled below it, taking a moment to stretch her back and gaze over some old medical equipment along the west wall. Kishiyama had said that decades ago, the site had also served as some kind of emergency medical center, maybe for the occasional farmer or others traveling through the Colorado boonies. An old wheelchair and an army-green gurney—relics of the era—now stood on display for museum visitors. Next to them was a pale-blue metal chair with a round, rotating seat that looked like it could have been used for dental work. Its headrest, supported by a bar attached to its backrest, appeared to be built more for restraint than comfort.

On a table in front of it all sat a glass display case. It held rusted scissors, pliers, and clamps. Beside them were injection needles, small boxes, and tin canisters. One of the boxes read "Family Radiation Measuring Kit." Another housed tiny tubes of sterile water. A can was labeled "Waterless Hand Cleaner."

To her left were large steel drums marked "Drinking Water" and some good-sized metal chests. One was labeled "X-Ray" in a stenciled font.

When she reached a short staircase, she climbed up to a steel platform and peered over a guardrail at the darkened exhaust pit below. *This will be home for a while. Hopefully not forever.* A dank odor drifted up from its depth, and a chill jetted up her spine. She latched onto the railing, finding herself feeling lightheaded for a moment.

She believed in her soul that the substructure would keep them all safe. Kishiyama assured them that it would. But at that moment, it felt like little more than a coffin.

"There's someone on the grounds!" The voice rang out behind her. "Inside the fence!"

Her heart leapt from her chest as she spun around. Her hand went to the Dan Wesson revolver holstered at the waistline of her cargo pants. She nearly dropped the gun when she pulled it out, leaping from the platform and racing after the brisk, echoing footsteps that funneled toward the doorway in the adjoining room.

Chapter 11

Gregory had one hand on the back of Sean's shirt collar and the other latched onto his bound wrists as he quickly escorted him up the north tunnel.

"Who's up there?" Kishiyama demanded, following closely behind. His gun was pointed at the back of Sean's head.

"I don't know," Sean muttered. "No one else was on the schedule tonight." Sean's thoughts raced to those who were there earlier in the day. *Sofia? Big Mike or Budweiser Mike? Could one of them have left something behind?* Another possibility was that Lumbergh had come back to talk some more. *He'd have a gun.*

"Morgan says he's inside the fence!" Gregory shouted in Sean's ear, spraying it with spit. "It's not just some camper looking for a roll of toilet paper."

"None of your friends have a key?" Kishiyama asked.

"I don't have any friends."

"Then who the fuck is it?" Gregory yelled.

Sean grunted and stopped in his tracks, planting his feet. The others bumped into him. He spun his head toward them and said, "Maybe Mitchell forgot to lock the gate when he brought the bus in. Did you guys think about that?"

The lone pair of footsteps following behind came to an abrupt halt as well. "No!" insisted Mitchell, out of breath. "I know I locked it. Both the entrances. Both gates. I double-checked!"

One of the twins made his way toward them, a rifle looped over his shoulder. He was out of breath.

"Morgan says it's just one guy," said the twin. "He hid down in the driveway when he heard the guy's car pull up. He didn't see what he was driving, but the guy opened the gate and came right on in." The twin lifted his finger and pointed it at Sean. "He's out there calling this guy's name. Morgan said he sounds pissed."

"Who is he?" Kishiyama asked Sean.

Sean grunted. "It's got to be my supervisor. The asshole drops by here unannounced from time to time to check on things."

"Everyone's back inside now, right?" Kishiyama asked of the twin, who answered with a nod of his head. "Good. Go to the bay, get everyone together, tell them what's going on, and tell them to shut up until you all hear from me."

The twin nodded and jogged back down the way he came, skirting the access tunnel and disappearing through the bay entry.

"Can you get rid of him?" Kishiyama asked Sean.

"Not if he saw your fucking bus in the driveway, and it's a safe bet that by now, he has."

"Would he call anyone?" Kishiyama pressed. "The authorities— upon seeing the bus?"

Sean knew the answer to be a definitive no. Instead, Mahan would look for him, find him, and chew his ass out. But Kishiyama didn't need to know that.

"Yeah," Sean answered, lifting an eyebrow. "He doesn't dick around when it comes to security. He's likely already called it in. I'd say you boys have about fifteen minutes before the cops show up."

Mitchell let out a gasp from behind them.

"Bullshit!" said Gregory. "Cellphones don't work out here."

"I didn't say anything about cellphones. He carries a satellite phone. There's a landline in my trailer too. He has a key to it since the county owns it."

Gregory's head swung to Kishiyama.

Sean kept up the pressure. "Fifteen minutes gives you all enough time to pile into that bus of yours and—"

"Sean!" The outraged call echoed through the facility. It was Mahan. He'd already entered the access tunnel.

Sean wasn't going to give the others time to react. He spun on his feet and sent a high knee squarely into Gregory's sternum. The henchman toppled backwards into Kishiyama, whose gun clanged across the floor. With Sean's hands bound behind him, there was no way he could grab the weapon. He turned—catching a glimpse of Mitchell paralyzed with fear—before he ran down the tunnel toward the access tunnel.

"What in the hell is going on?" Mahan's angry voice carried through the site again. "Whose bus is this? Why is it here?"

"Mahan, run!" Sean yelled. "Get out of here!" His shoulder bounced against the ribbed wall of tunnel as he fought to keep his momentum and balance. "They've got guns!" He slogged forward.

Sean's voice prompted the emergence of the twin from the bay doorway. With wide eyes, the twin grabbed for the rifle strapped over his shoulder. Sean left the first tunnel but didn't go for the access tunnel. Instead, he launched straight toward the twin, lowering his shoulder directly into the man's neck. Sean snarled as he smashed the twin's body into the wall behind him.

"Sean?" Mahan called, trying to make sense of what he'd just heard and seen.

The twin fell to the floor and Sean crumpled to a knee. Sean grunted and pulled himself back up to his feet. He sent a stomp into the twin's face, and then turned to see Gregory running toward them. He knew he didn't have time to make it outside himself. But Mahan did.

Sean lumbered forward into the access tunnel before falling back onto a knee. His supervisor was standing halfway down the passage on confused footing. The light above shone off thick-framed glasses and illuminated his button-up shirt and pleated pants.

"Run!" Sean shouted, just before something hard cracked against his skull.

He toppled forward onto his chest, pain rushing through his head as he fought to keep his chin up and eyes forward. Mahan, having finally absorbed the seriousness of the situation, was scurrying toward the door. Gregory was close behind him, with others in the group—including Tammy—racing past Sean to join the chase. The brisk footsteps reverberated through the tunnel.

When Sean heard metal hinges cry, he thought for a second that Mahan had made it out, but the weight of the door was likely what did his boss in. Mahan kicked and wailed as he was dragged back inside by the mob. The door slammed shut, and a gun barrel was pressed into the swell of Sean's back, commanding him to stay down on his chest. Sean did, but kept his head lifted and his gaze on the melee.

Sean thought for a moment that it was Kishiyama standing above him, but the leader soon stepped around his body and made his way toward his flock, his pistol in hand.

"Don't you dare move," came a woman's voice from above Sean, breath pouring from her mouth. It sounded like the mother of the baby.

"What do you want?" Mahan screamed, his trembling voice higher than Sean had ever heard it. "Oh God, what do you want?"

Between the shifting intruders, Sean glimpsed Mahan bleeding from his mouth, glasses crooked. Mahan was shoved to the floor on his back, the others standing over him with their weapons drawn. Gregory emerged from the pack and met Kishiyama halfway down the tunnel. He held what appeared to be a leather wallet in his hand, which he quickly riffled though.

"Lawrence Mahan," said Gregory. "Looks like he works for the county. Coleman was probably telling the truth when he said this guy's his supervisor. He doesn't have any phone on him, though. That was either bullshit or he left the thing in his car."

"Lawrence Mahan?" Kishiyama asked in a single breath. "You're sure?"

"Yeah," Gregory answered. "Why?"

Kishiyama didn't respond, glaring at the floor for a moment. He walked past Gregory with deflated shoulders, approaching the others. "Back away," he directed them in a lowered voice. "I need room."

His people complied, forming a wider buffer around Mahan—and giving Sean a better view. Mahan, facing slightly away from Sean, planted his elbows on the floor and lifted his head off the concrete. He adjusted his glasses.

"Wh-who are you people?" asked Mahan, his voice trembling.

Kishiyama stopped when he reached Mahan's feet, staring down at him. Mahan raised his hand in front of his face, using it as a visor against the glare of the lightbulb above. Sean could see his chest rising and lowering with each breath.

"You?" Mahan said.

Kishiyama raised his arm. A loud pop and a burst of light filled the tunnel.

Chapter 12

A woman's scream ripped through the tunnel. It was Tammy, toppling backwards and falling to her butt. She backed away on her elbows and heels, eyes bulging in horror. The others also receded from Mahan's body, their faces pale and mouths gaping as they exchanged glances, a dozen silent questions written on their faces. They clearly had no idea of what Kishiyama was going to do.

Sean stared forward as the room spun, his mouth open. All breath had left his body. His mind struggled to process what he had just witnessed. All of the qualms Kishiyama had expressed about killing—all of the talk about his people being there to *save* lives—was suddenly as empty as the chamber of the leader's pistol. He had murdered a man in cold blood, and that blood was now spreading evenly along the concrete beneath Mahan's head.

"My God," the woman above Sean gasped. The gun she pressed against his back trembled.

"You sons of bitches," Sean muttered before raising his voice to a roar. "You sons of bitches!"

"This man was sent here to stop us!" Kishiyama said loudly, his head shifting to different members of his tribe as he spoke. "This was part of the prophecy. This is why we came armed. This is what you've been trained for—what you've prepared for. If I could have spared this man's life, I would have."

"Bullshit," Sean snarled.

Kishiyama continued, raising his arm in the air. "It was either his life or all of ours. And I chose for *us* to live. This man would not have survived to see another sunset even if he had never stepped foot inside this shelter tonight. Remember that. What happened now was inevitable."

"You're a fucking murderer!" Sean shouted. "And the rest of you assholes are his accomplices."

Gregory scowled, raising his gun and turning to Kishiyama. "Let's take care of him too. It doesn't matter now."

"You'd better, dickhead." Sean growled. "If not, I'm going to shove that gun right up your ass and pull the trigger."

"No," said Kishiyama, approaching Gregory.

"We don't need him."

"No!" Kishiyama shouted, grabbing Gregory's wrist with one hand and using the other to send a wicked backhand across his enforcer's face.

Spit sprayed from Gregory's mouth and other members of the group flinched. Tammy pulled herself to her feet on shaky legs. She held her stomach, looking nauseous as she watched the exchange.

"It's not about *need*," said Kishiyama, his voice loud enough for all the others to hear. He glared daggers through Gregory, keeping ahold of his wrist. "What we do, we do for humanity. Never forget that." He turned to the others. "None of you ever forget that!"

"What we do, we do for humanity," a couple of voices chimed in. Others soon joined in. "What we do, we do for humanity."

Gregory's chest heaved in and out as he drew in breath, glaring back at Kishiyama until his face relaxed and he too joined in with the chant. All but Sean and the woman hovering above him were speaking the words.

Kishiyama released Gregory and turned to one of the twins. The blood under the twin's nose told Sean that he was the one he'd clashed with during his escape attempt.

"Get his car," Kishiyama instructed. "Take it down to the driveway and park it beside the bus. He should be alone, but make certain no one else is out there. See if there's really a phone in his car. If so, get it and remove the battery. If it's the type you charge, just break it."

The twin swallowed and nodded. He walked over to the body, skirting the blood and dropping to a knee. He began uneasily digging through Mahan's pockets, looking for keys.

"Mitchell!" Kishiyama called, eyes focused above Sean's body toward the other end of the tunnel.

Sean had forgotten about Mitchell. He wasn't one of the vultures surrounding Mahan.

"This man was our enemy, but he still deserves a proper burial," Kishiyama told him. "There's bound to be a shovel somewhere in the bay. Bury him to the north where you can't be seen from the road. Then clean up the tunnel. That will be your penance for earlier."

There was no reply.

"Mitchell!" pressed Kishiyama.

"Okay," Mitchell whispered, sounding out of breath. Sean heard him shuffle off.

Sean raised his head as best he could. "You don't think people are going to come looking for Mahan? You don't think people are going to figure out he's missing?"

Tilting his head toward Sean, Kishiyama confidently replied, "No, I don't."

"Why not?" asked Sean. "Because it's not part of *the prophecy?*" The seething sarcasm was followed by a shove of the gun barrel into his back.

"Tie him up where he had Mitchell," Kishiyama ordered. "It's out of the way, and he still has information to give us."

As Gregory approached Sean, Kishiyama handed him his gun. The unblemished twin appeared and wrapped his hands around Sean's arm, helping him up to his knees. The gun against Sean's back was removed. Sean's eyes slid to Tammy, who was still visibly shaken. She gazed vacantly at Mahan.

Behind Tammy, Sean noticed several large inch-thick metal

sheets leaning against the tunnel wall. Each looked at least eight feet long and maybe three feet in width. The one facing outward had some holes drilled into it. The group had to have brought them in from the bus, though for what purpose, Sean couldn't fathom.

"Get up," said Gregory, pointing his pistol at Sean.

Sean didn't comply at first. Instead, he glared at Kishiyama. He thought hard about charging the leader and making him pay for what he'd just done. But with his arms still secured behind his back, he knew he couldn't exact the kind of pain he desperately wanted to. He took in air through his nose, telling himself that the time would come, and for now he'd have to bide that time.

When Gregory repeated the command, Sean climbed to his feet, the twin assisting him. He winced from the pain racing along his skull. When he turned around, he saw the mother of the baby standing before him. Instead of holding her child, she was holding the gun that she'd use to pin him down. Her eyes were wet, and he could hear her sniff.

"Mother of the year," Sean told her, showing his teeth.

Her eyes further swelled with tears, and she brushed a long strand of her dark hair from her face before turning and walking away.

"Go," said Gregory.

Sean didn't say a thing as he exited the tunnel and entered the other. Multiple sets of footsteps followed him, echoing off the walls like the sound of Mahan's pleas that still rang through his mind. *Mahan was an asshole, but he didn't deserve what happened to him.*

His boss had been a single man, living alone with just a cat—information that had trickled out during their past meetings. Showing up at the site so late in the day meant that he was on his way home, his workday over. Perhaps Kishiyama was right in that he wouldn't be missed by anyone, at least not until he failed to show up at work the next day. Then again, Mahan's job kept him pretty mobile, visiting different locations across the county. Maybe his empty office on a Tuesday morning wouldn't strike anyone else in the building as being the slightest bit odd.

Kishiyama seemed to already know this, and the last word out of Mahan's mouth played over and over in Sean's head: "You?"

When they reached the mangled vault door, Sean lowered his head and squeezed his way through it. He kept his eyes forward as others followed. No one spoke until they reached the north wall.

"Go to the back corner of the room," said Gregory. It's where Sean was already headed.

When he reached the shelving post he had tied Mitchell to, Sean dropped to his knees and slid to his butt. He leaned into the post. The twin, who smelled of sweat, bound him to it with a rope he'd gotten from somewhere—first around his arms, and then around his chest. Duct tape was used to pin Sean's legs together at the ankles.

Once the twin was finished, Kishiyama dismissed him. Sean was left alone with Kishiyama and Gregory.

Sean raised his head, meeting their eyes. Their faces were as hard as his.

"Mahan knew you," Sean said to Kishiyama. "How?"

Gregory's eyebrows arched and his head turned to Kishiyama.

Kishiyama glared at Sean for a moment before responding. "He didn't know me. I didn't know him. What happened wasn't personal."

"You're a liar." said Sean. "He recognized you, and that's what got him killed. That's why you shot him." Sean narrowed his eyes. "What were you afraid he'd tell the others about you?"

Kishiyama's jaw clenched. He took in a deep breath. "I want you to tell us where the detonators are. And I want you to tell us right now."

"You know, I bet I'm not the only one who noticed that," said Sean, refusing to accommodate Kishiyama's change of the subject. "That Mahan recognized you. Something tells me that your boy Gregory here doesn't really give two shits either way, but I'm betting the others out there—the ones who've, up until now, bought all your bullshit—are starting to have some doubts about Dear Leader."

"My people are loyal, Mr. Coleman. They have complete faith in me, and—"

"Oh really? You must not have seen their faces back in that tunnel. But I did. They're losing that faith."

Gregory broke in, his eyes on Kishiyama. "I know I'm sounding like a broken record here, but this guy . . ."

"No," Kishiyama said, closing his eyes in annoyance. "And that will remain my answer until I say otherwise, understand? Don't ask again."

Sean scoffed. "I must have really endeared myself to you, Kishiyama. I guess I should feel flattered that you care so much about me. Hell, there are people who've known me for years that would've given Gregory the okay by now, but not you. What is it, my charming demeanor? My good looks?"

Kishiyama lowered his head to the floor. "Gregory, leave us."

"What?" Gregory asked in disbelief.

"You heard me. Leave us. Go help Mitchell or someone else. There's plenty of work to do, and we're behind schedule. Mr. Coleman's not going anywhere . . . And it's time he was told about the prophecy."

Chapter 13

"May 27th, 2003," said Kishiyama, sitting on the same box that Sean had used as a chair when he'd questioned Mitchell. With his arms crossed in front of his chest, he looked at Sean as if he expected the caretaker to find meaning in the date.

"Today?" Sean asked, brow furrowed.

"No," answered Kishiyama, shaking his head. "It's tomorrow. And if I and my people hadn't come here today, you would have gone to bed tonight believing that tomorrow would have played out just like any other day. Coffee. Maybe a morning show on television as you got dressed. Then a day of patrolling this property."

Sean listened silently.

"But tomorrow, unfortunately, will *not* be a typical day. In fact, everything will change tomorrow. And I mean *everything*. The people. The planet. Life as we know it."

"What are you?" Sean scoffed. "An insurance salesman?"

"Shut up!" Kishiyama yelled, standing straight up, his hands formed in fists. "Just for once, shut up!" His chest heaved in and out before he tempered himself. "I'm trying to explain why we're here, Mr. Coleman. If you don't want to listen to that explanation . . ."

"Go on," said Sean. He didn't trust Kishiyama to tell him the truth, but he suspected whatever he had to say might be helpful in better understanding the situation he was in. If anything, he'd get an idea of what type of story the older man had sold to his followers.

Kishiyama pressed a button on his watch and then reached

forward, holding his left wrist in front of Sean's face. It flashed "7:43." He lowered his arm to his side before the watch could snap back to the current time.

"At approximately 7:43 a.m. Mountain Daylight Time tomorrow morning, a large object—roughly four times the size of Earth—will pass dangerously close to this planet."

Sean sat stone-faced, biting the inside of his cheek. He'd figured that whatever tale of destruction the cultists were working off of had to be a doozy—perhaps something along the lines of a natural disaster or even a nuclear strike—but he hadn't seen the science fiction angle coming.

Kishiyama continued. "Some believe it will actually collide with Earth, in which case none of what we're doing here will matter. But we have it on good authority that that won't happen. Regardless, the close proximity of Nibiru will have a catastrophic effect on this planet."

"What's Nibiru?" Sean asked.

"It's the name that a prominent contactee has assigned to the planetary object that I'm describing. It's derived from mythology, but the name matters little. What is of enormous concern, however, is that the near miss will result in the Earth's rotation ceasing for 5.9 days, as well as a shifting of the planet's poles. This will lead to rapid, almost immediate global climate change and significant displacement of the planet's crust. Earthquakes. Tsunamis. Tropical jungles turned to frozen tundra, if the change in sea level doesn't put them all under water."

"Well that sounds as scary as shit, Kishiyama" said Sean, the sarcasm buildup in his gut finally oozing over. "And by taking up shelter underground, in a fortified concrete compound, the idea is that your people will ride out all of these changes—survive doomsday, and start over?"

"If we're lucky," said Kishiyama, dismissing Sean's snide tone.

"Colorado gives us a better chance of survival. This site sits approximately a mile above sea level. The earth is harder here, and the geographical positioning of Weld County should—"

"God," Sean scoffed. "You really have invested some time in this bullshit story."

Kishiyama stared at him for a moment before responding. "Mr. Coleman, I've invested *everything*. And it's not a *story*. It's the prophecy."

"Who *prophesized* it? Alfred E. Newman?"

Kishiyama's face tightened. "No." He took a breath before continuing. "Her name is Nancy Leider. She resides in Wisconsin."

"Wisconsin, huh? So what makes some cheesehead the be-all and end-all of . . . intergalactic crap-happenings?"

"Let's just say that her connections are sound and taken as gospel among my people and many others. Though her name may mean nothing to you, she has a wide reach. She is a person of influence. I believe others are heeding her words as we speak. The Pana Wave in Japan. Followers of Zecharia Sitchin's work."

"Inmates in mental asylums," Sean said, nodding.

Kishiyama ignored the remark. "Even some of those who've never heard the prophecy will make it through this alive—the lucky ones. We don't know who they are, or where they'll be—other than places where the geography will protect them. But Leider is confident that there will be smatterings of survivors who will rise up in this new, broken world and help put it back together." Kishiyama's eyes turned sorrowful. "The overwhelming majority of the human race, however, will perish."

Story complete, Kishiyama watched Sean through narrowed eyes, seemingly trying to gauge the thoughts running through his captive's mind.

Sean's chest rose and lowered. His nostrils spread as he glared up at Kishiyama. A good ten seconds crawled by before he spoke.

"You murdered a man over this fucking nonsense? Do you have any idea how insane you are—how insane *all* of you are?"

Kishiyama sighed. He shook his head and stood up, a vein revealing itself at the center of his forehead. "I am not expecting you to believe what I'm saying, Mr. Coleman. Your ignorance and skepticism on this matter is understandable. I'm telling you this so you'll understand what is at stake for those of us who *do* believe it. My people *know* this to be Armageddon. We know that tomorrow morning, the world will change. We know we must survive. We know that anyone who stands in our way is working against our very survival and the revival of mankind."

Sean shook his head.

"My people are fully committed," continued Kishiyama. "They will not let you or anyone else stop us. They have placed all of their faith in this mission—this crusade. If we survive, we will emerge from the rubble." His body tensed up and his hands slowly formed into fists. "But we cannot do that without those fucking detonators."

Sean nodded his head, sliding his tongue along his lower lip. "You know what, Kishiyama? I think there's a lot of truth in what you're telling me."

Kishiyama's eyes widened.

"Not about the giant rock from outer space, of course. That's all bullshit. But I think you're telling me the truth about what your people believe. I mean, Mitchell sure as hell buys it. Of course, no one's ever going to accuse that poor bastard of being the sharpest tack on the bulletin board."

"Mitchell's an important member of our—"

"He's a sheep, just like others. And they're being led by a con man . . . with the possible exception of your buddy Gregory. He seems a little brighter than the rest—a little more clued in."

Kishiyama shook his head, sighing.

"Be honest with me, you gutless piece of shit. There's no one else around to hear you. Neither of us believes the world is going to end tomorrow."

"You're wrong."

"No, I'm not. You're here for another reason." When Kishiyama said nothing, Sean asked, "What are the detonators for?"

"To free us."

"Let's try that again. What are the detonators *really* for?"

Kishiyama chuckled. "You're really not going to tell me where they are, are you?"

"No, and if your story weren't bullshit, you wouldn't care."

"Excuse me?"

"You already know the detonators are somewhere in this room," said Sean. "And according to your *gospelly-believed* prophecy, you have plenty of time to find them—you know, with all of that cataclysmic chaos taking place, over five-point-whatever days, while you're waiting for the planet to start spinning again and the Earth's crust to stop doing jumping jacks. Hell, that gives you almost a week before you even need to start *thinking* about trying to blast your way out of here. Surely you will have found the detonators by then. Right? I mean, this room's big, but it's not *that* big."

Kishiyama smirked.

"Unless you need those detonators faster than you're letting on," Sean added. "For whatever reason that might be."

The smirk disappeared. Kishiyama nodded and said, "You know what, Mr. Coleman? You're right. It's *not* that big of a room. And with enough of us looking, we *will* find them. I was just hoping not to have to pull the resources, because we really do have a lot of work to get done, and that includes me."

Kishiyama reached to his side and grabbed the roll of duct tape, tearing off seven or eight inches. He approached Sean, holding the piece at opposite ends. Sean twisted his head to the side, but Kishiyama managed to cover his mouth with it anyway, pressing the edges firmly against his skin. He then rubbed his hands together, backing away as Sean glared daggers at him.

"Speaking of work, Ms. Leider laid out a number of preparatory steps on her website," said Kishiyama. "Proper food storage. Room sterilization. Setting up a latrine—it's not like we can count on the plumbing in this place." He walked backwards, his eyes remaining on Sean as he made his way down the aisle. His lips began curling at their corners again. "Pet euthanasia."

Sean's pulse jolted. His eyes widened and he leaned forward, his body pulling at the ropes around him.

Kishiyama grinned, shrugging his shoulders. "It's right there on her website, Mr. Coleman. All of my people have read it."

Chapter 14

S ean had grunted and snarled until his face had burned red and his throat filled with bile, but his efforts hadn't kept Kishiyama from leaving the room. His arms and wrists sore from straining at his binds, he continued to dig his heels into the concrete, arch his back, and twist his torso. He hoped to stretch the rope and give himself some room to work with, but thus far, it hadn't gotten him anywhere.

Kishiyama might have been lying about Avalanche to try and soften Sean up, but taking the leader's story as a whole, killing a dog seemed like the least twisted part. Besides, Kishiyama had murdered a human being without batting an eye. Believing he'd have qualms about doing the same to an animal would have bordered on delusion.

Avalanche would be easy pickings too, stuck in Sean's trailer with nowhere to escape. It wouldn't help that the dog loved people and wouldn't put up a fight upon the door opening. Then again, there was something about the group that Avalanche hadn't liked from the beginning. The aggressive growls and barks when they'd walked through the gate proved that he'd had a better read on them than Sean had. Hopefully those instincts would give the dog a fighting chance.

Sean fought and snorted against his binds for the next thirty minutes before others entered the room. He could only hear them as they shuffled through boxes along what sounded like the first row of shelves. After a while, the clamor grew closer, suggesting that they'd moved on to the second. They exchanged limited conversation, and only in regard to their search efforts. They'd probably been instructed not to talk about anything else with him within earshot. He identified at least four different voices.

They slowly made their way closer to his row, and he grew nervous a couple of times when he heard the squeaky wheels of the mobile staircase and footsteps walking up and down it. He'd hidden the detonators well, but if the group was scouring the upper shelves, there was no guarantee they wouldn't find them.

About forty-five minutes after the search had begun, Tammy appeared from around the corner along with one of the other women. He glared at them, pressing air from his nose. They timidly glanced at him before turning their attention to the shelves. Another woman and a man—the father of the baby—emerged from the opposite end of the row. Pulling the mobile staircase beside him, the man positioned it and ascended as the woman began checking the floor-level shelves. Sean took some silent satisfaction in knowing that if they'd made it that far and were still searching, they hadn't found the detonators.

The four worked their way toward each other to where Sean was bound, careful not to get too close to him. Having gone through every shelf, they turned their attention to the boxes against the wall. While lids were opened and hands dug through boxes, Sean noticed Tammy glancing at him from time to time.

Once finished, the four exchanged depleted expressions. They had failed their assignment. The man glanced at Sean, then nudged the women toward the exit with a nod. As they left, Tammy turned to Sean, her eyes soft as if expressing sympathy. Sean glared back, shaking his head slowly to let her know he didn't want any from her.

As time crawled by, a torturous sense of helplessness further reduced Sean's spirits. It was compounded by his parched throat that longed for a drink, and sadly it wasn't water that he craved. Sean had been dry for almost twenty-four hours, and for a man who'd gotten reacquainted over the past several months with the practice of chasing his sorrows away with booze, his inability to do so at that very moment served as a cruel taunt. His head ached and his hands trembled. He hated what he'd become.

He had done so well after Zed's death. Sober for over a year, out of respect for the old man. That was, until he'd found out the truth about everything, and that truth had proven too much to bear. It left him hollow inside, and he'd filled the emptiness with the same companion that had reliably been there for him over much of his adult life. He had a real problem. And if he were to ever chase the demons back into their hiding places, he would need help—the kind of help that Lumbergh had offered. But that chapter would have to wait until he'd gotten himself out of his current predicament.

Sean's mind drifted back to the question of how Mahan could have known Kishiyama. He believed the answer was important to figuring out the leader's true reason for being there. Though Mahan didn't have much of a family life, it was possible that he'd traveled in social circles that would have somehow connected the two. That, however, seemed unlikely. Mahan was a workaholic. More realistically, he would have met the leader through his job. Sean wondered if Kishiyama had worked—or currently worked—for the county. Weld was the third largest county in the state, with plenty of people on the payroll. What hurt the theory, however, was the presumed location of where the group had traveled from. Their cover story had been Berthoud, but their bus had a Texas license plate.

His head continued to hurt, and his eyes felt the daggers of the bright lights above. A couple of times, Sean found himself nodding off. On the third spell, the image of a tall, straw cowboy hat formed in his mind. A gurgling sound came from it, and Sean realized it covered the face of a man lying on a wooden floor. The hand of a young boy removed the hat, revealing the bloody, wide-eyed face of Sean's father.

"Sean?" he said.

He heard the creak of wood behind him, and Sean opened his eyes to find himself strapped to shelving in the missile site's archive room. He turned his head to the right as best he could. He saw nothing but boxes. A scuff along the floor to his left pulled his head in the other direction. He caught the edge of a shadow just before it disappeared around the corner.

Sean grunted and squirmed, the tape across his mouth keeping him from asking who was there. Soft footsteps shuffled their way down the aisle behind him. Within seconds, he could no longer hear them. Sean wondered if he had been asleep longer than just a minute or two. He hadn't a clue what time it was.

No more than fifteen minutes went by before Sean heard footsteps again. They were heavier this time, faster paced. Gregory soon rounded the corner. There was purpose in his stride, and he held one of his hands behind his back, as if he were concealing something. His gun was holstered. His lips were pressed tightly, but they began to curl as he grew closer, elevating the toothpick lodged between them. He stopped within a few feet, saying nothing before reaching forward and tearing the tape from Sean's mouth in one brutal yank.

The move burned Sean's skin, but he didn't give Gregory the satisfaction of showing how much it hurt.

"What is it, monkey boy?" Sean asked, his voice coarse.

"So now you know," Gregory said, wading up the tape in a ball with his fingers, and tossing it aside.

"Know what?"

"What we're doing here."

"Yeah, hiding out from giant space balls. Or at least pretending to. Where's Kishiyama? Preparing the cloaks and tiki torches?"

"He's keeping us on schedule," Gregory replied, his smug face stretching at the cheeks. "He's a good organizer. A strong leader."

"He's a con man. Now, are you going to show-and-tell whatever it is you're hiding behind your back, or are you going to keep up the attention-starved-child routine?"

Gregory chuckled. "I just wanted to drop off a memento. A little keepsake you might appreciate."

"Let me guess. You made me a peanut-butter birdfeeder out of a pinecone and some yarn."

Gregory's face tightened. "Not quite." He whipped his arm from behind his back and tossed something red to the floor beside Sean. There was a light clank of metal when it landed.

At first, it looked like a short piece of rope, but when Sean's eyes adjusted, a red dog collar came into focus. It was stained with blood.

Sean's back shot straight and his soul filled with rage. "You mother fuckers!" he snarled, spray flying from his mouth and bound legs kicking.

Gregory took a step back. Sean leaned forward as best as he could, veins bulging in his neck. He glared at Gregory with clenched teeth, letting him know without words exactly what he planned on doing to him once he was free.

Gregory grinned, tapping the side of his pistol against his thigh. "Hey, don't blame me," he said, shrugging his shoulders. "Putting down pets is right there in the prophecy. Ease their suffering. One less mouth to feed."

"Nothing's going to ease *your* suffering, fuck-stick," Sean said, his heart hammering. "This game you assholes are playing. It's going to end with you and your boss in a world of hurt."

"We're *all* going to be living in a world of hurt," said Gregory. "But at least we'll be living."

Sean shook his head, his eyes still glued to Gregory.

Gregory continued. "You know, you could have at least delayed this by just telling us where the detonators are. We'd have let you say goodbye to your pooch."

"Go fuck yourself." When Sean shifted his shoulder, he heard a faint tear from behind him and felt the rope around his wrists unexpectedly loosen. His eyes widened, but he quickly tempered his expression, not wanting to alert Gregory. Gregory's unflinching smirk affirmed that he hadn't heard the rip.

"The good news," Gregory began, "is that like Mahan, your doggie earned himself a proper burial. In fact, the two are together— in the same plot. Man and man's best friend, keeping each other company."

"Do me a favor and keep the shovel handy."

Before Gregory could respond, Sean added, "You know, I've been meaning to ask you something, Gregory . . ."

"What's that?"

"That toothpick in your mouth. Does your dick ever get jealous of how big it is?"

Gregory's lips leveled. "Still the smart ass, even now." He shook his head. "Keep it up, because the sooner Kishiyama's charity runs out, so does your time." He offered Sean a fleeting gaze, and then turned to leave.

Sean glanced down at the collar again. Smudges of blood covered the nametag, but Avalanche's inscribed name was still visible.

"Who did it?" Sean asked.

Gregory stopped and turned his head. "Who did what?"

"Killed my dog. Was it you or Kishiyama?"

Gregory smirked. "Actually, it was your old roommate Mitchell."

"Mitchell?"

"Yeah. He may be an idiot, but he's a loyal idiot. They're all loyal." Gregory's smirk turned into a full grin before his face went deadpan. He left.

The second he disappeared around the corner, Sean began working his wrists. He forced one arm down and lifted the other one up. Within seconds, he heard another tear.

Chapter 15

The rope had been cut. Several strands of it, anyway. That was Sean's determination as he studied his unraveled binds from a knee behind the shelving. Stretching his neck in circular motion, he discounted the possibility that the damage to the rope had been there prior to being tied up. The twin had done a thorough job securing his wrists, leaving practically no give at all. It was the person who had snuck into the room as he slept who'd sliced through the rope—not all the way, but enough to let him work through the rest himself.

Could Kishiyama be setting me up? Sean thought. *Could he want me to try and escape?* If so, Sean couldn't decide why.

He rose to his feet, staring down at the bloody dog collar before retrieving it and stuffing it into his front pocket. He carefully made his way to the back end of the aisle. He stopped there for a moment, placing his arms on his hips and bowing his back until he felt a pop. His constraints had left his large body tight and achy. It felt good to be able to stand straight again.

His eyes rose to the shelving along the back wall. He hoped to spot something in storage that he could use as a weapon—something other than binders and cardboard boxes filled with documents, of which there was an ample supply. He knew there to be a handful of old adding machines an aisle over. They were made of solid metal and could do some damage, but they'd be hard to grip and swing. *Maybe as a last resort.*

Heart racing, he jogged to the rear of the next aisle, keeping his eyes on the other end of the hallway as he crossed it. He wasn't sure what he'd do if Kishiyama or one of his people suddenly appeared, but he wanted to see it coming and have time to react.

He peered around the corner, scanning the shelves. When he found nothing useful, he moved to the next aisle. Not far from the mobile staircase he'd used earlier was a mishmash of office chairs tucked beside each other along one of the floor-level shelves. His eyebrows rose as he looked them over. There were five or six of them—leftover furniture from upgrades in some county building. They'd been spared because they were in good shape and could eventually be used elsewhere. At least they *had* been in good shape . . .

One of them was now broken, the casualty of a sexual escapade between Sean and the woman he'd brought home from the bar, whose name had—again—escaped him. A heavily inebriated midnight tour of the facility had led to an impromptu lap-dance in the swivel chair, which proved unable to support the two's combined weight of roughly four hundred pounds. The backrest and one of the armrests snapped off at their bases, sending the slowly spinning lovers crashing to the floor in a heap of arms and legs.

It wasn't the failed stunt, however, that Sean was thinking about. Instead, what leapt to the forefront of his mind was a remark the woman had made afterward as the two of them were returning the chair—in multiple pieces—to its rack.

"Looks like a battle-axe," she'd joked, clenching her teeth and growling for a moment as she held the detached armrest with both hands above her head.

In fact, the armrest *did* resemble a battle-axe, with the support serving as the blade, and its two-foot base acting as the handle. It had good weight to it too, made almost entirely of metal. Sean carefully made his way to the chairs, keeping his eyes forward as he slid his arm along the shelf below them. He grabbed the armrest and then retreated back to the end of the aisle. He peeled the already cracked layer of vinyl from the arm-support and discarded the remaining foam cushion underneath it. He was left with a smaller instrument that resembled a pickax more than a battle-ax. Still, any blow he could land with it would get the job done.

He took in a couple of deep breaths, tensed his arms, and made his way for the vault door, weapon in hand.

Chapter 16

The air was cold at the bottom of the exhaust pit, at least ten degrees cooler than the floor above. To fight the chill, she'd crossed her arms in front of her chest, using her wrist to aim the flashlight at Dean, who was climbing down the fixed steel ladder. The twin had a good-sized box of canned fruit and vegetables tucked under his arm.

The pit's moist smell had been overbearing at first, but she was beginning to form a tolerance for it, which would hopefully make things a little easier over the next week. She was more concerned about claustrophobia, not just her own but also the others'. Being stuck in a dark and dreary cement cell for that long could drive people mad, especially with a fussing baby in the mix. It could feel like being trapped in purgatory—and for all intents and purposes, that's exactly what it would be.

Five-point-nine days. Then things would begin to stabilize, and the group could climb up to the main floor of the compound, which would then become their home indefinitely. In a sense, it would be like being reborn.

Kishiyama always expressed faith that the full structure would hold, but the Earth's pole shift would shake and alter the landscape above. The silo's walls were made of thick concrete, but that concrete was over forty years old, and the foundation likely hadn't been inspected since the site's deactivation. Moisture from four decades of weather, evidence of which were all over the walls, could have created weak spots. Sections or chunks could potentially fall from the ceilings and walls, crushing those beneath them. The lowest room in the building would provide the best protection.

Dean joined her at the bottom of the pit, his swollen face wincing at the bright light in his eyes.

"Sorry," she said, redirecting her beam at piles of boxes in the corner of the room.

Dean added his box to them and flinched when a loud voice from above shouted, "Heads up!"

Something large dropped from above, landing on the floor between them with barely a sound. She leapt back and lit up the object, revealing it to be a pile of dark military-style blankets.

"I found them behind the sluge tank in some dusty boxes," came the voice again. It belonged to Dean's brother Doug. "They're probably older than this place, but they'll work!"

"Behind the what?" she asked, not bothering to look up.

"The sluge tank. That's how it's labeled anyway. That huge metal tank in the liquid-oxygen room."

"Okay, thank you," she replied, remembering the big barrel-looking piece of equipment she'd seen earlier.

Dean picked up the blankets and sidestepped a stack of thin mattresses and some battery-operated lamps to place them on top of a pile of other blankets the group had brought with them.

The cell was filling up. Just about all of the food, water, clothes, and other provisions for the first week had already been brought down, along with some luxury items like decks of cards and board games to ease nerves and pass the time.

She swung her flashlight over to the empty baby's bassinet. It was pink and low to the ground, hanging from a thin metal frame with an automatic mechanism that let it rock by itself. A bag of disposable diapers sat beside it.

She gazed sadly at it for a moment before turning to Dean. She swallowed. "We're just all pretendin' like it never happened."

Dean turned toward her. He placed his hands on his hips. "The man in the tunnel?"

She tilted her head. "Of course the man in the tunnel."

He sighed. "What's done is done. None of us wanted that, but Kishiyama's right. The guy could have screwed it all up."

"How? We could have tied him up with the guard."

Dean stared blankly for a moment. "Just trust that the right thing was done. Like Kishiyama said, he'd have been dead in the mornin' anyway."

"But not by our hand," she said. "By God's. There's a difference."

"It looks good!" a different voice sounded out from above, causing the two to jump. "Well organized!"

She lifted her flashlight, exposing Kishiyama, who now stood on the platform high above them. Her chest tightened as she prayed that he hadn't heard her.

"Thank you," they both answered. She quickly lowered her flashlight, leaving only the leader's outline visible from some ceiling light behind him.

"It's not the Ritz," he said with his hands on the railing. "But it will do. Just a few more things, and we can start laying the planking over the opening."

"Yes sir," they both said.

Silence befell the three. Seconds crawled by before Kishiyama finally spoke. "Why are we doing all of this?"

"What we do, we do for humanity," they both replied, lowering their heads.

"Again."

"What we do, we do for humanity."

The silence returned for a few seconds before Kishiyama asked, "What is that?" His voice ticked up with curiosity.

She and Dean lifted their heads.

"Sir?" Dean asked.

"Those cans. The shiny ones. In the light."

She followed the beam of her flashlight to where she'd inadvertently been illuminating a row of three canisters beside the boxes of canned goods.

"I don't know," she said with narrow eyes.

"It's old candy," answered Dean. "Doug found it when he was rummagin' through one of the closets."

"Here, in the bunker?"

"Yes, it's really old, probably from when the site still had the missile. The canisters say somethin' about carbohydrates."

Kishiyama took a step back on the platform, his head lifting as if he were weighing a thought. "Hard candy, red and yellow in color? About the size of a penny?"

Dean paused. "Yes," he said, his tone one of puzzlement.

She too wondered how Kishiyama could have been privy to such a detail, but she knew better than to ask. It would come across as if she were challenging his authority.

"Throw one up here," Kishiyama ordered.

"A canister?" Dean asked.

"No, just a piece of the candy."

Dean complied, jogging over to the canisters, sliding his hand inside one that was open, and pulling out a handful of candies. When he tossed one of them up to Kishiyama, she followed it as best she could with her flashlight. It didn't go high enough, falling back down into the pit and skipping across the floor. Dean threw a second piece up. This time, Kishiyama caught it. He immediately brought it beneath his nose.

It was then the she witnessed a gesture that she had never before seen or heard from Kishiyama: a laugh. It began with a chuckle, then quickly raised in tone to what sounded like a cackle. Its awkward pitch compelled her to look at Dean. His gaze was already on her, mirroring her confusion.

In a flash, Kishiyama disappeared from view, the sound of his brisk footsteps echoing across steel and then concrete.

Chapter 17

Sean carefully slid his head around the edge of the warped vault door, peering into the landing area between the kitchen and control room. He listened quietly. After a moment, he heard a lone voice. It belonged to a man, but it was so faint that Sean couldn't make out who. The dialogue seemed one-sided, not part of a conversation. It was as if the man were recording a message or talking to himself. All Sean was sure of was that it was coming from the south side of the building—the living quarters. Sean's path to the outside would take him in the opposite direction.

He twisted his body around the door and stepped onto the landing area, armrest pickax in hand. Moving slowly across the linoleum, he kept quiet as he approached the doorway to the control room. Careful not to let himself become visible from the adjacent hallway, he peered inside the room. Other than some sleeping bags strewn on the floor, and some food and water, there wasn't much. Sean couldn't tell with absolute certainty that no one was inside, but from his vantage point, it appeared that way.

The south wing was like a ghost town, a sharp contrast with the flurry of activity he'd heard when he was tied up. Other than the voice down the hall, there was no sign of life. Sean worried again that he was somehow being set up, lured into doing something that benefited Kishiyama. But Sean couldn't for the life of him figure out what that might be. Unless they were hiding, the rest of the group had to either be outside or in the bay area.

He walked up the ramp and steps, the tunnel opening just a

couple of yards ahead on the right. If Sean could negotiate the tunnel's 120 feet without being seen, he'd have a straight shot—through the smaller tunnel—to the outside. If there were someone waiting at the other end, he'd have a big problem. There'd be nothing to duck behind in the tunnel if bullets started flying. Sean swallowed, tightening his grip on his weapon. But the moment he took a step forward, the situation changed.

He heard a shout from the other end of the tunnel. The voice sounded like Kishiyama's. Sean threw himself against the wall beside the tunnel's opening, pressing his back flat against the concrete. Another man said something back to the leader, and the two had an excited exchange. Within seconds, footsteps began echoing their way down the hallway, toward Sean.

"Shit," Sean muttered, squaring his jaw.

He weighed his options, trying to determine if it was just the two that were headed his way. From the scuffing feet and chatter, it sounded so. The second man wasn't Gregory. It might have been one of the twins. Both men were assuredly armed, but Sean doubted they had their guns in hand. As far as they knew, their only potential threat—Sean—was still tied up. That was, unless his escape attempt was all part of their plan. He decided that it was best to assume he had the benefit of surprise, and with only two men standing between him and the outside world, Sean knew he couldn't back down.

"Look for an open canister of hard candy," he heard Kishiyama say as his voice grew closer. "That's where they'll be."

Sean's chest tightened. They knew were the detonators were. He didn't know how, but they knew. Any leverage Sean may have had was now gone. He crossed his right arm in front of his chest, twisting his weapon in his hand so its "blade" was perpendicular to the wall. He planted his other hand against the wall behind him, fingers spread to steady himself.

Sean held his breath, and the moment the outline of a figure emerged, he sent a wicked backhanded strike through the tunnel entrance. He caught a glimpse of Kishiyama's wide eyes just before the leader dropped to a knee. The cusp of the armrest swung just above his head and impaled the sternum of the man next to him. It was the father of the baby, his eyes now bulging as his mouth gaped open. A loud gasp spewed from between his lips as his hand fumbled for the rifle slung vertically in front of his stomach.

Kishiyama had toppled to his rear and was scrambling backward. Sean saw no gun in his hand, so he continued the assault on the father. He lunged forward, letting go of the armrest and grabbing for the rifle. It was a Colt Commando semi-automatic, and his hands quickly latched onto its stock and barrel. He yanked the weapon toward him, its sling bringing its owner along for the ride, setting up a colossal head-butt from Sean. Then another.

The armrest clanged along the floor as Sean tried to pull the sling over the weakened man's head. That's when he caught Kishiyama, out of the corner of his eye, reaching for something at his side. It was a gun holster, a pistol inside.

The father's arms flopped around like a beat-up doll's as Sean yanked savagely at the rifle. Sean tried to unclip the sling from above its barrel, but when he saw a knife sheathed to the man's belt and Kishiyama's arm rising from the floor with a pistol, he knew he had to switch gears. He grabbed the knife from the sheath and yanked the man into him by the arm, spinning him so that he was facing Kishiyama. A human shield.

While Kishiyama bobbled the pistol, Sean hooked the man's arm behind his back and lifted the five-inch blade to his throat, guiding him a few steps backward.

"Let him go!" Kishiyama demanded, his pistol jerking up and down as he tried to line up a shot. He'd risen to a knee.

"Fuck you," Sean snarled, hunched down a bit to compensate for the height difference. "Get up and back yourself all the way down that tunnel. We're leaving."

"No one's leaving!" he shouted.

"P-please," the father pleaded, twisting his head as best he could toward Sean. "We're doin' this to survive. I want my little girl to live."

"She *will* live," snapped Sean, holding the knife steady. "Nothing's going to happen in the morning. Your leader's filled your heads with bullshit. He's using you."

"He's lying, Morgan," Kishiyama said calmly. He climbed to his feet, keeping his gun forward. "The prophecy said there'd be liars—non-believers who would try to stoke doubt in your mind. Who would try to stop us! You've known this longer than you've known me."

A whimper dropped from Morgan's mouth. "What we do, we do for humanity," he began whispering.

"Knock that shit off!" Sean snarled. Morgan stopped. "Back off!" he warned Kishiyama again.

"You don't have it within yourself to kill a man, Mr. Coleman," said Kishiyama. "You're not the type."

Sean sneered. "I've killed three men in the past two years, dickhead. They all had it coming, just like you assholes do." He edged forward. "And they probably didn't think I was *the type* either. Now back up!"

Kishiyama's face tightened, Sean's words seemingly having resonated. The leader took a few steps back, keeping his gun trained forward. He glanced over his shoulder at the other end of the tunnel. The junction was empty, the rest of his followers unaware of what was happening. He turned back to Sean, swallowing.

"That's good," said Sean, his knife still against Morgan's throat. "Keep moving."

The three men moved slowly. Sean kept his eyes on Kishiyama, ensuring the leader didn't try to motion instructions to Morgan. Kishiyama again looked behind him, searching for reinforcements but finding none. They had another hundred feet until the end of the tunnel.

Kishiyama gritted his teeth as he stared at Sean. The muscles in his face tightened and twisted so sharply that he almost looked like he was having a stroke. The display likely represented a dozen different scenarios flashing through his mind. His face glistened with sweat under the next lightbulb they passed beneath. He suddenly stopped, his hand trembling.

Sean halted, tugging back on Morgan. "Keep moving," he told Kishiyama, pressing the edge of the blade against Morgan's Adam's apple. He felt his captive swallow.

Kishiyama tilted his head, his eyes softening. "I'm sorry, Morgan."

When Kishiyama straightened his arm, Sean gasped at what he knew what was about to happen. He released Morgan just as the bullets began entering the father's body. Loud pops and Morgan's wails filled the tunnel as Sean sprinted in the opposite direction, tucking his head low. Sparks flew to Sean's left, and his right shoulder jolted as lead pierced it. He grunted and lunged through the tunnel's opening, crashing to the floor as bullets whizzed over his head. Sean pulled himself along the platform until he was out of Kishiyama's line of sight. He glanced at his shoulder where blood ran freely before scanning the area for the knife. It was nowhere to be found. He must have dropped it in the tunnel.

"Wait," Morgan moaned a half second before another shot rang out. Kishiyama had finished him off.

"He shot Morgan!" Kishiyama yelled, his voice echoing through the tunnel. "Help!"

Chapter 18

Out of breath, Sean made it down the steps and ramp, and onto the linoleum. His head swiveled around the room, his mind overloaded with the question of what to do next. Voices sounded from the other end of the tunnel. A man shouted. A woman screamed. The group was arriving on the scene.

Sean held his hand to his shoulder, applying pressure. He winced from the injury's burn. Blood oozed from between his fingers, but he didn't feel as though the bullet was still in him. It was likely a graze, perhaps from a ricochet off the tunnel's wall. He glanced at the vault door but knew he couldn't return to the large room beyond it. He needed to place a shield between him and the others.

Kishiyama was done protecting him. Whatever obligation he'd felt earlier had died with Morgan. The leader was framing him for the man's death, riling up his people into a lynch mob. If there had been any scattered dissent or reluctance among the group, it was quickly being washed away with the raw emotion of one of their own—the father of a little girl—being murdered.

The kitchen and control room didn't have doors, so Sean ran down the hallway toward the living quarters, checking the first and second rooms on the left. Both were locked, and Kishiyama's people still had his keys. A room further down the hallway was typically blocked by a locked chain-link gate, but its padlock had been removed. Sean crashed through the gate, swinging it open hard. When it collided with the adjacent wall, he caught movement inside the room he was barreling toward.

The lone voice he'd heard before—it had belonged to the tall figure that was now scurrying behind tall shelving overflowing with binders. The man was likely armed—all of Kishiyama's people were—but Sean prayed he'd caught the individual by surprise. The cement walls may have subdued the sound of gunshots. At least that's what Sean told himself as he skirted the open door and slid past the first row of shelves.

He kicked an expanded folding chair out of his way and rushed by an old desk covered with electronics and other clutter. His uninjured shoulder collided with the back wall as he tore around the third row of wooden shelving. With his hands out in front of him to cover his face from a potential gunshot, he lunged toward the figure who'd backed himself into a dead-end in front of two tall file cabinets.

But just as he was about to level the man, Sean's eyes bulged and his arms shot out to catch himself along the wall and shelving. Two tiny, alert eyes were staring back at him from the man's arms. They belonged to the infant daughter of the man who'd just been killed.

Holding the baby in a blanket in front of him and cowering against the file cabinets was Mitchell. His mouth gaped below his wide eyes. His frazzled hair covered the sides of his bruised face as his arms shook.

"Son of a bitch!" Sean snarled, clenching his fists and expanding his chest. He wanted to punish Mitchell right then and there, but he couldn't with the baby in his arms. "Where's your gun? Show it to me!"

"It's not here! It's in the bay!" he cried, tucking his head down lower.

"Bullshit! Hand it over!"

"I swear!" he said. "I've been watchin' the baby . . . while the others finish up!"

The little girl made a gurgling noise as Sean's eyes shot back and forth between the two. He didn't know if Mitchell was telling him the truth, but if he didn't keep the others—who were undeniably armed—from entering the room, it wouldn't matter. He pounded the side of his fist against the wall and spun around, running back to the entrance.

He heard fast footsteps along linoleum just before he slammed the wooden door and twisted the lock at the center of its knob. He knew the lock wouldn't keep them out for long, so he began looking around the room for objects to barricade in front of the door. The file cabinets might work, but they'd take forever to drag from the opposite corner.

He noticed some old radio equipment and bundles of wiring on top of the desk he'd run by earlier. He didn't know if it belonged to Mitchell, or if any of it worked, but he'd have to find out later.

"Mitchell!" he yelled, scanning the bottom shelves for something with good weight to it. "Get your ass out here so I can see you!"

Sean's eyes slid along the wall beside the door. Underneath some old picture prints were stacks of cardboard boxes, none of which were big enough to serve his purpose. Mitchell timidly emerged from behind the back row, the baby in his arms. She squirmed and began to fuss, her fingers latching onto some of his long hair. He hushed her.

"Sit down in that chair," Sean ordered, motioning toward the toppled folding chair.

Mitchell carefully moved toward the chair, leaning over and lifting it upright with his free hand. Sean could hear him swallow as he sat down.

When the doorknob rattled, Sean yelled, "I've got the baby! I've got Mitchell too! Think about that before you start shooting through the door!"

The warning would buy him some time, but likely not much. Kishiyama knew he'd entered the room without a weapon, and if it were true that Mitchell had left his gun elsewhere in the compound, one of the others would assuredly know about it. He had no more time than it would take his pursuers to put two and two together.

"What's happenin'?" Mitchell asked, out of breath.

"Shut up," Sean answered.

Sean wasn't all that familiar with the room he was in. The county's more sensitive archived documents were kept there, which was why it was closed to public tours. Though Sean's keys had granted him access, he'd had no reason to enter in the past, other than once when he'd assisted a county layman with a cart of boxes. If there were items inside that could help him with his current situation, he'd have to do some looking for them.

When he moved between rows, his shoulder struck the edge of the shelving, and a binder from one of the upper shelves fell to its side. The sound drew Sean's head upward where he saw dust floating below the overhead lights. Sean gazed at the swirling mist, blinking. The racks were extremely heavy, but they were also lanky. Up top, they could sway like skyscrapers in an earthquake.

There was only about four feet in between each row of shelves, narrow by most standards, but perfect for what Sean had in mind. He glanced at the locked door and then up at the top shelf of the first rack. He nodded his head and then turned to Mitchell, whose seated body jolted from the sudden attention.

"Put that baby under the desk behind you. On the floor, in her blanket."

"What?" Mitchell asked.

"She'll be safe there. I need your help."

"I'm not helpin' you," he said, shaking his head.

Sean stormed toward him. Mitchell shrank in his chair, eyes wincing as Sean grabbed him by his collar and brought his face in close. "Mitchell, you *will* help me, or you're not going to live long enough to survive the end of the world. Got it? People are dead and you killed my fucking dog. I'd be happy to return the favor right now, but that would put me in charge of that baby. Is that what you really want?"

Some spit slid from Mitchell's mouth as his body shook. "No," he muttered.

"Good," Sean said, releasing his collar and taking a step back. "Now do as I said."

As Mitchell rose from his chair and carried the baby to the desk, Sean stepped between the first two rows of shelves. He lifted his right foot and planted it on the second shelf of the first rack. He twisted his body and then did the same thing with his left on the second rack, straddling the aisle. Facing Mitchell and the baby, he held onto the vertical supports with his hands.

Having laid the baby in her blanket beneath the desk, where she began to fuss again, Mitchell approached Sean. His glare shifted between Sean and the ceiling. "Are you tryin' to climb out of here?"

"No," Sean grunted, going through the same motions as before to lift himself up to the next column of shelves. He then moved his right foot over to join his left on the second rack, doing the same with his hands on the first rack. When he turned to Mitchell, he read conflict in his steady eyes.

"If you even think about running for that door," Sean threatened. "I'll drop down there and beat your skull in."

"I wouldn't leave the baby with you," said Mitchell, his voice shaky.

Sean gritted his teeth and began pushing forward with his arms while pushing backwards with his legs. The wood from both sets of shelves creaked. He grunted as the bullet wound on his shoulder reminded him it was there.

"Do what I'm doing, Mitchell," Sean ordered. "On the shelves below me."

More binders began to topple. Sean could feel the space between the two structures widening. Mitchell moved into position below him, his hands on one row and his feet on the other. Sean flexed his arms and straightened his back, groaning. A cardboard box fell from above, bouncing off his hip, and crashing to the floor beside Mitchell. It exploded into a heap of manila folders and papers.

"Push harder, Mitchell!" Sean demanded. He watched Mitchell's body tighten in compliance below him. He heard his grunts.

There was a loud thud at the door, and then another. The others were trying to break in. The baby cried loudly now, nearly drowning out their efforts.

"Push!" Sean yelled, his arms and legs shaking as they straightened.

A sharp crack of wood, and another immediately after it, brought a sudden release of tension. The first row of shelves buckled and toppled forward. Wood splintered as boxes and binders found air. Sean lost his handhold and crashed down on Mitchell. The two landed with a sickening thud along the tile and debris below, Mitchell breaking much of Sean's fall.

The baby screamed as the crashing and banging continued. Sean lifted and twisted his head just in time to see the second row— seemingly in slow motion—falling in the opposite direction. Its top edge caught the bottom of an overhead light panel, knocking half of it from its fixture and sending sparks flying. Sean moved off Mitchell and scrambled toward the baby on his hands and knees. He lunged over binders and boxes and tucked his head under the desk, using his broad back to shield the wailing infant from the shattered glass that fell from above. He stayed put until the clamor came to an end, watching the baby's curious eyes examine him quietly for a few seconds before her face shriveled up and a new round of crying commenced.

Sean backed up and slid to his butt. He took in a breath before turning toward the door. Dust hovered in the air as a couple sheets of paper drifted to a rest on the floor. Beyond it was the collapsed shelving, propped diagonally against the top half of the door and most of the wall beside it. The others weren't getting in.

The room looked like a bomb had been dropped on it. All of the shelving had been toppled, including the third row that had been knocked against the back wall by the second, like a giant pair of dominoes. Half of the lighting panel above was still lit, swinging back and forth on wires from the ceiling. The archives were scattered everywhere. Some were in piles on the floor. Others were still cradled in the angled shelves against the walls.

The baby continued to cry as Mitchell coughed and slowly climbed to his feet. He held his hand to the back of his head. Though he was covered with dust and hair hung in his face, Sean could read softness in his sunken eyes. He peered around Sean at the baby.

"Thank you," he said, his eyes glazed over. "You protected the baby. Thank you."

Sean walked over to Mitchell. "Don't mention it," he said before forming a fist and sending a solid jab right between his eyes.

Mitchell's head snapped backward and he crashed to his butt on top of an open box. He moaned as Sean reached down and grabbed him by the collar. Sean yanked him up to his feet like a ragdoll and sent a hard fist into his stomach, lifting Mitchell off the floor. He followed up with a knee to the same spot, eliminating any air from his chest that may have remained. Mitchell's eyes were the size of ping-pong balls when Sean grabbed him by the collar again. With his other hand, he latched onto Mitchell's belt. Sean planted his feet and swung and tossed Mitchell like a discus. He flew through the air, only going a couple of feet before his back slammed into the wall beside them. He crumbled to the floor, on top of opened binders and papers, gasping and raising his arm up in front of him defensively.

"You sick fucks!" Sean shouted, his fists clenched.

All he could see was Avalanche. He jammed his hand into his

pocket and retrieved the dog's collar. When Mitchell tried to crawl away, Sean came up behind him and wrapped the collar around his throat.

"Killing a dog, you fucking cowards?" Sean snarled, pressing a knee into Mitchell's back as he pulled on the collar.

Mitchell's arms flailed before his hands went to the collar, tugging at it. "Didn't kill!" he cried. "Didn't—"

Sean pulled back harder, showing his teeth as his arms flexed. He kept up the pressure, peeling Mitchell's chest up off of the floor before removing his knee and using his foot to stomp his body back down to the tile. Sean growled, took a breath, and whipped the collar off Mitchell, throwing it across the room.

Mitchell gasped for air as the baby wailed. He erupted into a coughing fit his hands covering his throat.

"Didn't kill," he muttered.

"Sean Coleman!" a voice sounded out from the other side of the door, over the baby's cries. It was Kishiyama. "Let us in so we can talk this over!"

Sean scoffed, shaking his head. "Talk about what?" he yelled. "How you murdered Morgan and are pinning it on me because your people are stupid enough to believe whatever you tell them?" He knew the others could hear his voice.

"Morgan's . . . dead?" Mitchell whispered, his beaten body writhing along the floor. His head turned slowly toward the baby.

"You killed him in cold blood, Sean," lectured Kishiyama. "He was the father of that little girl. A husband." He took a moment, and when he spoke again, there was a crackle in his voice. "We've been trying to spare your life. We've protected you. And this is how you repay us?"

"You fucking weasel," Sean muttered under his breath.

"Open the door and give us the girl! There's no reason anyone else has to die!"

"The door's barricaded!" Mitchell shouted in a hoarse voice, clenching his ribs and neck afterwards. "We can't open it."

"You son of a bitch!" a woman screamed from the other side. "Give me my daughter!"

Sean's eyes went to Mitchell as her loudening sobs paralleled her baby's cries. She wept and pounded at the door.

"Give me my Diana," she cried.

Sean's stomach dropped at the revelation that the baby shared his sister's name. He shook his head, clenching his fists and imagining himself giving Kishiyama the same treatment he'd just given Mitchell, only not letting up until the leader stopped breathing. The baby wailed even louder, as did her mother. Sean sat stone-faced, waiting for the mother's crying to subside. It eventually did.

"Okay, everybody get back to your jobs," came Kishiyama's voice, his words muffled as if he now had his back to the door. "Let Gregory and me deal with this problem. We have a few hours left and we need to make them count. They're not going anywhere."

"No!" the mother shouted. "My baby!"

Kishiyama's voice lowered, and his words were hard to make out, but his tone suggested that he was trying to console the mother. Farther away now, Sean heard him bark an order to "Dean and Doug," probably to deal with Morgan's body. After that, there was only silence, though Sean assumed someone was probably close to the door, eavesdropping.

"How could you?" said Mitchell, his voice shaking. "He was a father."

"I didn't," said Sean, his eyes tracing what he could see of the doorframe. "Dear Leader shot him. On purpose. Just like he did Mahan."

Mitchell shook his head. "You're lyin'."

Sean's head whipped toward Mitchell. "And you're brainwashed," he said angrily. "If I'd had a gun, I would have shot Kishiyama, not one of his sheep." He raised his arms in the air. "You see a gun on me, Mitchell?"

"Either you dropped it, or you killed him a diff—"

"Oh, just shut up," said Sean, rubbing his knuckles against his own head in frustration. "Your head is wedged up Kishiyama's ass sideways, and it's not coming out. I get it. You don't have to keep reminding me." He glared at Mitchell as the baby continued complaining. "Make yourself useful. Get up off your ass and take care of that baby. Feed her. Change her diaper. Do whatever you were doing before I came in here."

Mitchell glared back for a few seconds before gingerly rolling to his hands and knees. He cringed and held his ribs as he climbed to his feet. Trudging over to the desk, he leaned down and retrieved the baby. He brought her up to his arms and began shushing her. When he reached toward a soft satchel on the floor beside the desk, Sean told him to wait.

Sean pulled himself up to his knees and then to his feet. He joined them and grabbed the bag from the floor, quickly digging through it. He searched for weapons but found mostly bottles, diapers, and formula. Satisfied that nothing inside was a threat, he handed the bag to Mitchell. Mitchell took it, glanced over the room, and then brought the baby over to a space on the floor that was free of debris.

Sean peered at his own shoulder, wincing as he moved his hand over his wound. He re-applied pressure.

"I didn't kill your dog," Mitchell whispered.

"Like hell you didn't," Sean said in a normal voice. "I saw the bloody collar."

"Shh," snapped Mitchell. "If you don't lower your voice, they *will* kill him."

"What are you talking about?" asked Sean, approaching him.

Mitchell kept his voice low. "I was supposed to, but I didn't. That was *my* blood. I took it from my shoulder." He nodded toward his right arm.

Sean's eyes narrowed as Mitchell continued attending to the baby. He pulled up Mitchell's sleeve until he found a large bandage just below his shoulder, held to his skin with adhesive. Some blood had soaked through, but it had long since dried.

"Bullshit," said Sean. "You wouldn't go against Kishiyama. You wouldn't go against your dumb-ass prophecy."

Mitchell clenched his jaw. "I've read the prophecy many times," he began matter-of-factly. "It says to kill *your* pets, not *other people's* pets. It's not the place of others to do what's the owner's responsibility." He swallowed and tilted his head. "The others interpret it differently."

Sean's eyes were glued to Mitchell as he weighed in his mind whether what he was hearing could be true, or if it was a story to keep him from receiving another beating. "If the others think Avalanche is dead, and he's not, where is he?"

"There's a metal shed northwest of here, on the other side of the campground. He's locked inside with food and water. No sense in him going hungry or thirsty between now and tomorrow mornin'."

Sean knew of the shed. It had been put up by a farmer who owned some adjoining land a few years back, or so he'd been told. The county allegedly bought it from him and now stored tools and some machinery there. Sean backed away, still unsure whether or not he could believe Mitchell. When he turned to the desk beside him, Sean noticed an '80s boombox sitting on a shelf above it. Below were miscellaneous electric parts and wiring, and a metal box with multiple knobs. Beside the box was a tipped over microphone with a short stand.

"Holy shit," he muttered, realizing that the box was a HAM radio. Its cord led down to an outlet on the wall.

He leaned in, still holding his shoulder, and found a switch in the back of the box. He flipped it on. When the face of the radio lit up, so did his eyes. He immediately began twisting knobs. When static poured out of a smaller box beside the larger one, he gasped and grabbed the microphone, pulling it upright and depressing a button at its base.

"Hey," he excitedly said, unsure of how to begin a cold radio call. "I'm at the Missile Site Park in Weld County, close to Greeley, Colorado. I need help."

Muffled laughter crept into the room from the other side of the door. It sounded like Gregory.

"It's not set up yet," Mitchell said calmly, keeping his back to Sean as he changed the baby's diaper on the floor.

Sean switched channels, listening for variances in the static but finding none. He repeated the exercise over and over, getting the same results, until Mitchell spoke up again.

"It won't work without the antenna."

"Where's the antenna?" Sean demanded.

Mitchell rolled up the dirty diaper and used its side tape to secure it shut. Sean waited for him to answer, but he didn't.

Sean dropped the microphone on the desk with a clunk. He approached Mitchell, grabbing him by the back of his neck and placing his mouth beside his ear. "Where's the antenna?"

His tense shoulders arching, Mitchell hissed, "Back in the bay, I . . . I think. I was just testin' that the radio was still operational. Someone dropped it in the tunnel when it was brought in from the bus. We weren't plannin' on using it until after the gestation period."

"After the what?"

"The gestation period. The reformin' of the earth. Once it's done, the plan is to start lookin' for other survivors."

Sean scoffed. Keeping one hand on Mitchell and the other on his shoulder, he leaned in close and lowered his voice. "Was it you?" he whispered, glancing at the door.

"What?" said Mitchell, cringing.

"Was it you? Who messed with my ropes, back in the other room."

Mitchell twisted his head as best he could toward Sean, his eyes sober and blinking. "I don't know what you mean."

Sean grunted and whipped his hand off Mitchell. He backed away, and when he felt the seat of the folding chair press into him from behind, he dropped into it, leaning back and taking in a deep breath. *If it wasn't Mitchell, who was trying to help me?*

The baby had quieted, and by the time Mitchell had hoisted her back up and was rocking her in his arms, her eyes were beginning to dry.

Sean opened his mouth to speak, but Kishiyama's voice suddenly sounded out from behind the door.

"It makes sense why you ran in there like a coward, Sean. You knew I could no longer protect you. Not after what you did to Morgan."

"No more *Mr. Coleman?*" asked Sean, leaning forward with his elbows on top of his thighs. "Are we on a first name basis now that you're pinning the man's murder on me? Is that how it works?"

"He's lying, Mitchell," said Kishiyama.

"You don't have to worry about Mitchell," said Sean, watching Mitchell. "You own his brain. You could tell him you're a thirteen-year-old Swedish peasant girl, and he'd still believe you."

Seconds that seemed like minutes ticked by before Kishiyama spoke again. "On an upper shelf inside a canister of old shelter candy, I'm being told."

Sean shook his head in frustration.

Kishiyama continued. "A pretty smart place to hide the detonators, I must admit. But as was the case with you barricading yourself in there, it was an ultimately pointless exercise. We now have everything we need, and you're isolated and unable to cause us any more problems."

"I have two of your people," Sean said. "You don't sound particularly concerned about them." He glared at Mitchell. "Imagine that," he whispered.

When Kishiyama said nothing, Mitchell spoke to Sean in a soft voice, keeping his eyes on the baby. "We're loyal and committed to each other, includin' this child." He raised his eyes to Sean. "Especially this child."

"Morgan would disagree with you . . . if he still could," said Sean.

Mitchell shook his head, biting his lip and lowering his gaze back to the baby.

Silence crawled by for several minutes, and Sean wondered if Kishiyama had left. He meandered around the room, concentrating on trying to figure out his next move. The baby eventually drifted off to sleep in Mitchell's arms, letting Sean clear his head. Still, no doable ideas were presenting themselves. The heavy, disfigured shelving had so thoroughly beset the doorway that it could take Sean a good thirty minutes with an axe and crowbar to even begin to clear it, and that was if he wanted to.

Though Sean was decidedly trapped, he knew that his safest play was to stay put—for now. Someone was assuredly waiting on the other side of the door with a gun, and the previous incident had made clear that ducking behind a hostage wasn't a strategy he could count on. Though Mitchell seemed to be more important to Kishiyama than the others in the group, save Gregory, he wasn't a reliable insurance policy.

Still, Sean needed a plan for when the others would eventually bust in, if not for Mitchell, then for the baby. Kishiyama's mind control over the group was impressive, but if there were anything that could challenge or even bend it a little, it would be the love of a mother. If the leader couldn't guarantee the protection of that child, he'd risk the beginnings of a mutiny. Kishiyama was savvy enough to recognize that and act accordingly.

The ceiling above was solid concrete, with the overhead wiring for the lights encased in metal. Remnants of a ventilation system hung from the south side of the ceiling, but the ducts were narrow and thin, and couldn't be crawled through even if they could be reached. Sean noticed a foot-wide hole along the back wall, where the toppled shelving had punched through drywall. He carefully began scaling the shelving as best he could, nostrils flaring when pain jolted up his injured shoulder. The damaged structure creaked from his weight. He'd barely made it to the second tier when the shelf under his foot split loose from its frame, dropping him back to the floor with a couple of boxes and splintered wood. Before falling, he did manage to catch a glimpse of a cement barrier behind the drywall.

"Fuck," he grunted.

"The door's the only way out," said Mitchell. "We're stuck in here until they get us out. We should just wait for that to happen."

Sean chuckled, brushing dust from his pants. "Thanks for the advice, mark." He checked his shoulder, confirming that the bleeding hadn't started again.

"Mark?"

"As in carnival mark—a sucker. The kind of person who believes in magic and thinks professional wrestling is real." He turned to Mitchell. "The kind of person who thinks a meteor is going to destroy the planet, just because some asshole with a dopey mustache tells him so."

Mitchell shook his head and muttered, "We knew this was comin' before we ever met him."

"What?" Sean asked, walking toward him.

Mitchell sighed, his eyes averted away. "The prophecy didn't come from Kishiyama."

"I know. It supposedly came from some Wisconsin chick. But you're saying that you knew about it before you knew Kishiyama?"

Mitchell turned and began walking away from him. "It doesn't matter."

Sean grabbed his shoulder, stopping him. "Then there's no reason not to explain it to me. How long have you and your people known Kishiyama?"

"We were blessed with his arrival last September."

"Less than a year ago?"

"Yes. It was very good fortune. Without him, we wouldn't have . . ." Mitchell stopped, catching himself. He took a breath. "I shouldn't be talkin' about this."

"Oh, I think you should," said Sean. "So you all were doomsdayers before he ever came into the picture. You already believed in this bullshit, and let me guess: he rode into town like a white knight and ginned you up on this idea of taking over a missile silo."

"That's not what happened," Mitchell said, frustration in his voice. "We were already talkin' about silos. Others were too."

"What others?"

"Others. From all over the world. Others who knew this day was comin'. People like us."

"How did you meet these others?"

Mitchell hesitated. He finally shrugged and said, "Prodigy, mostly. Some on America Online."

"America Online?" Sean said, recognizing the brand from several computer discs he'd received as junk mail over the years. "The Internet?"

Mitchell nodded. "Yes. Online communities. Chat rooms."

Sean's jaw tightened. He nodded as his eyes stared straight ahead. "Where anyone can read what you're talking about."

Chapter 19

Mitchell had been reluctant at first to reveal the group's origins, but some poking and prodding, along with Sean's reciting of the prophecy as it had been told to him by Kishiyama, soon opened him up like a spigot. The fact that the leader had already made Sean privy to the group's justification for being there seemed to leave little reason in Mitchell's mind for continued discretion. It was as if the revelation had lifted a burden from his conscience, and he was now free—and even eager—to get his side of the story out.

As Sean had suspected from the license plate on the bus, the group was from Texas. Fort Davis, Texas, to be exact—a small, isolated town about three hours southeast of El Paso. Most of the group had grown up in the nearby hills and had known each other since childhood. And judging by Mitchell's side ramblings about the US government and 9/11, it was clear that conspiracy theories and anti-establishment sentiment were tightly engrained in their culture.

The group had subscribed to end-of-the-world scenarios for some time, the community seemingly conditioned by town elders. Mitchell viewed them as mentors and talked about them endearingly—especially an old school teacher named Gus, who had false teeth and walked with a cane. Mitchell looked up to him like a grandfather until he'd passed on. It wasn't until the Internet became more accessible that they'd learned that they weren't alone in their beliefs—not by a longshot.

According to Mitchell, Kishiyama's presentation of Nancy Lieder's doomsday doctrine was pretty accurate. What Kishiyama had failed to mention, however, was that the Wisconsinite's prophecy had supposedly been relayed to her directly by aliens—as in, extraterrestrials—who referred to themselves as Zetas. Sean had to bite his tongue as Mitchell laid out the intergalactic communicative relationship, deciding that it was more productive to gain as much information as possible than to further berate Mitchell over his delusion.

It was Kishiyama's involvement with the group that was of particular interest to Sean, being that he had gone from being an outsider to the leader of the pack within the span of eight months. Mitchell said that they had met Kishiyama over the Internet. After weeks of messaging back and forth and a long phone conversation, Kishiyama drove out to Fort Davis to meet them. He'd brought Gregory with him.

"He got it," said Mitchell. "He understood, and agreed that a missile silo made the most sense. He told us why this one here would give us the best chance—you know, of survivin'. He'd thought of everything, had maps and blueprints. And with Gregory being ex-military, he was able to get us weapons and help train us on 'em."

"Wait," Sean said, leaning forward from his seat on a couple of boxes. "Gregory was in the military?"

"Yeah, he doesn't talk about it much. The government screwed him over somehow. That's what they do, after all. Anyways, he and Kishiyama had it all figured out. Without 'em, we'd have been lost. We owe 'em our lives."

Sean rolled his eyes. "Where's Kishiyama from? Colorado?"

"No. San Antonio. He'd never been to Colorado."

Sean was convinced that this wasn't true. Mahan had recognized Kishiyama from somewhere, and he highly doubted it was San Antonio, Texas. "What's his job? Does he have one?"

"Yeah, he's a retired scientist. That's why he's so smart."

Sean's eyes narrowed. "A scientist. What kind of scientist?"

"Just a general kind, I guess," Mitchell said, shrugging his shoulders. "He knows a lot about geography and the weather. Hell, he's knows a lot about lots of things."

Sean shook his head, sighing.

"You still don't believe me?" asked Mitchell.

Sean fixed his eyes on Mitchell's. "Mitchell, I believe you're being honest with me, but I also don't think you're telling me the truth." He leaned back and yawned, thinking about how much the words that had just left his mouth sounded like one of the fortune cookie sayings his father used to drop, back when Sean knew him as a wise uncle.

Mitchell gazed at him with a tilted head.

Sean's eyes stung from fatigue and increasing sensitivity to the light above. He rubbed them with his fists. "What about you?" he asked.

"What?"

"What's your job? Kishiyama's a scientist. Gregory's a soldier. What are you, an electrician?"

Mitchell nodded. "Partly. Mainly construction though. I learned it from my pop before he died. But over the past few years, I've been doin' more tearin' down than buildin' up."

Sean squinted. "What do you mean?"

"Blastin' mostly. Makin' way for roads. Tearin' into mountains. That sorta thing."

Sean nodded, drawing in a deep breath. "So that's why you're special."

Mitchell's head recoiled. "Huh?"

"It keeps coming back to the detonators. I'm betting that Kishiyama and Gregory don't know jack-shit about explosives, do they? But you do, and that's why you're so damn important to them. That's why they need you."

"Well yeah," said Mitchell matter-of-factly. "They're *all* countin' on me. If we get buried in here, I'm goin' to need to blast us out. If someone who doesn't know what they're doin' tries it, they could bury us for good."

Sean lifted his arms and spread his back out along the dented cardboard beneath him. Interlacing his fingers behind the back of his head, he squinted up at the ceiling.

"What are you doin'?" asked Mitchell.

"Thinking," Sean answered.

A sensation of nakedness overcame the boy. His front pocket was no longer sagging. His stomach dropped, and a gasp left his mouth. His hand quickly went to his chest. It was gone.

With his eyes wide and his breathing heavy, he subtly leaned forward in his seat. He searched the truck's floorboard as the cab bobbled from a washboard section of the dirt road. All he found was a candy wrapper he'd dropped there earlier and some pea gravel from his boots. He brushed his hands along the front pockets of his jeans, and then the back ones. It wasn't there either. He sank back into the cushion, swallowing and slowly turning his head toward the driver of the vehicle.

Uncle Zed was gazing out through the windshield, the rim of his straw cowboy hat hovering over his long silver sideburns and the toothpick that dangled out of his mouth. It didn't appear as though he'd noticed the boy's curious behavior until he spoke.

"What's the problem, Sean?"

The boy pursed his lips. Ashamed, he turned his head away, directing his glare through the side window.

"Lose my badge?" Zed asked.

The boy's shoulders deflated. His face pruned up and he felt tears forming in his eyes.

"It's no big deal, Sean. I have others." His freckled hand left the steering wheel, moving to Sean's shoulder. "Really, it's no big deal."

"But this one was yours," said the boy. "It wasn't like the others. It was special. It had your name on it." He turned toward Zed. "I don't know how I lost—"

"Hold on," Zed interrupted. He pulled over to the shoulder of the road and popped the truck into park. He twisted in his seat, turning to face the boy. He pulled the toothpick from his mouth.

"I'm sorry, Uncle Zed," said the boy, his voice crackling.

Zed's soft eyes offered a wink. His lips curled into a smile, looking upon the boy with unmistakable pride. "It's not the badge," he said. "It's the man behind it."

The boy let himself breathe. A smile began to form on his face, but before it could settle, he watched his uncle's jaw unexpectedly tighten. Zed's eyes widened with what looked like fear.

"Keep your eyes open, Sean," he said.

A half second later, a loud blast echoed off the inside of the truck. Glass shattered, and the boy's body convulsed, his hands covering his ringing ears. His jaw dropped as he watched smoke pour from a gaping hole in Zed's throat.

Zed's eyes floated aimlessly for a moment before they met the boy's gaze. A gurgling noise fell from his open neck before his body slumped against the door behind him. His dead eyes remained on the boy.

"Dad!" the boy screamed.

———◆———

Sean's body jolted forward. He slid off the cardboard boxes, spilling onto his butt on the tile floor. A stream of sweat ran down his jaw. The bright room was blurry at first. He blinked and whipped his head back and forth as things came into focus. The sight of collapsed shelves and a jumbled mess of boxes and binders put him back in the archives room.

His heart jumped when he didn't see Mitchell. He sprung to his knees and twisted himself toward the door. It was still pinned shut by the shelving case.

"You really were asleep?" asked a sober voice from across the room.

Sean followed the words, finding Mitchell sitting on the floor beside the desk, with his back against the wall. He still held the sleeping Diana in his arms. He looked tired, his eyes barely open.

"What?" Sean asked.

"I thought you were screwin' with me this whole time," said Mitchell, lowering his head. "Pretendin'. Waitin' for me to try something."

Sean rubbed his right eye with the palm of his hand. "Why the hell would I bother doing that?"

Mitchell shook his head. "I don't know, but your eyes were half open. They looked like they were followin' me. It was weird. I've never seen anyone sleep like that."

Mitchell's words hovered in Sean's mind for a moment. They not only echoed what the woman he'd slept with the night before had told him, but also fell in line with what his father had said in the closing seconds of his dream: "Keep your eyes open, Sean."

"Who's Uncle Zed?" asked Mitchell.

Sean glared at him before responding. "You heard me say that, when I was asleep?"

Mitchell nodded. "Right before you . . . woke up. Your uncle?"

"It doesn't matter," Sean said. He pulled himself to his feet and stretched out his back with his hands on his hips. "How long was I asleep?"

"I'm not sure. It might have been an hour."

"An hour?" Sean said, his eyes wide. "You thought I was fake sleeping for an hour?"

Mitchell shrugged his shoulders. He rocked Diana in his arms when she began to stir. "I fed her. She took the formula well."

Sean walked over to them, looking down at the baby. The delicate features of her face softened his eyes. "No one tried to get in while I was out?"

Mitchell shook his head.

Sean lifted his gaze and examined the room again, hoping for some fresh perspective. He wasn't sure what he was looking for, having earlier checked the walls for flaws and finding none. Still, his father's words from the dream kept repeating themselves in his head: "Keep your eyes open, Sean." And so he did.

He skimmed the ceiling before lowering his gaze across the oversized photographs on the wall—old black-and-white pictures of the inside of the facility from when it was operational. One of the photos was of some bunkbeds against a wall and a footlocker in a corner of a room. Another showed a janitor mopping a tile floor. The third was of a lounge chair with a lamp next to it, and the fourth was mostly covered by a section of collapsed shelving.

"They'll get through that door before it's time," said Mitchell, blinking sleepily.

"Before it's time for what?"

"You know, when everything changes at 7:43. They'll want to make sure we're safe. Diana, anyway. And the others. Maybe even you."

"We're not *safe* in here?" asked Sean raising a hand in the air. "This room's just as good as the others."

Mitchell lifted his eyes. "It's not as good as the exhaust pit in the bay. There's more protection there." He pointed up at the damaged light fixture that dangled above. "Less chance of somethin' like that or worse fallin' and hittin' someone. Less chance of a wall cavin' in."

Sean shook his head.

"We're talkin' about major changes to the earth's crust," Mitchell added.

"Whatever."

Sean moved in closer to the pictures when something in one of them caught his eye—the floor in the photo of the janitor. It matched the tile beneath Sean's feet. The photos had been taken in the very room he was now trapped in. The same tile was visible at the bottom of the fourth picture, the top section of the photo obscured by boxes on a shelf that had been parked in front of the image.

Sean leaned forward and crawled across broken wood, binders, and cardboard until he was able to push the boxes aside.

"What are you doin'?" Mitchell asked.

Sean ignored him as he stared at the fourth photograph, now fully visible. His eyes widened, and a grin slowly developed across his face. "Keep your eyes open, Sean," he said to himself.

The image was of one of the silo's old crew members—Collins, the man who'd later killed himself inside the facility. As with the photo back in the control room, there was sadness in his face, and the uneasiness in his eyes suggested that he'd been photographed by surprise. This time, however, Collins wasn't posing. Wearing a short-sleeve shirt and a pair of tense biceps, he was pulling himself up out of an open panel in the floor. There was some type of crawlspace below the room. How far it went, Sean aimed to find out.

Sean twisted his head back toward Mitchell, his grin having morphed into a sly smile. That smile quickly flattened, however, when Sean noticed a stark paleness in Mitchell's face. With open mouth and trembling arms, he was glaring right past Sean.

"What?" Sean asked.

Mitchell's body wobbled. He awkwardly pulled himself up to his feet by sliding his back up against wall behind him. When he stumbled forward, nearly looking as though he was about to pass out, Sean lunged toward him. He reached for Mitchell's chest and snagged Diana from his arms just as he collapsed back down to the floor.

"What the hell's a matter with you?" Sean gasped as he juggled the baby in his arms.

Sean dropped to a knee, and once he had the baby's head

supported above his forearm, he turned his attention back to Mitchell who was now on his butt, still staring at the wall. His body continued to shake.

"No," Mitchell gasped.

"No, what?" Sean followed Mitchell's eyes to the wall where the pictures hung. "What's your problem?"

"You had to have . . . have p-put that . . . there."

"Oh, Christ," Sean said. "You'd better not be having a stroke. I'll get blamed for that too."

"But . . . you couldn't have." Mitchell's words were garbled.

"Just breathe, Mitchell. Calm yourself down. This kid doesn't need me taking over as her nanny. Compose yourself."

Mitchell mumbled to himself as he grunted and pulled himself up to his feet. All Sean caught was "be sure." The man ran toward the pictures, climbing up the shelves in front of them the way Sean had, but without the caution. Facing the image of the janitor mopping the floor, he shook his head and brought his hands to his face, breathing in short gasps. Sean moved closer, still holding the baby.

The young man in the photo was dressed in a janitorial uniform, and his eyes were pointed toward the camera. As was the case with the crew member in the other photo, the shot seemed to have been taken without his knowledge. He had short black hair, arched brows, and narrow eyes. When Sean stared deeper into those eyes, a sense of familiarity stewed in his gut. A few seconds later, his stomach dropped. He lowered his gaze to the stenciled lettering just above the man's chest pocket. It read "Kishiyama."

Chapter 20

"Never been to Colorado, huh?" Sean chided, standing below Mitchell with the baby. He watched as Mitchell's eyes continue to glaze over. "Except for when he worked here, in this very building, mopping floors."

"There has to be . . . there has to be an explanation," Mitchell whispered.

"There is," Sean said, lowering his voice. He didn't want whoever might be outside the door to hear what they were saying. "It's what I've been saying. Kishiyama's been lying to you. He's using you and your friends for something, and it's not to survive the apocalypse."

Mitchell shook his head. "The prophecy is real."

"Fine. Believe it's real. But don't believe for another second that Kishiyama does, or that it's the reason he's here." Sean moved in closer. "You were there when he shot Mahan. Did you see what I saw, right before he pulled the trigger?"

Mitchell slowly twisted his head toward Sean, blinking.

"Yeah," Sean said, nodding his head. "You saw it. Mahan knew who Kishiyama was. He recognized him." When Mitchell shook his head and opened his mouth, Sean cut him off. "You forced yourself to believe you'd seen it wrong. That you'd heard it wrong. That maybe Mahan had confused him for someone else. Well, now you know that your instincts were right."

Mitchell carefully climbed down from the shelving, his legs wobbly when he dropped to the floor, enough that he slid to his knees. He swallowed and said, "Do you think your boss just recognized him from the photo?"

Sean lowered himself to a knee in front of Mitchell. "A stranger from a decades-old photograph? I doubt it. It's got to be more than that. They had some kind of history."

Mitchell glared at the floor. Seconds ticked by before he spoke again. "Could Mahan have worked here, at the silo, back when it was still active?"

"No," Sean said, his lips curling at Mitchell's slow but steady awakening from his leader's mind control. "He was too young. It had to have been more recently."

Sean stretched out his arms and handed Diana back to Mitchell. He wasn't prepared for the handoff but complied.

"This explains the candy though," Sean said. "How he knew."

"Candy?"

"The shelter candy. The *carbohydrate supplements* in that old canister, where I'd hidden the detonators."

Mitchell's face tightened. His eyes were riddled with confusion.

"Kishiyama figured out where I'd put them because he recognized their smell on my breath, back in the other room. I imagine everyone ate those things when they worked here, even the janitor."

Mitchell's expression didn't change.

Sean lowered his shoulders, sighing. "The candies have a very distinct smell—one that sticks with you. I'd be able to recognize it anywhere, too."

Mitchell nodded, though Sean suspected he wasn't quite following what he was saying. There were too many other things clouding his mind.

"Listen, Mitchell," Sean began. "I'm done harping on you for buying into the Wisconsin alien-whisperer's *X-Files* crap. On that, we're going to have to have a gentlemen's disagreement. I think you're an honest man, and I get that you and your Texas friends believe in this crap, and nothing I can say is going to change that."

Mitchell gazed emotionlessly at Sean as he spoke. Sean continued.

"And *because* you're an honest man, I believe you when you tell me that Avalanche is alive and well, and waiting in that shed. And if that's *not* the case, there's going to be hell to pay."

"It's true," muttered Mitchell.

"Good. Now in case I'm not making myself clear, I don't have a beef with you or any of your people. Just Kishiyama and Gregory. And I think it's becoming pretty obvious, even to you, that those two *aren't* your people. As God is my witness, Kishiyama murdered this baby's father. He shot right through him to get to me, as if his life and his family's lives meant absolutely nothing."

Mitchell took his gaze off Sean to look at Diana's face. His eyes began to water. He swallowed and nodded.

"Whatever those two are up to, I'm going to put an end to it," said Sean. "I'm not going to let them kill anyone else." He leaned forward and climbed to his feet, his knee popping as he did. Looking at Mitchell with the baby, he added, "And when I'm done with them, you and your people are welcome to stay here and see what happens at 7:43. If it turns out you're right, and all hell breaks loose, you'll be in the safest place I know."

Mitchell's eyes fell to his side, seemingly in contemplation.

Sean climbed along the shelving and grabbed the photograph on the end from the wall, tearing it off at the corners where the adhesive wouldn't give. Mitchell sat on the floor as Sean climbed back down and held the picture out in front of him, one hand at the top and one at the bottom. Sean peered around its edge, comparing scenes. Determining that the removed panel in the photo lined up with an area of floor between the first and second rows of toppled shelves, he walked over to it, dropping to his knees. He set the picture down and began sliding his hands along the floor. It only took a few seconds to find a seam, along with the glue or clear calking that sealed it. The panel was about four feet wide by three feet long.

Sean grunted and stood up, looking around the room. His eyes stopped on the folding chair.

"It'll work," he said under his breath. "But it will be loud."

"What?" Mitchell asked, thinking Sean was talking to him.

Sean glanced at the desk and then turned to Mitchell. "Does that radio work?"

Mitchell's face tightened. "No. Remember? The antenna isn't set up."

"Not the HAM. The ghettoblaster."

Chapter 21

As Ron Oldhorse walked along the shoulder of the cold, lonely highway, his father weighed heavily on his mind. He couldn't shake the image of the old man's cold eyes sunken deep inside his heavily wrinkled face. They'd revealed nothing but bitterness and years.

He pulled his denim jacket higher up over his shoulders to fend off the early morning cold and the stewing guilt that had hitched a ride on his conscience. The sun wouldn't rise for a few hours, leaving him with only darkness and darker musings to fill his attention. Desperate for a distraction, he imagined the sun cresting the plains along the eastern horizon, exposing every detail of the long blades of grass that would cushion its ascent. He hoped the imagery would rid his thoughts of his father's glare of betrayal, but like the oscillating winds that pressed against his back from the northwest, they wouldn't let themselves be ignored.

When a pair of headlights lit up the road from behind him, Oldhorse turned, noticing that the vehicle's lamps were uneven. That meant they likely didn't belong to a police car. He lowered the bottom of his jacket over the large hunting knife sheathed at his side and lifted his opposite arm at half-mast, extending a thumb.

A pickup truck flew by, maintaining its speed, just as the other vehicles had. Nighttime drivers weren't willing to take a chance on someone with his appearance—a long-haired drifter type whose dark complexion, tall moccasins, and beat-up pack made him look like he'd just strolled off a reservation. Oldhorse nodded, at ease with the driver's decision, though a little company would have been welcome.

You're getting soft, he thought to himself as the truck's taillights disappeared over a short hill ahead. *You'll get there when you get there.*

He reached into his jacket pocket and pulled out a strand of homemade deer jerky, gnawing off a bite as a stray gust of wind blasted his worn face.

Chapter 22

"Wouldn't have pegged you for a Fogerty man, Mitchell," said Sean, a half grin on his face.

He held the boombox by its handle in his right hand. In his left was the cassette tape he'd just pulled from its face. Its label read "Creedence Clearwater Revival."

"And the batteries work?" he asked.

When Mitchell nodded, Sean plopped the cassette back inside. He brought the radio over to the door, stepping over boxes and other items. He reached around the shelving and placed the radio on the floor, speakers pointing toward the door. Sean turned the volume all the way up and pressed the play button.

"Now when I was just a little boy," the lyrics belted out, even louder than Sean was expecting. A guitar and drumbeat followed suit. He nodded his head.

"Are you sure this is going to work?" asked Mitchell.

"It worked on an episode of *The A-Team*."

Mitchell's eyes thinned as Sean walked passed him and the baby. Sean grabbed the folding chair, collapsing it as he made his way toward the floor panel. He stopped halfway between.

"He's right," Sean mumbled to himself. "It's loud, but not loud enough."

"What?" Mitchell asked as Sean approached him.

"Get her to cry," Sean said.

Mitchell's eyes shot wide. "What? Why?"

"Because she's loud. And right now, I need things to be loud."

"But she's sleeping."

Sean lowered his shoulders. "Look at the door."

When Mitchell turned his head, Sean pinched Diana on the outside of her thigh. She squirmed for a second before her face shriveled and her mouth opened. She let out a piercing scream that brought Mitchell's focus back to the forefront.

"What the? What did you do?" he asked, shifting to put himself between Sean and the child.

"Nothing," Sean said, feigning ignorance. "I guess she's not a Fogerty girl. Now bring her closer to the door and remember what I said: Kishiyama and Gregory aren't your people. They're liars. They're not here for the same reason that the rest of you are. In order for things to work out the way you want them to—"

Sean was interrupted by a loud voice from the other side of the door. "What the hell's going on in there?" It was Gregory. "Mitchell, what's happening?"

"Don't answer him," said Sean shaking his head. "If you care about your people—and I know you do—you'll keep your mouth shut." He placed his hand on Mitchell's shoulder as Diana continued to scream. "Okay?"

Mitchell glared for a moment before nodding his head. Sean patted him on the back as he made his way over to the door. Standing at the edge of the panel, he spun his chair upside down and waited until an uptick in the music. When it came, he drove the chair's backrest into the floor along the seam. The calking cracked, along with some of the tile. Sean got in a few more shots before the song ended and the next one began. He then resumed work, pounding away as Diana's wailing carried on.

"Mitchell!" came Kishiyama's voice, along with a fist on the door. He could barely be heard above the clamor. "What's happening?"

Mitchell stared at Sean, saying nothing. Sean nodded and delivered some final strikes to the last stretch of seam, sending chunks of calk and tile into the air. He then set the chair down and dropped to his hands and knees, clearing away the shards. He traced the outline of the panel with his hands, looking for a chink wide enough to slide his fingers in. When he found one, he pulled back on its edge until the panel began tearing its way through the remaining glue. Sean smelled dust as he lifted what amounted to a wooden board.

A crawlspace presented itself, the lights above revealing it to be a little deeper than three feet, down to a cement floor. He set the panel to his side, and then slid to his chest, pushing binders out of his way. He stuck his head into the hole and arched his neck, trying to determine how far the crawlspace went. It was dark, and Sean could see no vertical barriers, though some assuredly existed in the foundation. What he did see, at least twenty feet in front of him, was a sliver of light, a beam shining through the floor from somewhere else. It was far enough away that it had to be coming from another room—its positioning suggesting the control room.

When Sean lifted his head, Mitchell was standing just a couple feet away, holding the baby. She was still crying, but his rocking was drawing it down. The music still blared.

"We're coming with you," he said. "I need to get her back to her mother."

"No," Sean said, pulling himself to his knees. "We'll get them back together, but right now, it's best that they think we're all stuck in here. If they stop thinking that—if they hear a baby's cries from underneath their feet instead of in this room—we'll lose the advantage."

Mitchell took a deep breath. "And what happens if they bust in here? They'll know I helped you. They'll know I kept silent as you escaped."

"You'll come up with something, just like you did with Avalanche." When Mitchell opened his mouth to protest, Sean cut him off. "Just tell them I knocked you out or something. Your face should convince them. Don't say anything to them until I come back for you two, even if it takes a while. Just keep playing that tape, switching sides when you need to."

With that, Sean slid to his rear and then carefully lowered himself into the crawlspace. With his feet on cement and the top half of his body still above the floor, he grabbed the panel, dropped to his knees, and pulled it back over the opening. It snapped back into place, leaving Sean in almost complete darkness. There was a strong, musty odor in the air.

"They'll figure out where you went, even if I don't tell 'em," said Mitchell, his voice suppressed. His bobbing shadow blocked a corner of the panel's subtly lit outline.

"No sense making it easy on them. And Mitchell," he said through the floor, then hesitated. "Thank you."

Chapter 23

Sean stayed put in the darkness under the panel for a couple of minutes. He worried that Mitchell might have been exaggerating his willingness to defy Kishiyama. The leader had been fueling and honing the tribe's apocalyptic fears for the better part of the year, commanding their loyalty and faith. There was ample reason to suspect that Mitchell might suppress his doubts over the photograph, try to trap Sean under the floor, and alert Kishiyama. Instead—judging by the creaks and scuffs above—Mitchell kicked some binders over the panel to camouflage it and walked back over to the desk. The boombox continued to blast music. He wasn't warning anyone.

As was the case with Avalanche—assuming that what Mitchell said about the dog was true—his loyalty to the prophecy was greater than his loyalty to Kishiyama. He'd been ordered to kill the dog, but his interpretation of the doctrine allowed him to choose a different course of action. He may have been brainwashed, but the ultimate architect of the con job wasn't Kishiyama. It was a woman from Wisconsin. Her rules came first. Kishiyama's power had come from confidence, intelligence, and the autocracy he had created within the group.

Confident enough that Mitchell wasn't going to sell him out, Sean began crawling toward the light under the adjoining room. It seemed fainter than before, but it was still visible. Unable to see much else, Sean made it only about six feet—over dust, wood shavings, and concrete debris—before his forehead collided with a steel girder.

"Fuck," he whispered, teeth aching.

A metallic echo buzzed through the shaft. He waited for it to settle. It was soon replaced with a different noise—one that was sibilant, like pressurized air from a compressor. It was coming from the direction he was headed, rising and lowering in volume but consistent in tone. Though there was some familiarity to it, Sean couldn't place what electrical or plumbing instrument it might belong to.

The noise continued, but after a few moments, Sean chose to ignore it. He lowered his head and proceeded forward, moving slower while stretching his arms out farther in front of him. He hoped to identify any more objects before his head did. Even with the new tactic, his face managed to sweep through more spider webs than his hands. He slid over a family of ribbed steel rods—likely rebar that was used in laying the cement foundation decades earlier. The sound grew sharply louder as he got within a few feet of the light. He cautioned his movements when he heard what sounded like someone's voice above the floor.

Light gleamed through a gash in a floorboard, in between wooden studs. The thin opening was less than a foot long. It looked like the result of the corner of a heavy piece of equipment being dropped long ago. Splintered wood beneath the hole protruded toward Sean, and he carefully rolled to his back on the cement to peer between it and some damaged tile. With his head positioned beside the bottom of a concrete column, he found that he had a straight view of one of the bulbs hanging on the ceiling above. He was definitely beneath the control room. He could tell by the dropped ceiling.

His pulse leapt when a floorboard creaked loudly just above him. He remained still as a shadow crossed in front of the light. The hissing air seemed to rise in intensity with each movement of the shadow.

Sean lifted his head up a little in hopes of getting a better look through the hole. When he did, the hiss sharpened. And Sean realized that the sound wasn't coming from above the floor, but rather below it, where he was—mere feet away.

His heart stopped. He slowly twisted his head in its direction, the light from above lending him just enough visibility to make out a coiled object on a small slab of concrete. A few seconds labored by before he saw it move. *Shit.*

It was a snake, agitated from its territory having been invaded.

Sean controlled his breathing, lying still as his mind sped a hundred miles an hour. What he was hearing wasn't a rattle. It was a hiss, which likely meant a bullsnake. Sean had encountered a few in the fields around the campground. One had even made it into the bay once. They fed on mice and voles, and though they weren't venomous, they were large enough—around five feet in length when full size—that getting bit in the face by one would be nothing to scoff at. The thought also entered his mind that if one of them had managed to slither in through a crack in the foundation, others may have as well.

Sean began slowly scooting his body away from the snake, but stopped when he heard what sounded like a whimper from above, followed by a whisper. The voice sounded as if it came from a woman, but he couldn't tell who. The whispering was repetitive, as if the woman were reciting the same sentence over and over again. He listened intently, trying to decipher her words as he kept an eye on the snake.

A huge thud suddenly rattled the floor above, sending Sean's stomach into his throat. The snake lunged forward, sinking its fangs into Sean's left arm, just above the elbow. He grimaced and crossed his opposite arm over his chest, wrapping his hand around the snake's throat. He squeezed it, prying it loose from his arm. Its body writhed, trying to coil around his wrist, but he used his other hand to keep it taut. With a muffled grunt, he swung his arm and tossed the snake far to his side. He heard it land several feet away in the dark.

Shot in one shoulder and bit in the other, he thought as he ignored the sting and positioned himself back under the hole in the floor. He tasted dust on his lips as the shadow again hovered above, partially eclipsing the light. He made out the outline of a long mane of hair. The woman appeared to have dropped to her knees.

"Forgive me," she moaned. "Forgive me."

Sean's face tightened. The rest of him remained still. The chances of her seeing him through the floor were very low, but they'd increase if he moved . . . even a little.

The woman sobbed and continued to plead for forgiveness. When she began slapping her hand against the side of her head, Sean cringed. He thought he might be watching the baby's mother, torn over the loss of her husband and the captivity of her child, but the voice was off. The thick hair didn't look right either.

The woman stopped talking, but the whimpering continued. She choked on her own breath and pulled at her hair. When Sean heard what sounded like the clicking of a pistol's action, his chest tightened. *Was this woman planning to shoot herself?*

His mouth gaped and his soul struggled with what to do. He didn't want to give away his position but also didn't want the woman to die. She, like her cohorts, had been duped into believing delusional ideas and taking extreme actions, but they weren't killers—not like Kishiyama. Still, any intervention from Sean could result in a quick call to the others, or a bullet through the floor at the man most of them believed had murdered Morgan.

Sean's arms shook and he gritted his teeth. His mind flashed back to a couple of years earlier when he was unable to stop a man from taking his own life back in his hometown of Winston. He watched helplessly that day as the man sent a bullet through his skull, and he quickly concluded from under the floor that he wasn't going to let it happen again.

But just as Sean opened his mouth to cry out, another voice stopped him.

"What are you doing?" It belonged to a man—one who'd apparently entered the room unnoticed. His tone was one of concern.

There was some shuffling above as the woman scrambled upright. "I . . . I just . . ." she began. "I dropped my pistol . . . and I thought I had broken it." A loud sniff shot from her nose. "And I know we only have so many guns . . ."

Sean finally recognized the voice. It was Tammy.

"It's okay," the man said. It sounded like one of the twins. "We'll get through this. They'll get us through this." He seemed to buy the woman's explanation. "Besides, I just found another gun—up in the security guard's trailer. Check this baby out. He had it clipped under a dresser drawer, along with another set of keys. Mitchell somehow missed it."

The twin must have tossed the keys to Tammy, because her arm suddenly shot up as if to catch something. A second later, he heard the metal jingle in her hand. The keys were mostly duplicates that went with the facility. Of more sentimental attachment to Sean was the Colt Python. The silver pistol had been given to him decades earlier by his uncle, back when he was believed to be Sean's father. Sean stewed over the idea of the twin flashing it around.

"Everything's goin' wrong," Tammy muttered, unimpressed with the twin's findings. "The guy in the tunnel. Morgan. Diana."

"They'll get Diana," said the man. "Mitchell's in there with her. He'll protect her."

"He can't protect her," she said, her voice straining. "He's weak. He's always been weak. Gregory was right. Maybe we should have just killed the security guard."

A few seconds floated by before the man responded. "We didn't come here to kill anyone."

"I know we didn't, but two people are dead anyway, aren't they? And maybe more before Nibiru hits."

"They'll figure it out. Kishiyama and Gregory. They're smart. By the time Nibiru comes, we'll be down there, all of us together, ridin' the storm out . . . just like when we were kids."

A reluctant chuckle spilled from Tammy's mouth. "The tornado."

"Morgan's mom's basement. The wind tearin' apart their upstairs. I'd never been so frightened in my life. I thought *that* day was going to be the end. I think we all did. But we survived it, and we'll survive this."

"I thought about that day for years," said Tammy after a few seconds. "I still do. It was just one storm, and lasted only a few minutes, but all of that destruction . . . Half the town was wiped out. Those people who died . . . "

For a moment, the two sounded almost normal, like Sean and his sister when they would share memories from the past. Sean didn't realize until just then how much he had, over the past months, missed those conversations. His more penetrating thoughts, however, were drawn to how otherwise ordinary-sounding people could have let themselves be steered into adopting such a perverse belief system. Seconds later, Tammy seemed to offer some insight into that question.

"Everything our parents and the others warned us about became clear after that," she said, her voice cracking a bit. "We're like an ant colony building a hill. Living our lives and doing our work until, one day, we get stepped on. And everything changes."

"That's what Gus used to say," said the man.

"And he was right. But if we dig down deep enough, and survive the day, we can rebuild. Same as the ants."

Sean and his sister had grown up hard, and they had been dragged through a web of deception he wouldn't wish on anyone, but at least the community they were brought up in hadn't filled their heads with dangerous delusions—delusions they couldn't come back from. For the first time in a long time, Sean felt fortunate.

"How's Heather?" Tammy asked.

"The same. She hasn't stopped cryin'. Dean's with her." Some silence drifted by before he spoke again. "I think . . . I think she blames me."

"Blames you? What would she blame you for?"

"For . . ." He paused. "I was the one who tied up the security guard. And I tied him up good. Real good. He shouldn't have been able to get out of those knots, but somehow he did. And if he hadn't . . . Morgan would still be alive."

After a moment, Tammy said, "Don't you dare blame yourself, Doug. Don't you dare do that."

"I can't help it. I can't—"

"It wasn't you that screwed up."

"What? What do you mean?"

She took a few seconds. "I wanted him gone. I wanted him out of here."

"Oh, Tammy."

Sean listened intently, leaning up on his elbows.

"He watched us kill his boss, Doug," said Tammy. "And Mitchell put down his dog. He would have never come around to our way of thinkin'. He would have never become one of us." She held back her weeping.

"Nibiru would have changed his perspective."

"Maybe," she said. "Or maybe he'd have decided that ridin' out the end of the world among killers wouldn't have been a life worth livin'. Maybe he'd have cut our throats down there in the pit, as we slept. We've been preparin' for this day for a long time. The guard hasn't. How could he have wrapped his mind around all this?"

The twin let her tension settle a bit before speaking up again.

"You thought he would have just left us alone once he got loose?"

"Pretty much, yeah. He knows this place. He knows the hidin' spots. He knew he was unarmed and way outnumbered by people with guns. I was countin' on him slippin' out through the tunnels when the coast was clear."

"But that would have jeopardized everything—all that we've been preparin' for."

"No it wouldn't have," she snapped back. "Mitchell took care of the phone lines and his car early on. We never found any cellphones."

"He had this gun, though. Out in his trailer."

"Yeah," she said, her voice waning. "I know that now. We didn't know it at the time. I figured he would have had no choice but to walk all the way to town to get the police. And if the cops somehow showed up before Nibiru, we'd be able to keep them out, holed up in a place like this. We would have just had to stall long enough for—"

Tammy stopped at the sound of approaching footsteps. There was some quick muddling and the moving of items along the floor, as if the two were cleaning up evidence of their candid conversation. The light above Sean suddenly went away, an object having been pushed over a gash in the floor.

"Is it just you two in here?" came Gregory's voice.

"Yes," they answered together.

"We have you all set up in here," Tammy added, a remark that aroused Sean's curiosity.

"Okay," said Gregory. "We've got only a couple hours till sunrise. Sync-up meeting in the bay in five minutes. Tammy, get everyone together for it. Doug, you watch the room where Mitchell and Diana are. They've got a radio or something turned up loud in there. We don't know what that's about, but if Coleman tries to get out, call me on this right away. The channel's already set. I'll catch you up to speed in the meeting."

With that, there was some loud movement along the floor, and after a few seconds, it sounded as though everyone had left the room.

"Five minutes," Sean whispered.

The missile bay was at the other end of the compound, far out of earshot from any noise that would come from the control room above. Doug would be much closer, but with CCR still blasting through the radio, he wouldn't hear anything either. Sean's opportunity was approaching quickly.

He raised his arms and slid his fingers through the slit in the floorboard above, wincing when splintered wood poked into the palm of his hand. The object covering the hole felt like nylon. It might have been the sleeping bag he'd seen Tammy with earlier. Sean gritted his teeth as he tugged at the edges of the gap to try and widen it. His arms flexed as he pulled in opposite directions. The tile above the wood twisted inward a bit, but the wood itself was the true obstacle. Despite the previous damage to the floorboard, it was mostly solid and wasn't budging. It would take more than raw muscle to widen the hole enough for Sean to pull his large body up through it.

He took a breath as he relaxed his arms. He then worked the tips of his fingers along the nylon, slowly tugging it along the floor, an inch at a time, until light again shined through the hole above. He twisted his body until he was back on his stomach, digging his elbows and the tips of his boots into chunks of concrete and shards of wood. He crawled back to the rebar he had gone over earlier, his face softening when the guitar riff from "Fortunate Son" came into range. Mitchell was keeping up his end of the bargain.

Sean grabbed a couple of the inch-thick rods, and at four or five feet long, he tried not to let their opposite ends drag too loudly along the ground as he made his way back to the hole in the floor. He waited there for a few minutes with his ear close to the opening, counting on the meeting beginning on schedule.

Convinced enough time had passed, he positioned one of the rods nearly vertically, shoving its top end up about a third of the way through the hole. He then grabbed the lower end with both hands, planting one foot against the cement column beside him and the other along one of the wooden studs under the floorboard. His face taut, he straightened his legs and pulled back on the bar, arching his back and grunting as wood cracked and tile tore.

Chapter 24

*T*wo, *maybe three more hours,* Oldhorse thought as he continued west. The mountains in the distance were still cloaked by darkness, but there was something mildly comforting about at least being headed in their direction. Far beyond the range that would come into view with the sun was Oldhorse's home.

He had dwelled in the mountains outside of Winston for years. His place was a secluded, bare-bones cabin, without a phone or electricity. He lived off the land, growing and hunting for his food, and largely closing himself off from the outside world. It was a life he'd found after some time in the US Army infantry, part of it brought on by a deep fascination he had with the history of the Lakota Native American tribe, of which he was a descendent. The other part came from a run-in with the law in South Dakota, for which a federal warrant was still out for his arrest.

Oldhorse's biological parents had died in a house fire when he was just an infant. The only remaining family he had was his adoptive father, a retired small-restaurant owner. Oldhorse's life on the run had kept him a stranger to that family for years, to the extent that he hadn't heard of the passing of his adoptive mother—automobile accident—until she'd been in the ground for two years. With news of his father on his deathbed, Oldhorse wanted to make amends, and let the old man know that he loved, appreciated, and thought of him often.

But as he'd discovered just hours earlier, too much time had passed. Even under hospice care, at death's very doorstep, his father would have nothing to do with him.

Oldhorse had snuck into his room after dark to avoid the off-chance of federal surveillance, had the feds been aware of his father's condition. He'd knelt beside his father's bed and held his hand. Under the dim glare of a single lamp, he asked for forgiveness. With wet eyes, he tried to explain what had happened so many years ago up north, and how he hadn't a choice but to disappear.

With what was left of his fragile strength, his father pulled his hand away and spoke only two words: "Leave . . . Now." The rest of his response was etched across his father's face.

It wasn't the way Oldhorse wanted to leave things, but the more he persisted, the more upset his father grew, erupting into a coughing fit that took minutes to wind down. Oldhorse ultimately decided that he had cost his father enough pain over the years, and that he could best honor him now by abiding by his wishes.

But that was yesterday. With the beginning of a new day came a new objective. A new mission. If he couldn't repair his own relationship, he was determined to try and save another.

Chapter 25

She sat silently on a steel folding chair at the back of the group, a jacket draped over her low shoulders. Her tears spent and her gaze empty, Kishiyama's words were unable to penetrate her thoughts. He was like a talking head on a muted television. The others were standing, nodding attentively as he spoke. A blurred head or two turned to her from time to time to speculate on her mental state. Their concerns were little more than an abstract backdrop to the image of her husband lying still on that cement floor, blood flowing from his chest.

When she thought she heard her baby's cry, she sat up straight and snapped her head to the side. The bewildered expressions told her that the sound wasn't real.

"Heather?" Kishiyama said.

She slowly turned to him. "I'm s-sorry," she stuttered. "I just—"

"I know," he interrupted. "*We* know. Diana will be fine. You have my word."

She opened her mouth to speak, but he had already turned his attention back to the others.

"We're within the final hours," he said, squaring his jaw and gazing across his audience with gleaming pride. "This global fate that none of us ever wished for but have diligently prepared for will soon be upon us." He crossed his fingers in front of his stomach, taking a breath. With a half grin, he continued. "It hasn't been easy. It hasn't been without sacrifice. But as history has taught us, the preserving of our humanity and the advancement of life on Earth has never been easy. It has never been without sacrifice."

His people nodded.

"I'm very proud of you all—of each and every one of you. Your faith in the prophecy and your commitment to mankind will not go without recognition. Your journey and your efforts will be recognized and celebrated by future generations. Children will learn of you, their founding fathers, through books and their teachers—chapter one in this quickly approaching era of new-world history." He raised his hands in the air as if he were preaching a church sermon.

Heather watched the uplifted faces of the others. She could share neither their confidence nor sense of hope. She understood the big picture and the role they would play in rebuilding the planet, but the enthusiasm she witnessed further sickened her stomach. Her husband was dead. Their daughter was being held by the man who'd killed him. And Kishiyama seemed content on treating the situation as an afterthought. *Maybe he's right. Maybe true leaders stay focused on the long game.* But to Heather, he couldn't have felt more wrong.

"I need her with me," she blurted out, again drawing the room's attention. She lowered her head in reverence but kept talking. "I can't be down in that pit without Diana. She needs her mother. She needs to be safe. I can't go six days without knowin' whether or not she's safe."

Kishiyama watched her, stone-faced.

"Please," she continued. "Please let me stay up here, on the main floor, with you."

All eyes went to Kishiyama.

"No," Gregory interjected, shaking his head. "That's not the plan. That's never been the plan. Three of us up here—him, me, and Mitchell. The rest of you down there. Anything else is an unnecessary risk."

"But . . ."

"This isn't about *you*, Heather! It's about survival!" Gregory's tone grew sharper as he spoke. He threw his arms in the air and gazed across the group. "Why are we doing this?"

"What we do, we do for humanity," half of them chimed in.

He pulled the toothpick from his mouth and widened his eyes. "What?"

"What we do, we do for humanity." This time, the rest of the group joined. Heather followed suit, but only with the movement of her lips.

"That's right." Gregory slid the toothpick back between his teeth. He turned back to Heather. "Diana's fine. Mitchell's there to protect her. We'll get them both out, safe and sound, but if it doesn't happen until after lockdown—"

Kishiyama raised his hand and flashed Gregory a glance, bringing his diatribe to a screeching halt. He then turned to Heather, picking up where Gregory had left off.

"If it has to wait until after lockdown, Diana will be in good hands over the gestation period with the three of us. We will take extra measures to protect her. But we need the rest of you to be safe when the times comes. This is imperative and not subject to debate. The stakes are too great. The new world will be dependent on you." His voice and eyes softened when he added, "Don't let Morgan's sacrifice be in vain."

Kishiyama turned his attention to the rest of the group. "Don't let Morgan's sacrifice be in vain!" he shouted, raising his fist. "The new world will be dependent on all of you!"

The mantra generated head nods and applause from seemingly everyone but Heather. She lowered her trembling hands to her side, her eyes filling up again. "She's all I have. Please . . ."

"You have all of us," he said. "We're a family and we need to work together. And when this is over, all of us—including Diana—will rise from the ashes. Together."

Chapter 26

With an apple-red face and veins bulging from the sides of his head, Sean forced his shoulders up through the fractured wood. He squirmed and cringed as it scraped his wounds and tore at his sleeves. Once his shoulders were free, he knew the rest of his body would come easier. He needed to hurry, as time was truly of the essence.

If the instructions he'd heard were being followed, everyone but the twin was in the bay area. That would mean that no one would be standing between Sean and the tunnels. He'd have a clean shot to the outside, but that opportunity would only last as long as the meeting. And he'd already used up several precious minutes punching through the floor.

He grunted and snorted as he twisted his body, shoving one of his arms entirely through the hole. His elbow bumped against the steel rod he'd pushed through earlier. He lowered his opposite shoulder and stood up straight, guiding it through as well. He then took a deep breath, fighting back the urge to cough as he spread his forearms along the floor. Sweat poured from head, and his eyes burned from the dust that had built up on his face.

He blinked and gazed around the control room, finding not one but three spread-out sleeping bags with pillows along the floor. Beside them were clothing and food—mostly canned goods stacked in neat piles. Some of the office furniture had been moved, but most of it had been left in place.

Planting his hands and spreading his fingers, Sean flexed his arms and lifted himself upward. Once he managed to bend his leg and get a knee onto the tile, the extra leverage let him pull the rest of his body out. He rolled to his side, sliding his tongue along his dry lips before rubbing his face with his arm.

He glanced at his bloodied shoulders before grabbing the rod, climbing to his hands and knees. He took a moment to slide the closest sleeping bag over the hole. Once he'd covered it, he twisted his neck with a pop and cautiously made his way toward the door.

The music still played down the hall, and he peeked his head around the doorframe to look for the twin. When he didn't see him, he stepped out of the room and jogged on his toes to the edge of tunnel. He blew some air through his mouth and craned his neck around the corner.

No one was inside the tunnel, but Sean's nostrils flared at the sight of the closed chain-link gate blocking the opposite end. "Don't be locked," he muttered as he entered the tunnel.

A few feet ahead, a towel had been thrown over the area of floor where Morgan had been killed. Sean guessed that his blood had stained the cement, and that one of the others had covered it to spare his wife the sight. He side-stepped the towel, choking up on the rod as he moved forward. His head shifted back and forth from one end of the tunnel to the other. He knew there wouldn't be much he could do if he was spotted, but he wanted to be ready for the situation if it came. He heard voices as he got closer to the gate. He was sure they were coming from the bay; the meeting was still in progress.

When he reached the gate, he saw that it was padlocked in the same way he'd often left it after tours. Even with his rod, it wouldn't come open easy, and certainly not without enough noise to draw attention from the bay. If he could hear the others talking, they would certainly be able to hear the snapping and bending of metal on his end. What discouraged him even more was the sight of the other tunnel's gate, also closed and locked. He had not one but two barriers to contend with to get outside.

Kishiyama had learned from the experience with Morgan. He'd figured out that even if Sean were somehow able to bust through the archives door and make it past the twin, the tunnel gates would ultimately keep him from escaping. Like sealing compartments in a flooding submarine, the damage would be contained.

He'd have to come up with a different play, but he couldn't do it there by the gate, fully exposed from both sides. He turned and headed back down the tunnel, again twisting his head back and forth to look for incomers.

He needed a hiding spot—somewhere where he could clear his mind, think through the situation, and act at a moment's notice. He was convinced he had some things working in his favor, like the group's belief that he was still barricaded in the archives room. Something told him that the advantage was worth more than just him getting a jump on the twin. Even if an ambush worked, and he got the twin's weapon, he'd still have the gates to contend with. Real life wasn't like in the movies, where you can bust through padlocks and thick chains by firing bullets. And on the other side of that first gate were more people with more guns. The twin couldn't be used as a hostage either, not after what had happened with Morgan.

Sean left the tunnel and rested his back along the wall beside its opening. From there, he couldn't be seen from either the tunnel junction or the living quarters.

He thought about where to go. Back under the floor in the control room was an option, but he knew from experience that it was tough and took time to squeeze through; he put the idea aside as a last resort. The doors in the hallway between him and the twin were all locked; he'd confirmed that earlier when running from Kishiyama. The vault room certainly had places to hide, but returning there would back him into a corner and place him too far away from the tunnel. There had to be a better alternative.

Sean leaned forward, placing one hand on his thigh as he took in a deep breath. Holding the rod like a walking cane, he unthinkingly let its bottom tip slide to the floor. It created an echoing thud on the steel platform below him. His eyes went wide and his body shot up straight.

He held the rod with both hands, ready to use it as a weapon as the reverberation held longer than seemed logical. Sean remembered the question from one of the cub scouts he'd led through that same corridor a good eighteen hours earlier: *"Is this a trap door?"*

Sean's eyes slid to the ring pull handle embedded at the edge of the metal platform.

Chapter 27

"**I**t's the same songs over and over again," said one of the twins to someone else as the two crossed over the hatch. Their footsteps were thunderous above Sean's head—a sound Sean had grown used to over the past hour. "It doesn't make sense why Mitchell's not saying anything, but it's him that's flipping the cassette in there. I could see his shoe when I peeked under the door the last time he did it. I even heard him shush Diana before the music started up again. But he wouldn't answer me."

The twin continued talking but his words grew faint and eventually inaudible as he reached the opposite end of the tunnel.

Mitchell was hanging in there, but Sean worried about how much longer his nerve would hold out in his absence. Sean hadn't expected to be under the hatch for so long, crammed into tight quarters with old piping and spare buckets of paint, while he waited for his opportunity. He'd figured that once the meeting was over, the gates at the tunnel entrances would be unlocked and reopened. Instead, they remained secured by one of the group's women who served as a gatekeeper.

Sean checked on her from time to time when he heard no one approaching, carefully raising the hatch no more than an inch to see her sitting in a folding chair in the tunnel junction. Armed, she unlocked and relocked the gates whenever members of her group required access to the other side of the facility.

Sean wondered if the effort was entirely about keeping him in, or if Kishiyama also wanted an accounting of where each of his people were at any given time. Perhaps he worried that some of them were losing their will to follow through with their mission and instructions, and the added measure would keep any weak knees from abandoning ship. It could also explain why everyone who'd passed through his side of the facility had done so accompanied by someone else. They were moving in pairs—a buddy system, or perhaps a support system.

Regardless, the predicament was testing Sean's patience. Though some light from the ceiling of the tunnel lent dim visibility to his surroundings through small, grate-like holes in the hatch door, Sean was otherwise in the dark. He checked the gate after every exchange at the junction, hoping for a moment of carelessness. Thus far, one hadn't presented itself. And with those crossing above him moving increasingly faster as time ticked down—perhaps due to last-minute preparations for Nibiru—he sometimes wasn't aware of their approach until they were right on top of him. It was unnerving and left him with little time to assess any split-second opportunities.

As much as he resisted it, his mind kept floating back to the hostage idea. It had gone terribly wrong before, but there was one scenario in which he believed he could possibly pull it off, a situation in which there'd likely be no loss of life: if Kishiyama himself were the hostage.

As demonstrated earlier, Kishiyama was willing to sacrifice members of his group for whatever his real reason was for being there. But the same would not be true of his followers. They wouldn't play games with their leader's life just to keep Sean from escaping. One of them—Tammy—had even been willing to let him escape when she believed it was in the interest of the larger operation. Gregory was there for a different reason, but he wouldn't dare hurt Kishiyama either. He was a subordinate. He was just as dependent on the leader as the others.

The trick would be to catch Kishiyama off guard, just as he was passing overhead, preferably at a time when he was by himself. Luck would have to be on Sean's side for such a situation to present itself, but if it did, Sean would have to be willing to commit. Thus far, however, he'd been given no such opportunity. Kishiyama hadn't even entered the north side of the facility since the bay meeting had let out. Gregory had gone back and forth a couple of times, but not Kishiyama.

His eyes weary, Sean silently yawned and thought about what time it might be. He guessed around five in the morning, which meant that the doomsday prophecy would be exposed as a hoax in less than three hours. The premise compelled Sean to ponder how Kishiyama planned on handling the revelation.

Once 7:43 comes, and the ground doesn't so much as quiver, what will keep the others from figuring out that they've been duped? Sean wondered. *Or will their purpose have already been served by then?*

Before Sean could get much more than a foothold on the thought, a loud whistle blew from the other end of the tunnel. It sounded like it came from the coach of a gym class. Sean's body tensed and he wrapped his fingers around the steel rod.

"All right, everyone!" a voice shouted from what sounded like the junction. It was Kishiyama. "It's lockdown time!"

Sean's eyes narrowed. He wondered if his time estimate could have truly been that far off.

"No!" a woman screamed out from what sounded like the same location. "Please! You must get Diana! I need her with me!" It was Heather, the baby's mother.

Kishiyama shouted something back at her, but Sean had trouble making out what he said. Other voices chimed in. Their words were difficult to decipher, but they seemed to be urging Heather to comply with the leader's order.

"I won't go down in the pit, not without Diana!" she wailed, her cries echoing down the tunnel.

"The exhaust pit," Sean muttered.

The logic that an open pit would be the safest place to ride out the end of the world had struck Sean as ridiculous at the time. But now Sean remembered the large metal sheets he had spotted in the tunnel, just after Mahan had been killed. They were thick and long enough to spread out, side by side, over the top of the pit. Kishiyama was getting ready to seal them all down there.

At first, the thought brought a grin to Sean's face. If they all below the floor on the other side of the building, they wouldn't be able to hear him pry open the gates and make his escape. His lips straightened, however, when his mind floated back to the food and sleeping bags he'd seen in the control room.

Sean nodded at the genius of Kishiyama's scheme. Isolating the others wasn't being done for their protection. It was being done to keep them locked away and out of his hair while he conducted whatever operation had *really* brought him there. Gregory and Mitchell would stay above with him—Gregory because he was in on it, and Mitchell for his expertise with explosives. Kishiyama had been in no hurry to free Mitchell because he knew he wasn't going anywhere. He and Gregory could, and probably preferred to, retrieve him later . . . once the others had been properly confined.

There were still many questions that didn't have answers—including Kishiyama's ultimate goal—but it was clear that the others were no longer needed. They'd already fulfilled their purpose. Whether or not that was limited to capturing the facility, keeping word from getting out, and hauling in supplies and equipment was hard to say.

A pair of footsteps passed over Sean's head, the individuals above casting a quick shadow as they made their way toward the junction and the continued sound of Heather's sobbing. By Sean's count, they were the last two on his side of the facility, other than Mitchell and Diana. Once the rest of the group was isolated, Sean would have only Kishiyama and Gregory to contend with. And the next one of them that passed overhead on their way to retrieve Mitchell would be in for one hell of a surprise.

Chapter 28

When a pinprick of unfettered sunlight revealed itself to the east, Oldhorse's weathered face tightened. Tall grass swayed in the wind on both sides of the road as sand and gravel crackled beneath his boots. A lone hawk glided low in the distance, searching for breakfast.

Having crossed an overpass he recalled Lumbergh driving over the day before, Oldhorse scanned the fields until he spotted a telephone pole. He made his way toward it, leaving the road and cutting through a meadow wet with morning dew.

Two barn swallows—one seemingly chasing the other—darted through the air above as he reached the top of a short hill. In the distance, he made out the perimeter of the chain-link fence that enclosed the property that Sean looked after, and then the trailer. It was early in the morning, and Sean might well be asleep, but Oldhorse didn't care. Driven by the failings with his father from the night before, he had to at least try and make a case to Sean about the importance of family, and how a young teenager named Toby desperately needed to be part of his life again.

Though Oldhorse's relationship with Toby Parker's mother, Joan, had ended a few months back, he still kept in touch with the autistic teen. They'd run into each other from time to time when Oldhorse would go into town to sell wood carvings to local shops. Toby and Sean had formed a strong bond prior to the revelations about Sean's father—revelations that led Sean down a dark path that took him outside of Winston. Toby, whose own father had left him long ago, hadn't been the same since.

As abrasive as Sean had been over all the years that Toby had known him, the boy had always had a soft spot for the uncouth security guard. Much to the chagrin of Toby's mother and pretty much everyone else in Winston, Sean had become somewhat of a mentor to the boy—a relationship that both of them seemed to benefit from.

Back when he was still with Joan, Oldhorse had somewhat envied that relationship. Joan had hoped that Oldhorse could be the type of father figure that Toby needed in his life, but the survivalist's fierce independence and detached nature didn't fit the bill. For that, he had regrets. It was one of the unspoken factors in him and Joan ending things.

Sean, even if he didn't realize it, had filled that void. And when he left Winston, it was as if Toby had been abandoned by his father all over again.

Lumbergh didn't know how bad things had gotten. He didn't know about the defiance and the incidents of acting out in school. He didn't know about the emotional meltdowns that required multiple doctors' visits. Thus, Sean didn't know about them either.

After leaving his father's bedside in Kersey, Oldhorse had tried to call Sean from a payphone at a nearby gas station, using a number for the site's campground that he'd found in the phonebook. He'd gotten no answer, so he'd taken to the road. It was a long walk—hours in the cold and dark—but Oldhorse had plenty of time to kill. Besides, the fresh air would help his clear his head. Or so he'd hoped.

The low sun was beginning to warm his face by the time he reached the south end of the fence. It cast a long shadow off Sean's trailer inside the compound. Oldhorse rattled the locked front gate, cupped his hand to his mouth, and called out Sean's name. When he received no response, he did it again. Still nothing.

It didn't surprise Oldhorse that Sean wouldn't have heard him from inside the trailer. If he had been drinking as much as Lumbergh had described, he may have been sleeping hard. What Oldhorse did find curious was that he hadn't heard a peep from Sean's dog, the white pit bull he'd met and played with a day earlier. No barking. No whining. Not even a scratch at the trailer door.

"Avalanche!" Oldhorse shouted, remembering his name. He heard nothing but the wind and the swaying of the chain-link.

Sean's car was parked behind the trailer, so Oldhorse knew he couldn't have gone far. He did notice that the Nova's hood was open a couple of inches, suggesting that Sean may have been having car problems.

He left the gate and walked over to the camp area. He saw no tents or trailers, and no sign of Sean. The American and Colorado flags flapped high above on a steel pole, their clips clanging as they bounced against metal. It was awfully early for them to be hoisted, not by military standards but for most government institutions. Oldhorse approached the pole and dropped to a knee along the sand and gravel at its base. He leaned forward and brushed the tips of his fingers along the ground. The turf hadn't been walked on that morning, which meant the flags had been left up overnight.

It might have meant nothing, other than that Sean was lazy or careless, but government-run parks and campgrounds tended to take their flag displays seriously. And with no lights set up below to illuminate Old Glory during hours of darkness, it should have been lowered at sunset.

Oldhorse checked the campground's bathrooms, and then circled around to the north side of the acreage. Peering through the fence, his eyes traced the land and the ventilation ducts that stemmed from it. With still no sign of Sean or the dog, he deduced that they had to be inside the silo.

He couldn't see the silo's entrance from his vantage point, which was how the site was specifically designed decades earlier. He scaled the fence, dividing a section of barbed wire at its rim with his arms. He stopped when his eyes homed in on a patch of land on the other side where two long mounds of fresh dirt rested. He narrowed his eyes, focusing on the shovel lying between them.

As he was about to pull himself up and over, a gust of wind against his back brought with it a sharp noise that gave him pause. He twisted his head and listened for it again. After a few seconds it returned—a dog's bark, he was sure of it. It was traveling from a distance, and was definitely outside of the fenced-in area. He dropped back to the ground, turned, and gazed across the terrain. The barking continued, and Oldhorse was certain that it was coming from behind a ridge to the northwest.

He made his way toward it, picking up the pace as the barks grew louder. From the top of the ridge, he spotted a metal storage shed at the edge of a pasture. It looked like it may have once been white, but its walls were now stained orange with rust. The shed had an arched, weather-beaten roof and couldn't have been more than ten feet wide.

He jogged across the pasture, slowing when he got to a muddy area in front of the shed. There, he saw a man's shoeprints, along with a dog's. The man's led in and out of the shed. They were too small and shallow to belong to Sean. The dog's only led inside. The barking grew more excited.

Oldhorse noticed a metal hasp sitting in the mud with a closed padlock still securing it shut. It had been forcibly knocked from the door and frame to gain entry to the shed. A long, triangular piece of scrap wood had been wedged beneath the door to keep it closed. Oldhorse kicked it loose and swung open the door.

Immediately, Avalanche launched toward him, his front paws landing on Oldhorse's stomach while his tail wagged excitedly.

"Good boy," he said, letting the dog lick the side of his coarse face. He rubbed his fingers behind one of the dog's ears as he glanced around the inside of the shed.

It was filled with little more than dusty tools and old farming equipment, though Oldhorse did notice an overturned bag of dry dogfood in the corner. The multiple piles of excrement on the wood floor indicated that Avalanche had been trapped inside for a while.

Oldhorse stood up and the dog followed him inside. On top of a workbench was a nylon leash. The red collar Avalanche had been wearing a day earlier was neither with it nor around the dog's neck. However, Oldhorse did see some splotches of reddish-brown on the workbench—dried blood, he'd guess. Lying next to it was a coping saw. A portion of its thin blade and some of its handle were stained red as well.

He turned and went back to a knee, quickly checking Avalanche's body for cuts. He lifted each leg and examined his underbelly but found nothing. When he rose, he took a breath and walked back outside, the dog following. His gaze met the top of the ridge he'd just come over.

Oldhorse wasn't sure what to make of the situation, but it was clear to him that whatever had gone down had done so without Sean's involvement. And being that Sean was the sole caretaker of the property, something had to be wrong.

Looking down at Avalanche, whose tail was still going a mile a minute, he said, "Let's find Sean."

Chapter 29

The world spun and faces and lights fluttered in and out of focus as she fought against the multiple sets of hands wrapped around her arms and legs. She whipped her limbs, screaming as the voices around her pled unsuccessfully for her calmness. They were soon in the shop area, one person after another spilling in from the junction.

For a moment, she saw Kishiyama standing in the doorway, shaking his head. He turned to Gregory to tell him something. A second later, Tammy's face eclipsed her view, hovering just inches away from her own. It appeared disfigured and disproportionate, as if Heather were glaring into a circus mirror. Tears rolled down Tammy's cheeks.

"It's going to be okay, I promise," Tammy whispered, her lips now pressed to her ear as they moved across the shop. "Just do as I say. Do *exactly* as I say."

Heather's heart was beating through her chest and she choked on her own breath. Still, she managed to feel Tammy shove something into the tight front pocket of her jeans. The object poked against her thigh.

"Help me," Heather begged.

"I *am* helping you," Tammy whispered, their faces touching. "I promise. Stay close to me."

Tammy suddenly whipped her head away, nearly bouncing it against Dean's. The twin had his arms wrapped under Heather's shoulders.

"Okay, stop!" she shouted. "Everybody stop!" She latched onto Dean's arm and tugged on it. "Put her down and just give her some room! It doesn't have to be this way. Let me take her down."

Dean and the others stopped, perhaps waiting for the okay from Kishiyama.

Tammy leaned in again, this time putting her hands on the sides of Heather's face. "I need you to calm down, honey, okay?" She spoke loud enough for those around to hear.

Heather complied, letting her body go limp, ending her fight. She took a couple of deep breaths.

All heads were pointed toward the doorway. Seconds labored by before Kishiyama spoke.

"Tammy, take her below," he said.

Heather was tilted vertical and returned to her feet. Her legs shook as Tammy turned and guided her in the direction of the bay. She put her arm over Heather's shoulder and pulled her in close.

"Walk with me," said Tammy.

They did as the others followed behind. Heather turned her head, watching them collect themselves and exchange subtle discourse and weary gazes. All were tired. All were anxious to move on to the next step.

"Walk faster," whispered Tammy, bringing Heather's eyes forward again. "Not like you're running. Keep it discreet." Tammy picked up her stride, setting the pace.

"What are we doing?" Heather asked.

"Not we. You," she answered as they left the shop and entered the bay.

Once in the bay, Tammy pulled her to their right, temporarily out of view of the others. Ahead, between them and the exhaust pit, was a short staircase and a steel observation platform. To the left was the doorway into the liquid-oxygen room.

Whenever members of the group had gone down into the pit with supplies, they first had to negotiate themselves around the left side of the observation platform—a tight squeeze between it and the wall separating the bay from the liquid-oxygen room. Heather's nerves heightened as Tammy quickly led them toward the narrow gap.

"I'm going down. You go in there," Tammy said, pointing to the liquid-oxygen room. "Hide behind the sluge tank. Don't make a sound. Go now."

"They'll know I'm missing," Heather gasped.

"No they won't." With that, Tammy shoved Heather toward the room's doorway.

Heather slid into the room and swung her body around to the other side of the wall, pressing her back against the concrete. She did her best to control her breathing as she listened to the others funnel into the bay.

"It's going to be okay, honey," Tammy said loudly, from the other side of the wall. "Just keep going down. That's it."

Tammy's instructions were intended for the ears of the others, a ruse to convince them that Heather was already working her way down the exhaust pit's fixed ladder, out of their view. As best Heather could tell, no one was questioning the premise. It was a smart play. If any of them happened to walk up the staircase to the observation tower, all they would see below were the steel sheets the group had laid over the pit earlier to serve as a protective roof. The only sheet that had yet to be slid into place was the one by the ladder. The rest of the pit was totally covered.

The rungs of the ladder echoed as Tammy made her way down.

"I want to say some things to the rest of you before we say goodbye for the next few days," began Kishiyama, bringing an end to some chatter among the group. "Please gather around."

Heather turned to the metal tank at the end of the room. Shaped like a giant barrel turned on its side, the head facing her was no less than six feet in diameter. The tank itself looked about eight feet long. She cautiously made her way toward it, sliding around some collapsed folding tables and chairs that had been placed there in storage. Stepping over some old boxes, she reached the backside of the tank and dropped to a knee. The bulb that lit the room was almost directly above her, and she worried that it could cast her shadow against the floor or a wall. She'd have to keep perfectly still and silent.

Kishiyama's voice carried in from the other room. "The time is approaching quickly. The event that we have been preparing for over many days, weeks, months—and for some of us, years—will begin within two hours." He took a moment before continuing. "None of us asked for Nibiru. None of us wanted Nibiru. Nevertheless, Nibiru is our fate. All that matters now is . . ." He waited.

"Humanity," the others answered.

"That's right. Humanity. We were given a gift—an early warning of this day by Nancy Lieder and the Zetas who've been communicating through her. Only, it wasn't a gift to *us*. It was a gift to anyone on this planet who was willing to listen—to hear the truth. And unfortunately, few were. That's what makes every one of us special. We listened. We heard the truth. And most importantly, we've acted."

Heather timidly nodded her head. Despite Kishiyama's methods—despite his tactical decisions—she knew in her heart that what the leader was saying was true. She had been told that this day was coming since as far back as she could remember. What she and her community of fellow believers hadn't anticipated over the years was one day receiving a literal date of its arrival. That information changed everything, and without Kishiyama miraculously entering their lives, and his leadership keeping them focused and organized, they never would have made it as far as they had. They were in as safe of a place as they could conceivably be, and if there were to be survivors of Nibiru, she would be among them.

But she needed to be with her daughter, and she knew her daughter needed to be with her. Tears returned to her eyes as she listened to Kishiyama talk about the sacrifices they had all made. Her mind went back to the sight of her dead husband's body lying back in the tunnel. Morgan was a good man. A good provider. A good father. She hoped that her daughter would somehow manage to retain some memories of him, as improbable as that was at her age. Diana would have to get to know him through stories and a family photo album stored with the rest of their items down in the pit.

Heather covered her mouth as her body shook, worried her sobbing would turn audible. She bit the inside of her cheek, hoping the physical pain would, for the time being, temper her emotional pain. It seemed to work, though the strain drew her thoughts back to the man who'd killed her husband—the man who now held her daughter captive. She hated him. She wanted him dead. And she wasn't sure, if presented with the opportunity, that she could stop herself from ending his life.

"As I said before, I'm very proud of you all," said Kishiyama from the other room, his words drawing her back. "And I'm honored to be among you and stand alongside you. In just over five days, we will rise from the rubble, and together we will help breathe life back into this planet!"

The others cheered. Some clapped.

"What we do . . ." Kishiyama shouted.

"We do for humanity!"

"What we do . . ."

"We do for humanity!"

Shoes scuffed along concrete and shadows stretched along the wall to Heather's right as her people made their way to the exhaust pit. She lowered herself to the floor and pulled herself partially under the tank, worried she'd be detected. When she did, a prick against her thigh reminded her that Tammy had shoved something into her front pocket. Her fingers went inside to retrieve it, pulling out a single key. It had to belong to the gate in front of the tunnel that led to the living quarters—the one way to access where her daughter was being held.

The rungs reverberated as one individual after another descended into the pit. Heather didn't understand how Tammy believed she could keep the others from realizing she wasn't down there with them. Perhaps she felt she could win over their silence. What was of immediate importance was that—with a ratchet and heavy chain attached to the adjacent wall—the last metal sheet was slid into place. The loud screech of metal on metal ended with a thud. That pit had been sealed, and it had been done without Kishiyama and Gregory figuring out she wasn't in it.

She eased out a sigh of relief, and then listened to the two negotiate themselves from behind the steel platform and back out to the center of the missile bay.

"Can we stop dicking around now, Hiro?" asked Gregory in a tone Heather had never before heard him use in addressing the leader. Her eyebrows narrowed.

"Go outside," replied Kishiyama. "Bring in Hammer Jack."

Chapter 30

Returning to the fence, Oldhorse told Avalanche to stay. The dog complied.

He tossed his backpack over to the other side where it landed with a thud and some dust. He then climbed up the chain-link, effortlessly pushing the barbed wire aside with his arms. He flipped himself over the other side, landing squarely on his feet with a grunt. Keeping low, he grabbed his pack and hurried over to the two mounds of dirt he'd spotted before. They were larger than he'd thought, their length and width now drawing deeper concerns. One mound was older than the other, the dirt having been displaced hours earlier. An area of long grass beside them had been flattened, as if something heavy had been laid there.

Around the mounds were multiple sets of shoeprints, some overlaying the others. One of them matched what he'd seen by the shack, but both were too small to be Sean's. Oldhorse swallowed and began sliding his hands through the dirt, but stopped a second later when he heard a loud bang. He went flat to his chest.

The noise had sounded like two pieces of metal slamming against each other, and it had come from the south. He crawled across the ground to some tall weeds, dragging his pack beside him. He slithered behind wet grass and scrub where the land leveled out, peering through it.

Below he saw the back end of an old white school bus, parked along an inclined driveway. Next to it was a white GMC pickup. In front of both vehicles was a large steel blast door carved inside of a raised area of earth. A regular-sized door was on the cement wall to the right of it.

A man in a dark shirt and camo pants, with short, bleach-blond hair and an athletic build emerged from the front of the bus. Oldhorse noticed what looked like a toothpick in his mouth, before his eyes lowered and widened at the sight of a radio hooked to his left side. On his other side was a holstered revolver. Oldhorse reached back and grabbed his sheathed hunting knife from his belt, thinking of his own firearm left at home, deemed unnecessary for a trip to visit his ailing father.

The man walked up to the rear of the bus, which was an old enough model that its two back doors took up nearly the entire width of the vehicle. He reached up and unlatched the doors, swinging one of them open. Its dry hinges screeched. He did the same with the other.

Inside the bus was a large yellow steel contraption that looked like a piece of construction equipment. The top of it nearly reached the bus's ceiling. The machine was mobile, with a tank-like caterpillar track at its base and an upper half comprised of a hydraulic arm, similar to a crane. Instead of a hook at the end of its jib, there was what looked like a drill or a spike. Oldhorse had never seen anything like it.

The man reached into the back of the bus and began dragging out a long metal ramp from under its floorboard. Probably once used for school kids in wheelchairs, it shrieked loudly as it extended. There was a click, and he dropped his end to the pavement. He walked up the ramp and into the bus, leaning over the equipment and twisting some knobs along its base. The machine began to hum. The man grabbed a small object from the floor next to the machine. Holding it with both hands, he walked backward down the ramp, his eyes still pointed toward the rear of the bus.

Oldhorse remained perfectly still, carefully following the man's movements as he would a deer's.

The machine began moving, jostling on its track. It jerked its way forward a couple of times until it was on the ramp. When the man reached the driveway and turned his body a bit, Oldhorse saw that the object in his hand was some type of remote control with an antenna sticking out of it. He was guiding the machine's movements. The machine steadily made its way down the ramp until it reached the pavement. There, the man turned it to the west a few feet before flipping some switches and putting it in reverse.

A high-pitched beeping noise rang out from the machine, and Avalanche started to bark. Oldhorse had to force himself to stay absolutely still. The noise grabbed the man's attention.

The man spun, glaring to the south for a few seconds before turning his body and flipping off the machine. He appeared to be listening. Avalanche continued to bark, and the man quickly set his remote control down on the ramp. He pulled his revolver from his holster.

Oldhorse remained still, knowing any sudden move could reveal his hiding spot. The man held his weapon the way Oldhorse had been taught to with a service pistol, elbows retracted to expose less of his body. He appeared to have combat training. Likely a military man.

Avalanche was still barking as the man slowly made his way up to the edge of the driveway, and then into the grass. He was headed right toward Oldhorse.

Oldhorse knew the armed man wasn't going to turn back, not until he got to the bottom of the barking. He likely wasn't the individual who had locked Avalanche in the shack—too big to leave such shallow, small footprints—but he clearly hadn't been expecting to hear the dog now. Oldhorse kept his eyes trained on the man's, looking for any hint that he'd been spotted. So far, there hadn't been one, but it was only a matter of seconds before his closing proximity would change things. He tightened his grip on his knife and tensed his body.

The barking suddenly seemed to shift directions, as did the man's gaze, following it. He stopped and turned his head toward the northwest corner of the grounds, where the land was lower. His eyes widened, and he holstered his weapon.

Oldhorse let himself breathe, otherwise remaining still.

The man reached across his belt and grabbed his radio. He quickly adjusted a knob and brought the receiver to his mouth. "Alpha One," he said. "Come in."

A few seconds floated by before there was an answer. "I said I'd call you, not the other way around." The voice belonged to a man.

"I know. Just a quickie. Listen, are you sure Mitchell's still on board with us?"

"What do you mean?"

"Coleman's dog. It ain't dead. It's running around outside the fence."

There was silence for a few seconds before the voice returned. "That . . . is very disappointing. But it changes nothing. He and Coleman are isolated down here. They can talk all they want, but they aren't going anywhere—not until we're ready to go in after them."

It was a relief for Oldhorse, hearing that Sean was alive and not buried under one of the mounds of dirt. Oldhorse remained prepared, however, to spring into action if the situation called for it.

"Which we'll need to do very soon," said the man standing just feet away from Oldhorse. "So Mitchell can complete his work."

"Of course. So take care of the dog, finish your business up top, and get back down here so we can proceed."

The man nodded. "Over and out," he said, shaking his head and returning the radio to his side. He retrieved his gun from his holster and began walking—almost casually—toward the northwest corner, away from Oldhorse and toward the barking.

"Come here, boy!" he shouted, mockingly. "Uncle Greg's got something for you."

Oldhorse lifted his head up a little, turning his attention to the door beside the driveway. It had to lead inside to the silo, where Sean was. With the man focused on Avalanche, Oldhorse was sure he could make it down the incline and in through the door without being seen. But that meant the dog would have to die, and Oldhorse wasn't about to let that happen.

He stuck the knife in his teeth and carefully crawled to his hands and knees, and then to his feet. When he retrieved the knife, he held it by its blade rather than the handle. He followed after the man, mirroring his pace, but being more cautious with his footing. Oldhorse was careful not to let his long shadow come within the man's line of vision.

Avalanche continued to bark. Upon seeing the man and Oldhorse behind him, the dog jumped up against the fence, his front paws pushing against the chain-link. Oldhorse raised his arm, bringing the knife up with it. He lifted his other arm for balance. The man slowed his pace until he came to a halt. Oldhorse did the same, steadying his breathing.

When the man raised his arm to level his gun at Avalanche, Oldhorse planted his left foot, clenched his teeth, and threw the knife. Almost simultaneously, the man spun toward Oldhorse. His gun fired, its blast echoing across the plains.

Chapter 31

His heart had been beating against his chest from the moment he'd heard the hinges of the gate. He slowly moved his body from a horizontal posture to a tucked position, feet planted on the cement and back pressed against the hatch above him. He was careful not to knock over any of the surrounding paint cans in the transition. Breathing through his nose, he continued to listen carefully to the approaching footsteps. They were light and definitely didn't belong to Gregory. If the others were now in the exhaust pit, the individual could only be one person—the person Sean had been waiting for.

The footsteps slowed as they grew closer, and Sean began to worry that he had somehow been detected. He was certain he hadn't made a sound, but the movements he heard felt cautious and deliberate. Still, they continued forward.

When Sean heard the hatch above him creak, and watched a shadow spread across the holes above, there was no turning back. He gritted his teeth and thrust his body straight, snapping open the hatch door. He felt weight on it before a small body came crashing onto the floor just in front of him in a pair of thuds. Soles of shoes in his face with their tips pointed to the ceiling, Sean grabbed the person by the ankles and yanked the body toward him, down into the hatch. Reaching for a collar, Sean already had his other hand shaped into a fist. But when he saw a woman's eyes and delicate features glaring back at him, he gasped.

It was Heather, the baby's mother. Her eyes wide and panicked, she opened her lips to scream. Sean quickly covered her mouth with his hand and forced her body down to the cement. She didn't go easily, kicking and trying to claw Sean's eyes with her fingers. He raised his chin to avoid her nails and lowered his body, the door descending down along his back until it closed shut.

Heather's body buckled along the floor, her legs knocking over paint buckets. She sent a knee close to Sean's groin, and her teeth sank into his palm. He clenched his jaw, fighting through the pain as he lowered himself horizontally across her, pinning her flat.

"Stop it!" he snarled, limiting his voice. "I'm not going to hurt you, but I need you to shut up!"

His words carried no weight. She fought even harder, biting his hand with all of her might. He managed to restrain her left hand, but her right made it to his cheek where her nails tore into his flesh. He grunted and forced her left arm over her right, pulling both of them down to her chest.

He moved his face in close to hers, nostrils flaring as sweat fell from his chin. "I didn't kill your husband, goddammit. Kishiyama did. He's been lying to all of you!"

Her body strained to break free, but his weight and size proved too much. Her struggling finally came to an end and her body went limp, her teeth letting up on Sean's hand. Her face was partially lit up by the light cast through the holes above, enough for Sean to see a lone tear running down her cheek.

Sean kept his hand there, not convinced that she wouldn't yell out if given the opportunity. "Listen, I'm not bullshitting you. I'm not going to hurt you. Your daughter's safe. She's with Mitchell."

There was nothing but hopelessness in her eyes as she gazed back at Sean.

"Where is everyone right now—the others in your group? How did you get down here? Do you have a key to the gate?" Sean raised his hand up a half inch, giving her room to answer.

Heather said nothing, her lips remaining shut and her eyes unchanged.

"I know you hate me," said Sean, nodding his head. "If I were you, and believed the things you believe, I'd hate me too. But I promise you that Kishiyama shot your husband, the father of your child. Not me. He and Gregory aren't who you think they are."

When her eyes shifted to the side, Sean knew he had struck a nerve. He arched his neck and pushed open the hatch just an inch or so to look down the tunnel. The gate was closed and appeared to be locked. She must have reached through the mesh after coming through and re-secured it. No one was in sight. He lowered his head back down.

"You have a key, don't you?"

She didn't react.

"Listen, I don't want to have to tie you up and gag you," Sean said. "But I will. Trust me, I'd rather just put you back with your daughter."

Her eyes slid to Sean's.

Sean continued. "And I can make that happen. I promise. Not later, but right now."

Her eyes narrowed.

"All I want is to get out of here. You and your people can have this place." He took a moment before continuing, letting Heather absorb his words. "Here's the deal. You're back with your daughter, and I'm gone. I just need to know where everyone else is. And I also need that key."

Sean could feel her body trembling under his touch, and he hated the trauma he was subjecting her to, but it seemed to have paid off when she nodded her head.

"Good," Sean said.

He raised his head, opening the hatch to take another look at the gate. The junction behind it was still clear. He quickly lifted it the rest of the way open. With one hand still pinning Heather's hands to her chest, he grabbed the steel rod and placed it on the platform beside him. He then stood up straight and carefully helped Heather upright by her arms before moving his hands to her waist and effortlessly lifting her onto the platform into a seated position.

Sean kept his eyes on her as he climbed out of the trench, worried she might try to scream, but a softness in her gaze suggested that she wouldn't. She appeared surprised by how gentle he was now being with her.

Sean lowered the door back down, grabbed the rod with one hand, and helped her up to her feet with his other. Holding onto her wrist, he guided her down the steps that led around the corner to the control room.

"Your baby's fine," Sean assured her as they entered the room. "She's beautiful. Mitchell's been taking good care of her." Just in front of the sleeping bag that covered the hole he'd made in the floor, Sean stopped and turned to face her. "But before I take you to her, I need that key."

She glared at him for a moment. "You know I have the key on me," she said, a crackle in her voice. "You could have just taken it from me by force. Why haven't you?"

Sean nodded, his face softening. "Because I'm not the man you think I am." The words echoed what he had said to Lumbergh the morning before.

She swallowed, her jaw tightening.

He glanced down at the floor before raising his eyes again to meet her gaze. He continued. "My sister's name is Diana. It's a good name."

Her lips straightened for a moment. "You'd better be for real," she said. "Everyone except Kishiyama and Gregory are sealed in the exhaust pit."

"With their guns or without them?"

"What?"

"I need to know what I'm up against. Do Kishiyama and Gregory have access to an arsenal, or—"

"No. They just have whatever's on them. The rest of the guns . . . They're with the others, under the floor."

"Okay. Where are the two now?"

She hesitated. "Kishiyama sent Gregory outside to get something. Kishiyama is down in that room east of the missile bay—the one with the stairs."

Sean's eyes narrowed.

"It's labeled something having to do with skids," she added.

"Skid Pad Guards," Sean said, his face taught.

The room to which she was referring used to house a large liquid-oxygen tank, back when the facility was operational. Over the years, it had been renovated to better facilitate the storage of heavy county equipment—everything from archaic computers to large office furniture. A cement ramp, along with gravity rollers and a pulley system, had even been installed to assist with the stockpiling process.

"What's he doing down there?" Sean asked.

"I don't know," answered Heather. She took a breath and then opened her mouth to say something else but stopped herself.

"What?" Sean pressed.

"Just that . . ." she began. "In all of our months of preparing, that room had never been brought up. Not once. But he's been down there a few times since we got here. I don't know why."

Sean nodded, unsure if he was being played. She reached into the front pocket of her jeans and pulled out a single key.

"Believe me," Sean said. "Kishiyama has kept *lots* of secrets from y—"

A loud pop sounded from the other side of the room. As if in slow motion, Sean watched Heather's eyes bulge and her mouth gape open as she fell forward into him, her face landing on his chest. The rod fell from Sean's grasp, his arms instinctively wrapped under her shoulders to keep her from collapsing to the floor.

When Sean raised his head, he saw Kishiyama in the doorway, his eyes intense and a pistol clenched in his hand. He moved in close.

"All you had to do was stay in the goddamn pit, Heather!" Kishiyama screamed. "That's all you had to do!"

Sean's heart pounded as he dropped to a knee, easing Heather down to the floor with him. Her eyes floated and a groan poured from her mouth.

Sean expected the next shot to come fast and enter right through the center of his skull, but Kishiyama hesitated. His nodding head and burning eyes suggested he had to get something off his chest first. Sean rolled Heather onto her side, looking for where the bullet had entered her body. When he spotted a tear in her clothes and blood above the left side of her ribcage, he placed his hand over the area, applying pressure. She grunted in response.

"You . . ." Kishiyama said, his nostrils flaring. "I gave you every opportunity to get out of this alive."

"Why?" Sean said, seething as he lifted his head and glared back.

"What?"

"Why was it so important for you to keep me alive?" Sean asked, spit spraying from his mouth. "You had no problem killing the others."

"I didn't want to kill *anyone!*" Kishiyama yelled, his mouth stretched wide as his voice echoed through the room. "Not Mahan! Not Morgan! Not the old man!"

Sean's face tightened. "What old man?"

Kishiyama squared his jaw and breathed through his nose. "It doesn't matter. Just know that it's because of him that you were spared."

"Just like you *spared* Mahan? Why did you kill him?" Sean subtly slid his free hand toward the steel rod on the floor. He hoped Heather's body was keeping Kishiyama from seeing it. "How did he know who you were? Did he know you used to work here?"

Kishiyama's eyes widened.

"Yeah, I know about your history with this place," Sean said, having learned from countless detective television shows over the years that keeping the bad guy talking was a good way to buy time. "What brought you back after all this time? Did you miss mopping the floors?"

Kishiyama said nothing but the fire in his eyes spoke volumes.

Sean continued. "Or maybe all that mopping pissed you off so much, you felt you had to come back here one day and blow the place up. Disgruntled employee . . . to the extreme." His hand finally found the rod.

"How did you get out of that room?"

"Magic," Sean answered, tightly gripping the rod.

Kishiyama clenched his teeth. "You don't think we'll figure it out, with or without you? You being here just means that Mitchell's much more accessible than we'd thought. That's only good news for us."

"Hey," a voice came out of the blue, followed by brief static.

Sean froze.

Kishiyama backed up a few steps, keeping his gun trained on Sean. He reached behind his back and pulled out a hand radio. He lifted it to his mouth. "What?"

Sean swore under his breath. Kishiyama was no longer close enough for Sean to take a swing at him with the rod.

"We've got a problem up here." The voice from the speaker belonged to Gregory.

"What kind of problem?" asked Kishiyama.

A few seconds ticked by before Gregory answered. "It's hard to explain. You're gonna have to see it for yourself."

Kishiyama's face recoiled. "*Try* to explain it. I'm a little busy at the moment." He released the transmission button and waited. Gregory's voice didn't return. "Gregory?" Nothing.

Kishiyama's eyes slid to the floor, and then up to Sean. His mind looked to be moving a mile a minute. "Get up," he growled. "You're coming with me."

Sean stared at him for a moment before his eyes fell to Heather. She was returning his gaze, taking in shallow breaths. Her face was pale but she was still conscious.

"Go," she mouthed to him, her lower lip shaking as a tear slid from her eye.

He lifted his hand from her back just long enough to slide a finger through the hole in her shirt. He tore it wider, checking her wound. Blood surrounded the bullet's dime-sized entry in her skin, but the amount wasn't excessive. Her injuries could well be bad, but it didn't seem she would bleed out in his absence.

"Now!" Kishiyama screamed, straightening his arm.

Sean's eyes shot back up to Kishiyama. He held them there as he reluctantly removed his hand from the rod. He leaned forward, reached his arms over Heather, and pulled one of the sleeping bags toward him. He was careful not to choose the one covering the hole in the floor. He quickly crumpled the bag into a large ball and slid it behind Heather's body, propping her up at an angle. She silently watched him, perhaps unable to speak. Her eyes expressed a hint of gratitude before they narrowed in pain.

"I swear to God . . ." Kishiyama began.

"I'm coming, asshole!" Sean snarled. He pulled himself to his feet where Kishiyama ordered him to raise his hands and walk toward the doorway. Sean complied.

"We're going outside," said Kishiyama. "Do anything besides what I tell you to do, and you're . . ."

When Kishiyama's threat ended abruptly, Sean glanced over his shoulder to see the leader glaring at the large color photo on the wall—the one of the site's former crew members. With his gun still trained on Sean, his face had gone blank. Only his eyelids moved as he examined the picture. It must have been the first time he'd seen it. He swallowed and quickly turned his attention back to Sean.

"Just see a ghost?" Sean asked in mock seriousness.

Kishiyama's eyes narrowed. "Just do as you're told or you're dead."

"Yeah, I know the drill," said Sean, facing forward.

The two left the room, Sean glancing back at Heather before they made their way toward the tunnel. Kishiyama followed a few feet behind Sean with his gun nudging him forward. Something about Gregory's cryptic broadcast had Kishiyama spooked. Sean hadn't any idea what was waiting for them outside, but he'd spent the last several hours trying to get to where they were now headed. In a way, it was progress. He just hoped Heather could hold on in the meantime.

"Which old man did you kill?" Sean asked as he walked up the steps beside the tunnel. He heard some keys jingling behind him as they entered the walkway.

Kishiyama sighed, but to Sean's surprise, he answered the question.

"Your predecessor. The old man whose job you now work." His voice reverberated through the tunnel.

Sean tucked in his chin. "Yeah right. That poor son of a bitch was killed by a tornado. Are you going to tell me that you conjured up that twister with a wizard's spell, maybe at one of your cult meetings?"

"No, I'm going to tell you that that poor son of a bitch would have survived that twister if he hadn't been up top trying to help *me* survive it."

Sean said nothing, his mind struggling to process the remark.

Kishiyama continued. "His sacrifice bought you my grace, Mr. Coleman. Charity might be a better word for it. But that decision turned out to be an enormous mistake on my part, and other people have paid for that mistake with their lives."

He ordered Sean to stop when they reached the gate. He tossed his key ring on the cement in front of him and told him to pick it up. Sean did, and seconds later he was opening the gate.

"Now the next one," said Kishiyama shortly after he'd unlocked it and stepped onto the junction.

Again, Sean complied. The gate swung open to the second tunnel. Sean made his way down it toward the entrance with Kishiyama close behind.

"His body was found in the campground," Sean said. "Notestine was his name. It never made sense to me how his dog managed to make it all the way down to the compound when he didn't even get as far as the fence. He had to have seen that twister coming."

"He most certainly did," said Kishiyama matter-of-factly.

Sean nodded. "I see. You were here casing the place that day, weren't you? From out in the campground?"

"More than casing it," answered Kishiyama, his voice sober. It seemed as though he was finally dropping any pretense of him being there for a reason that wasn't purely self-serving. "I was ready to take it that day. Mother Nature had other plans. I realized later that I wasn't *really* ready. There were things I hadn't thought through sufficiently. I would need more time. More man power."

"So you duped these delusional bastards into helping you."

Kishiyama didn't reply.

"You should have just applied for the open caretaker's job after Notestine died," Sean said sarcastically. "You'd have had all the time in the world. Believe me, I know."

Kishiyama was silent. Sean stopped walking. Mere feet from the door, he slowly turned around to face the leader, his hands still in the air. Kishiyama was glaring at him, his gun pointed directly at his face.

"Holy shit," Sean said, glaring back. "You *did* apply for the job, didn't you? That's how Mahan knew you. Hell, he probably interviewed you face-to-face—just like he did me. But you didn't know he was my direct supervisor until he showed up in the tunnel, did you?"

"Turn back around," Kishiyama said. "And unlock that door. Slowly."

Sean offered the hint of a smirk before doing as he was told. "Must have been one hell of a shitty interview, man," he continued. "I was hung over for mine and I still beat you out for the job? Hell, even my resume sucked."

"Oh, I'd be willing to bet that mine was worse. Slowly now."

Sean's eyes narrowed as he lowered his hand to the keyhole. "Even with your past work here?"

"Even with that," Kishiyama said, pressing the muzzle of his gun into Sean's back. "Slowly. Only open it a crack."

Sean slid the key into the keyhole. With a hard twist, the door unlatched from its frame. Bright sunlight poured in around its edges, forcing Sean to wince. The smell of dew slid in around it, bringing in fresh air up through Sean's nose. It was crisp, but the sun felt good on his face. Kishiyama leaned forward and grabbed the key ring from Sean's hand, sliding it into his pocket.

"Gregory!" Kishiyama shouted from behind Sean. "You out there?"

A good six seconds dragged by before there was an answer.

"Yeah!" Gregory shouted. "I'm having some trouble with Hammer Jack. His remote's doing some weird shit."

Hammer Jack? Sean wondered. *Remote?*

"Okay," Kishiyama told Sean, releasing some air from his lungs. "Open it all the way. Slowly." He kept his gun in Sean's back and raised his voice to address Gregory. "We're coming out! Don't be alarmed, I've got Coleman with me!"

Sean pushed open the door, taking in his first full view of the outside world in over twelve hours. Before him was the front of the school bus, its grill pointed toward the blast door. Still squinting, Sean poked his head through the entryway. He saw Mahan's white pickup parked beside the bus. Sean walked onto the driveway with

Kishiyama following closely behind. Gregory was nowhere to be seen.

"Gregory?" Kishiyama shouted.

His voice returned a few seconds later. "Behind the bus!"

"Go," Kishiyama directed Sean.

Sean's face tightened. Sean didn't know what was going on with Gregory, but something was off. He didn't sound like his cocky self, and if Kishiyama's swiveling head—visible from his long shadow cast along the pavement beside them—was any indication, the leader sensed it too.

"Stop," Kishiyama told Sean about halfway from the rear of the bus. Sean did. "Gregory, show yourself!"

Gregory didn't reply. The only sound came from a light breeze along tall grass, rolling in from the north.

"Back up," Kishiyama whispered, his voice shaky. "We're going back in."

A quick whistle streamed through the air from somewhere above them. Sean and Kishiyama twisted their heads in its direction, over and to the left. Above the cement retaining wall that separated the driveway from the enclosing hill stood a statuesque male figure. He was clad in denim, and his long hair blew in the breeze. Between his hawkish eyes were the sights of an aimed pistol. By his side stood a white pit bull, its tail wagging.

Chapter 32

Sean's breath had left his body. Ron Oldhorse was the last thing he was expecting to find. He couldn't fathom his reason for being there, but the corners of his lips curled at the sight.

"Who the fuck are you?" Kishiyama wailed, the muzzle of his gun bouncing up and down between the swell of Sean's back and back of his head. All but half of Kishiyama's face was concealed behind Sean's large body.

Avalanche barked at the leader's voice. He showed his teeth and snarled until a quick word from Oldhorse silenced him.

It was clear why Oldhorse hadn't taken the shot. He had good aim, but Kishiyama had positioned himself behind Sean from the moment they'd left the bunker. Oldhorse wasn't going to risk catching Sean in a crossfire—even though Sean's offhanded insults of Oldhorse over the years might have made the decision a tough one.

"Let him go," said Oldhorse, his voice monotone.

Sean could feel Kishiyama shake his head. "No, you put down your gun or I'll kill him." He leaned in closer to Sean. "Who is this?" he whispered. "Where did he come from?"

"You're so fucked, Kishiyama," Sean said. "You don't want to mess with this guy. He's a real savage—a mad man."

Oldhorse's eyes narrowed as he listened to Sean's description, otherwise maintaining focus on the situation. His gun was steady and so was the rest of him. Avalanche's head bobbed back and forth between him and the men below, his tongue now draped out of his mouth.

Sean continued. "This land we're on belonged to his people back in the 1800s, until they were slaughtered by the US Calvary. He vowed to one day return here to stake his rightful claim, and to take scalps from the occupiers . . ."

"Shut up, Sean," Oldhorse interrupted, his mouth barely moving.

Sean sighed, tilting his head.

"They're friends!" came Gregory's voice from somewhere behind the bus. "He got the jump on me and got my gun. He said he'd kill me if I didn't call you out here."

"Are you okay?" asked Kishiyama.

"I'll live, but I'm tied up behind the bus."

"I don't know what all he told you, Oldhorse," said Sean. "But these men are murderers."

With a nod, Oldhorse acknowledged that he understood. "There are two bodies up the hill."

No one spoke or moved as seconds that felt like minutes ticked by, all understanding that the situation was at a stalemate. Sean finally broke the silence.

"It's over, Kishiyama. It's just you now. Your people are all either dead, isolated, or onto your bullshit. Whatever all of this has been about . . . It's over."

"You're forgetting that I have a gun pointed at your head," Kishiyama said through his teeth. "You and I are going back inside. Right now." He tugged on the back of Sean's shirt with his free hand.

"I don't think so," answered Sean, lifting his gaze toward the sky. He had confidence in Oldhorse. "It's too damned nice of a day."

Sean closed his eyes, planting his left foot on the pavement. In an instant, he lunged to the right, breaking free of Kishiyama's grip before crashing to the ground. A shot fired off. Another quickly followed. Chunks of asphalt pelted Sean's face as he twisted his body and rolled underneath the bus. Avalanched barked loudly as another shot rang out. Sean kept rolling until he was on the other side of the bus.

He heard rapid footsteps. A second later the steel door slammed shut.

"Shit!" Sean snarled, pulling himself to his feet as Avalanche continued barking. "Oldhorse!" he yelled over the bus.

"Yeah!" Oldhorse shouted back.

"You okay?"

"Yep."

"Is he back inside?"

"Yep."

Sean cringed. "What the fuck's wrong with you?"

Avalanche stopped barking.

"Are you serious?" Oldhorse asked.

Sean jogged over to the front of the bus, peering over the hood at the closed door.

"He's got the keys," Sean moaned, leaving the vehicle's cover.

He ran toward the door, stumbling as he reached it. He grabbed the handle and tried to twist it. It wouldn't budge.

"Dammit!" he growled, dropping to his knees and taking in air. "A woman's been shot. We need to get in—"

A large white object flew into him, knocking him to his butt. Sean clenched his fist, ready to throw a punch, but his fingers uncoiled the moment Avalanche's thick, wet tongue engulfed his face. The dog's paws were soon up on Sean's shoulders. Sean raised his hands to push him off, but when Avalanche wouldn't relent, Sean opened his arms and let the tongue-bath proceed. He winced from the sting it caused to the cuts Heather had left, but a half grin formed on his face. His fingers went behind the dog's ears to give them a scratch.

"I missed you too, buddy," he said.

Oldhorse dropped down to the driveway from the hill, gun still in hand as he approached them. Sean twisted his shoulders to let Avalanche slide off of him. He took the extended hand of Oldhorse, who helped him to his feet.

"I thought you were supposed to be a crack shot," said Sean, his eyes narrowing.

"I thought you were supposed to be locked in some room," Oldhorse answered. "You're alive. Stop bitching."

Sean scoffed as Oldhorse's eyes skimmed his appearance: ragged clothes, both shoulders marred from bloody wounds, and parallel claw marks down the side of his face.

"Next time, wink or something," Oldhorse added. "So I know your play. Haven't you learned anything from all those detective shows you watch?"

Sean frowned, unsure of how Oldhorse knew what he watched on television.

"Toby still talks about you," Oldhorse affirmed.

Sean nodded. He didn't want to think about Toby right now. It just reminded him of how bad he had screwed up. "All that shooting and the guy gets back inside without a scrape," he said, eyebrows raised.

Oldhorse's face loosened. "Without a scrape?" With a nudge from his eyes, he directed Sean's gaze to the pavement where splattered drops of blood decorated the driveway leading up to the door. "He looks worse than you do now."

"Okay," Sean said, nodding. "I stand corrected."

"Guys!" Gregory shouted from behind the bus. His voice cracked. "Things don't have to be like this. We can all work something out! We can make a deal!"

Sean and Oldhorse glanced at each other before making their way toward Gregory. Avalanche followed, tail bobbing.

Behind the bus was a steel ramp that extended far out of its open rear. When they rounded the vehicle, Sean found Gregory strapped to its top by rope around his legs, waist, and neck, his swollen face forced toward the sky. It wasn't all that different from how Sean had been bound earlier, back in the storage room. Dried trails of blood led from Gregory's nostrils to under his chin. His wrists were bound by more rope. The upper left thigh of his pants was soaked with blood. A shirt or rag had been tied around it to stop the bleeding.

"Jesus," Sean said, walking up to Gregory. He placed his hand on Gregory's thigh. "What happened here? Did Oldhorse get you with his tomahawk?"

"A knife," answered Oldhorse. "I don't own a tomahawk, asshole."

Sean smirked, giving Gregory's thigh a squeeze. Gregory howled in pain, his back arching as much off the ramp as the ropes would allow for it. Avalanche barked until Oldhorse quieted him again.

Sean let up but kept his hand close by. "Keys," he said, glaring down at Gregory.

Gregory took in some deep breaths, his eyes wide. "Don't have any," he blurted out. "They're inside."

"I didn't find any on him," concurred Oldhorse. "Not even for the vehicles."

Sean grunted, his eyes sliding over to the large, peculiar looking metal construction tool parked just a few feet away. It was yellow, sat on caterpillar wheels, and was equipped with a crane-like arm. Sean examined the contraption from top to bottom.

"Listen to me," said Gregory. "There's a lot of green in this for everyone if we can call a truce. We can all walk away rich."

Sean ignored him, his eyes lowering to a phrase written in black marker on the bottom right corner of the piece of equipment: "Hammer Jack."

"Come on, Coleman," Gregory pled. "I know a lot has gone down, and there's bad blood between us, but you, me, and Tonto here can work out—"

Sean snarled and grabbed Gregory's thigh again. Gregory screamed, his mouth opening wide as Sean felt warm blood ooze under his fingers.

"You don't call him Tonto, you hear me?" Sean yelled, his face just inches from Gregory's. "His name is Oldhorse! Or you can call him sir."

Sean let go. Gregory withered in pain, his eyes watering and drool sliding from his mouth. He let out a few coughs. Oldhorse stood there with his arms crossed in front of his chest, his face emotionless.

"You call me Tonto sometimes," Oldhorse said to Sean.

"Yeah, well *he* doesn't get to," Sean retorted.

Sean gathered himself for a moment and then wrapped his large hand around the captive's neck. Gregory's eyes bulged and his mouth dangled open, his body squirming under the ropes.

"Enough of the bullshit, Monty Hall," said Sean, teeth bared. "I want to hear all of it, right now—why you really came here and what you're really after. And if you try to pay me off again, it will be time to dig a third grave."

Chapter 33

She drifted in and out of consciousness, intermittently hearing what sounded like a baby's cries. *It can't be Diana. She is too far away, behind concrete walls.* Heather convinced herself that the wails were in her imagination, and that the louder they grew, the closer she was to death—a sick taunt from the afterworld.

When the cries suddenly rose so loud that her ears rung, she opened her eyes to meet who she hoped would be an angel. Instead, she found a green object mere feet from her face, swaying and arching like a whale's tail rising up from the water. Only, the water was the floor, and when her eyes focused, she found that the tail was the lower half of a sleeping bag.

The bag flopped back over on itself, the crying now piercing. The next thing she saw was a man's head slowly rise from the floor. She gasped.

"Mitchell?" Her eyes fluttered.

"Heather," he said, his eyes wide and receding in concern as he examined her.

"Diana," she muttered. "Do you have Diana?" She turned her body to better meet his gaze.

Mitchell nodded and hunched forward, lowering his head. He then grunted and lifted his arms through the floor, holding the baby in his hands—a small blanket wrapped around her. Diana screamed, her mouth wide and a tear rolling down her tight, reddened face.

Heather's face shriveled, tears building in her eyes as well. "Oh thank God," she said with a gulp, extending her arms in front of her along the floor.

Mitchell nodded and handed Diana to her, making sure she had a good hold before removing his own hands. Heather held Diana close, pressing her lips to the baby's cheek and shushing her. A grin on her teary face, Heather watched as Mitchell pulled the rest of his lanky body out of a hole she hadn't noticed before.

"Thank you, Mitchell. Thank you."

Mitchell nodded and crawled over to the two, his clothes dusty from the passageway he must have traversed beneath the floorboards. He circled behind Heather, pushing aside a stack of canned goods and a steel rod that were in his way.

"What happened?" he asked. "Have you been shot?"

"Uh huh," she murmured, her eyes still glued to Diana.

"God. Tell me Sean didn't do this," he said, peeling off his shirt.

"No. Was Kishiyama. Sean . . . Sean tried to . . . help."

He quickly folded the shirt and held it against Heather's back, causing her to wince.

"How bad?" she asked.

"I don't know," he said. "I don't know. Where's Sean now? Did he get out?"

"Kishiyama has him. Took him outside."

"Shit," Mitchell said. "Kishiyama. He's been lying to us. He used us."

She nodded, humming into her baby's ear.

"He . . . he killed Morgan."

She continued nodding, her eyes shrinking with sadness as she brought Diana closer. Within seconds, the comforting took hold. The baby's wails began to taper off.

"Where are the others? Are they down below?"

She nodded.

"We've got to get you down there with the first-aid kits. They can help you. Nibiru will be here soon."

"What are *you* going to do?" she asked as Mitchell slid his arms under her, prepared to lift her and the baby.

Before he could answer, lumbering footsteps could be heard from through the doorway. They were quickly drawing closer. Heather could feel Mitchell's heartbeat racing against her shoulder.

Someone barreled into the room on sloppy footing, the man almost unrecognizable with the palm of his hand pressed against the side of his bloody face. Heather screamed. Mitchell fell to his butt behind her and the baby.

The man shook his head as if to clear a bout of lightheadedness. His deranged eyes quickly homed in on the room's occupants, focusing on the sight before him. His lips twisted into a maniacal grin, blood showing between the lines of his teeth.

"Just the man I was looking for," said Kishiyama, raising his gun toward the three.

Chapter 34

"Diamonds? Buried inside the silo? That's bullshit!"

"It's not bullshit," Gregory said, a fly landing on his nose. He shook his head to shoo it away, swearing. A bead of sweat ran from his hairline down his raw forehead. "They've been there for forty years."

"Where?" Sean demanded.

Gregory clenched his jaw, hesitating. He closed his eyes. "In that room off of the missile bay, with the stairs, buried under a shit-load of cement."

Sean turned to Oldhorse, his arms crossed in front of his chest. "That's where Heather said Kishiyama was, right before he brought me outside."

Oldhorse took a step toward Gregory, causing the captive to flinch. "These diamonds. How did they get there?"

"That's a long story," he said, the same fly buzzing around his head, dividing his attention. The smell of his blood seemed to be attracting it.

"Well you sure as fuck aren't going anywhere," said Sean. "So let's hear it."

The fly hovered above Gregory's eyes for a second before landing on his forehead.

"This fucking fly," muttered Gregory.

Sean grunted and slowly raised his arm high in the air. He then snapped his palm down hard across Gregory's head, bouncing the back of his skull off the ramp.

"Ow, you fuck!" Gregory cried.

When Sean removed his hand, the flattened insect lay there, one of its wings twitching in the breeze. His fingers quickly went around Gregory's throat, squeezing until the man's eyes bulged.

"We're not fucking around, asshole!" Sean yelled. "Now answer the man! How did the diamonds get there?" He squeezed Gregory's neck for another few seconds before letting go.

Gregory took in air, coughing. After a moment, through gritted teeth, he began. "One of the crew members that worked here back then—his wife . . . his wife was a Rockefeller. She . . ."

"A what?" asked Sean.

"A Rockefeller."

Sean turned to Oldhorse. Oldhorse shrugged.

"Jesus, they're a rich family, okay?" said Gregory. "Super rich. And famous."

"Go on," Oldhorse calmly said.

"She died in a car accident. So did the guy's kids."

"Collins?" said Sean.

Gregory squinted, not expecting Sean to be familiar with him. "Yeah, Collins. Well, he was all fucked up after his family died. Spent all of his time underground, here in the silo, even when he wasn't working. Guy didn't want to go back to an empty house. Hated being alone. Moved a bunch of his shit here. His bosses okayed it because he knew his stuff and they felt sorry for the guy."

"Wait a minute," said Sean. "How do you know all of this?"

"From Kishiyama. He worked here back then. He was a fucking janitor. He talked to the guy, and sometimes overheard what the others said about him."

"The diamonds," said Oldhorse, keeping the exchange on point.

"Okay. Like I said, his wife was a rich broad. An heiress. She thought she was marrying an astronaut. Probably figured her husband would end up walking on the moon someday, and they'd end up as one of those celebrity power couples. Socialites. Only reason a woman like her would fall for a working man."

Sean's face twisted in anger. "Get to the fucking point."

"Collins fucked up his knee!" Gregory yelled. "During training! And he wound up here—still serving his country, but not the way he wanted to. No prestige. No fame. You know . . ."

"The diamonds!" Sean demanded, slamming his fist down on the ramp, just above Gregory's head. "Enough of this *Lifestyles of the Rich and Famous* bullshit! Get to what Kishiyama's doing!"

"Okay, okay. God. I told you guys it was a long story! I'm getting to it!" He took a breath and clenched his jaw before continuing. "Collins's wife had kept a dozen blue diamonds in a safe at their house. One carat each. Rare cut and tone. They were a gift from her mother, or maybe a grandmother. I don't remember which. You know, family heirlooms. They were worth a shit-load back then, and a hell of a lot more now. After she died, Collins didn't want to leave them at the house, not with him never there. So he brought them to the safest place he could think of."

"A top-level security missile site," said Sean, nodding. "But how did they wind up under the cement?"

"Because there didn't *used* to be cement there. There was a duct, for ventilation, on that west wall. It led up to the outside."

"Where the gravity rollers are?" asked Sean. "You're talking about the big triangle block—the cement wall below it?"

Gregory nodded.

Sean turned to Oldhorse. "He's telling the truth. That was an add-on by the county, years after the site was deactivated. It was for lowering heavy items into storage. They concreted the hell out of that thing. Sloppy ass job too."

"Collins kept the diamonds inside the duct, a few feet behind the vent cover," said Gregory. "He didn't trust the other guys enough to store them in the living quarters. They were in a metal box the same color as the vent. Barely noticeable to anyone who would've bothered to take a look inside."

"This Collins," said Oldhorse. "He told Kishiyama about the diamonds? Why?"

Gregory swallowed. "Well, no. Not that part. Kishiyama happened to see him hide the box one day, from up on the bay floor where he was doing some mopping. It looked suspicious as hell. Collins didn't see him there. Kishiyama went back later and opened up everything. He found the diamonds. Even held them in his hand. And then he put them back."

"Why?" asked Sean.

"He was a young guy with a good, steady government job—really rare for a Japanese immigrant back then. He wasn't above stealing—you know, stuff that wouldn't be noticed. Believe me about that. But diamonds? Those would've been noticed by Collins. Plus, Kishiyama didn't know dick about jewelry. He half suspected they weren't real—maybe fakes that Collins had some sentimental attachment to. He didn't know, and he didn't want to take the risk."

"But at some point, he figured out that they *were* real," Sean said.

"Yeah. It wasn't until after Collins hung himself that Kishiyama found out his wife was filthy rich."

"A Rockefeller," said Oldhorse.

"Yeah," replied Gregory, rolling his eyes a bit. "A Rockefeller." He turned his attention back to Sean. "Kishiyama was told to box up Collins's belongings in the living quarters. That's when he found the guy's journal. Collins had done a lot of writing after his family died. He talked about the diamonds. Even mentioned that it was in his wife's will that they were to stay in the family."

Sean nodded.

Gregory continued. "Kishiyama pocketed the journal, and that was a big-ass mistake. He should have just torn out the page."

"Why?" asked Oldhorse.

"Whoever had told Kishiyama to box up Collins' things had fucked up. His shit should have never been touched. I guess when someone who's watching over one of our nuclear sites offs himself, the government worries that he might have been compromised—maybe by a foreign agent. When the MPs showed up, they sent home all non-essential personnel and opened an investigation. Didn't take them long to figure out that Collins's journal was missing. Everyone who'd worked with him had seen him writing in that damn thing—just about every day. With it nowhere to be found, the MPs wondered what was in it—maybe codes or descriptions of protocols. They showed up unannounced on Kishiyama's doorstep, asking questions. They strong-armed their way inside his place."

"And they found the journal," said Sean.

"No, they didn't. Kishiyama had burned it. All he cared about was the diamonds. He knew where they were, and he didn't want anyone else finding out about them. The problem was that the MPs found other shit in his place—junk he'd swiped from the silo over time. Batteries. Hand cleaner. A Geiger counter he'd smuggled out in his lunch pail." Gregory shook his head. "Even some kind of candy he liked—from shelter food rations. Stuff that wouldn't have been missed."

"Once a thief always a thief," said Sean. "So they fired his ass?"

"More than that. They charged him. Threw the book at him. Made him do some time. They never found the journal, but they always believed he had taken it. Tried to use it as leverage, but he never copped to taking it. Once he got out, they blacklisted him. Made his life hell. At some point, they probably figured out that he wasn't a security threat, but either way he was never getting back in the silo again. Hell, he was never getting a decent job again. Stealing from a top security nuclear site stays on a record."

"Mitchell said he was a scientist," said Sean.

Gregory shook his head. "Hell no. He worked in the science department of a community college . . . as a janitor. Only job he could get when he got out of prison the second time."

"Second time?" said Oldhorse.

"Different beef all together. Like I said, his life had turned to shit. Desperate times lead to desperate actions. He tried to rob a bank down in Amarillo and was put away for a long time."

"Sounds like it," Sean said. "This place hasn't been *top security* for decades. Prison must have been what kept him away all these years. Sitting in a cell, thinking about those diamonds."

"How do you play into this?" asked Oldhorse, looking down at Gregory.

"You know what? Don't worry about me. Worry about Kishiyama. He's the one who's got . . ."

In a flash, Oldhorse's knife appeared in his hand, Gregory's blood still decorating it. He moved in close, grabbing the captive's hair with one hand and placing the knife to his throat with the other.

"How do you play into this?" Oldhorse repeated. "And why are you being so helpful now?"

"Jesus! Okay!" Gregory cried, his entire body stiff. With his eyes fixed on the knife, the words flowed quickly. "We met at the college where Kishiyama worked. I took some classes there after I was discharged from the military."

"Discharged?" said Oldhorse. "Honorably or dishonorably?"

"Jesus, who gives a shit?" Sean asked, cringing as he turned toward Oldhorse. "We already know he's an asshole." He turned back to Gregory. "Get back to you and Kishiyama."

Gregory glared at Oldhorse for a few seconds before continuing. "So, Kishiyama told me his sob story when he was drunk one night, including how the county had buried his fortune under a ton of concrete, and how he'd tried just weeks before I'd met him to get to it. He'd planned to use Hammer Jack that day, but . . ."

"Hammer Jack," Sean interrupted, looking at the nearby machine. "What is it?"

"An RDM—a robotic demolition machine. That chisel on its nose—it chips away at concrete like a jackhammer, but faster and easier. But like I told him, *just* using Hammer Jack still would have taken forever. It would work for the delicate stuff at the end, but we needed explosives, and someone who knew how to use them."

"Mitchell," said Sean. "And you used the others to help you secure this place and buy you the time that you needed."

"And to take the fall afterwards," added Oldhorse.

Gregory nodded his head feverishly until Oldhorse let go of him and took a step back.

"Wait a minute," said Sean, his face sour. "You wouldn't worry that they'd finger you two?"

"They don't know our real names."

"Kishiyama *is* his real name. It sure as hell was when he worked here."

Gregory shook his head and pressed some air from his lips. "He legally changed it in the '70s, because of the blacklist. Didn't really help with that situation, but it worked well for the con. Plus, I think he liked hearing his old last name spoken with respect for the first time in a long, long time. Pride and shit."

Sean and Oldhorse exchanged tight glances.

Gregory continued. "I'm telling you guys this so you'll understand that there's good money in it for you if you just let us finish the job. Twelve diamonds split four ways."

"How much," asked Sean, drawing a sharp glare from Oldhorse.

"Now we're talking," Gregory said, his lips curling a little. "Roughly two million total—a half million for each of us! Do you get it now? You couldn't make that much in a lifetime as a security guard."

"I'm not asking for me, dickhead," said Sean, his eyes burning a hole through Gregory. "I just wanted to know the cost of two, maybe three lives."

"Oh come on! None of that was supposed to happen!" Gregory shouted.

"Bullshit!" Sean said. "You've been threatening to kill me since the moment you walked in the front door!"

"It was just talk—to scare you into cooperating! It wasn't supposed to be like this. I haven't killed anyone. I haven't even shot anyone! It was all Kishiyama!"

"You tried to shoot me," said Oldhorse, taking a step forward.

Gregory swallowed. "Listen, guys. All of this can be water under the bridge. We can all come away rich! We can make this deal w—"

In a flash, Sean clenched his fist and slammed it onto Gregory's wound, drawing a piercing cry. Gregory withered, drool trickling out of both corners of his mouth.

"Here's *my* deal. You can shove those diamonds right up your ass! There's a woman—a mother of a baby whose father you guys killed—in there right now with a bullet in her back."

"It was Kishiyama . . ." Gregory gasped.

"Shut up!" Sean snarled.

Oldhorse put his hand on Sean's shoulder, drawing Sean's attention. "I think I can get the pickup started," he said, looking at the truck.

Sean squinted. "Without a key?"

Oldhorse nodded.

"You can hotwire a car?"

He shrugged, eyes empty. "Some kinds."

Sean's eyebrows arched. He was impressed. He'd seen the operation performed on countless crime shows but hadn't had a clue how to do it in real life. "Okay, let's say you get it started. Then what?"

"I'd get to a phone. Call the police."

Sean took in a breath. "It'll take too long. We need to shut this whole thing down now. Heather may not have much more time, and the others aren't safe either. Kishiyama's unhinged. Who knows what he'll do to them—especially if he thinks there's no way out of this." His hands went to his hips. "There's got to be something we can . . ."

His words ended when his eyes drifted along the dent toward the top of the blast door. His hands left his hips and he looked to his right before turning his attention back to Oldhorse.

"You think you can hotwire the school bus instead?"

Chapter 35

Sean stepped on the gas pedal, sending the bus into reverse. The shriek of metal ramp grinding into concrete poured through the open back doors of the bus.

"Wait!" Gregory screamed, his voice high in pitch.

Sean glanced through the side mirror just in time to catch the back corner of the bus collide with Hammer Jack. There was a loud crash, and the machine toppled part way to its side. Only the retaining wall kept it from falling entirely over. Sean slammed on the brakes, giving way to a piercing squeal.

"Jesus Christ!" Gregory yelled. "What are you doing?"

"Should we unhook him from the back?" asked Oldhorse from the first bench adjacent from Sean.

"No," Sean said, taking some satisfaction in watching Gregory through the rearview mirror, squirming against his binds. "We'll get him later. You ready?"

Oldhorse nodded, leaning forward in his seat and wrapping his arms around a metal frame in front of him. "Sure this will work? The door looks thick."

"I guess we'll find out. Inside, those assholes got through a vault door with a small forklift. Same concept. Aim for the weak spot. Now hold on."

Sean fastened his seat belt and gear-shifted into drive. He slammed his foot on the gas. The bus lunged forward, the vehicle quickly building up speed as it surged down the driveway. Avalanche barked from the hill above as Sean gritted his teeth and put a death-grip on the steering wheel.

"No! No! No!" Gregory cried.

Sean turned the wheel to the left, picking the side opposite the blast door's motor. The bus built up speed until it collided with the door, bringing everything to a dead stop and sending a horrific calamity of metal on metal echoing through the air.

Sean was thrown against his seatbelt, teeth snapping together painfully, but it hadn't been as rough a collision as he had anticipated. He slid his tongue along his jarred teeth before turning to Oldhorse, whose chest was pressed against the frame in front of him. Oldhorse's head was tilted downward, but he soon righted himself and extended a thumbs-up to indicate that he was okay.

Sean stood up in his seat to assess the damage as Oldhorse pulled himself to stand and slogged his way around the frame and down the steps to the bus's open door. He hopped outside.

The bus's hood had jackknifed upward, twisting at an angle. Sean backed up the bus a few feet at Oldhorse's urging, the movement causing metal debris to trickle through the engine to the ground. Oldhorse yanked at the hood until it crashed down, giving Sean a better view of the damage.

There was about a foot of space between the lower side of blast door and the cement that encased it, a large dent at the middle of the door accounting for the disparity. The gap was clearly too narrow for either of the men to fit through.

"I'm going at it again," shouted Sean, earning a head nod from Oldhorse. Oldhorse dragged the hood along the pavement, removing it as an obstacle.

"You fucking . . . fucking . . . assholes," groaned Gregory.

"How you doing back there, Greggy?" Sean taunted as he began backing up the bus again. "Hope the ride's not too bumpy!"

Gregory said something in reply, but Sean couldn't hear it over the grinding of the ramp across the pavement. Sean drove backward a little farther than he had the first time, leaving the driveway and entering the grass and grade of the hill behind it. He sized up the damaged blast door for a few seconds before popping the bus back into drive. He pushed down on the gas and pressed his back into his seat. Oldhorse had backed out of the way. Avalanche barked. Gregory screamed something unintelligible.

"Come on!" Sean snarled as the bus sped forward.

The nose of the bus crashed into the same section of the blast door, smashing it harder than the first time. Sean's body jolted forward before he collapsed back into his seat. The bus slowly coasted backward from the blow. The engine was dead. Sean placed the bus in park.

He unbuckled the seatbelt digging into his hips, ears humming. A quick headshake did little to focus his thoughts. He twisted the key, hoping to restart the engine to back the vehicle up more, but he was met with only a low whining sound—no crank at all. He staggered to his feet and pulled himself down the steps and through the open bus door. There he found Oldhorse's leery gaze and an extended arm.

"I'm fine," Sean grunted, waving off Oldhorse's gesture.

Avalanche continued to bark until Oldhorse shouted something to him, commanding his silence.

The smell of antifreeze now filled the air as the two men squeezed their way between the bus and blast door, Sean taking the lead. When they got to its side, they both stared down at the bottom corner where more of the door was caved in. The buckled metal had formed a gap between two and three feet wide. It would be tough opening for Oldhorse to squeeze through, let alone someone of Sean's size.

A series of clicks brought Sean's head to Oldhorse, who was checking the action of his pistol.

"Give me that," said Sean, holding out his hand. "I'm going in first."

Oldhorse's eyes narrowed. "Find your own gun," he said,

sidestepping Sean and lowering himself to his hands and knees with his pistol pointed forward.

"I'm serious, Oldhorse, this isn't your fight," said Sean, hovering above him.

Oldhorse twisted his head back toward Sean, looking the large man up and down. "The only fight would be getting you unstuck from this hole."

Sean glared at him. "You asshole. You don't even know the layout in there."

Oldhorse turned his head back to the opening, scrutinizing. "I'll figure it out. Be ready out here. If he gets past me, he'll come out the same door he did last time. Don't let him get past you."

It was the most Sean had ever heard Oldhorse speak in one sitting. Before Sean could begin another protest, Oldhorse angled his shoulders and began twisting his body around the metal. His head and arms went through, but the rest of him got hung up. His back rubbed along the cement behind him, knocking fractured bits of it to the ground. The heels of his boots worked to find traction.

As the lean man made little progress, Sean resisted heckling his efforts. But Oldhorse's maneuvering suddenly resulted in the right calculation, and the rest of his body slid through the opening.

With wide eyes, Sean dropped down, squinting as he worked his head through the hole. His broad shoulders prevented him from advancing any farther. He could see part of the inside of the bay, but not much else. He heard Oldhorse's footsteps scurry off to the right.

Sean twisted his body, doing his best to emulate the movements Oldhorse had made, but it didn't take more than a few seconds before it was clear that he was an oversized, odd-shaped peg that just wasn't going to fit through the slot.

"Dammit," Sean grumbled, backing himself out. The helplessness of the situation killed him.

He pulled himself to his knees, and then his feet. He took in a breath and brushed off his pants, looking back toward the driveway.

The school bus was totaled, engine parts and fluids littering the pavement. He squeezed his way back around its front and examined the ground, searching for a piece of wood or metal that he could use as a weapon—an object he could swing at Kishiyama if he popped through the door.

When he found nothing of use, he made his way to the bus's side door. Just inside, there was a short stair railing with one end that looked loose. Sean grabbed it and began to twist it when he heard a voice from the rear of the bus.

"H-h-hello?" It was Gregory. He sounded disoriented.

"Still with us, champ?" Sean mocked, continuing to work the rail. He placed a foot up on the bus's first step for leverage.

Avalanche jogged over to him, his nails pitter-pattering across the pavement.

"What's happening?" yelled Gregory. "Where's your Indian friend?"

"Inside," Sean said, twisting and turning the rail, prying at its mounts.

"Doing what?"

"Probably carving your boss up like a totem pole. Wish I had a front row seat."

Avalanche sat beside Sean, staring up at him as he repeatedly yanked on the rail. Sean grunted, gritting his teeth. He leaned forward and then yanked back on it with all of his might. There was a loud pop and the rail broke loose, sending Sean stumbling backward into the side of Mahan's pickup. When he pulled himself up straight, he noticed a couple of army duffle bags in the back of the pickup truck. While the truck's liner was dusty from the ride in, the bags weren't. In fact, they looked brand new.

Sean leaned the rail from the bus up against the truck and grabbed the closest bag. He unzipped it to find neatly folded clothes—shirts, pants, shoes, socks, and more. Some of the shirts were Hawaiian style and didn't seem to match Mahan's tastes. The sizes looked small too.

When he pushed a pair of boxers aside, he discovered a dark blue passport. He pulled it from the bag and flipped to the first page. There he found a portrait shot of Kishiyama staring back at him. It looked to have been taken recently. The name below the photo wasn't his.

"Hiroyoshi Tenzan," he awkwardly read aloud.

"Ah fuck," Gregory groaned from inside the bus.

"That's what he changed his name to?" Sean called, tossing the passport aside. "Where were you guys planning on going after this?"

Gregory didn't answer.

"This was going to be your guys' getaway car, wasn't it?" added Sean. "Makes sense, I guess. Hell of a lot better than a shitty school bus. More subtle too."

A loud explosion suddenly went off somewhere behind him. The ground rocked, spinning Sean around. The rail fell to the pavement as Avalanche bolted up the driveway, instinctively fleeing. Chunks of cement fell from the surrounding walls.

"What the fuck?" Sean roared. The blast had come from inside the compound, on the north end.

"Jesus Christ," he heard Gregory say. "That crazy son of a bitch."

Sean jogged over to him, his heart pounding. Though the metal ramp was still attached to the bus, it was twisted at an angle. Gregory was still strapped to its face, now at about a 45-degree angle. His eyes were glazed at the center of his swollen, dirt-covered face.

"What the hell was that?" Sean demanded.

"Kishiyama got to Mitchell . . . and that skinny bastard finally earned his keep."

"They're blasting?" said Sean. "You said the diamonds were buried on the bay side!"

"They are," said Gregory. His eyes now homed in on Sean's. A subtle smirk twisted across his face. "You guys should have just taken my offer."

Sean grabbed Gregory's injured thigh and squeezed it. The smirk vanished, replaced with a painful howl from Gregory's mouth.

"What just happened?" Sean yelled.

"That blast wasn't for digging," cried Gregory. "It was for caving in the ceiling above your friend's head."

Chapter 36

"How do you know that?" Sean yelled, squeezing Gregory's thigh again.

"Fuck!" Gregory cried, his voice rising several octaves. "Because it was the backup plan!"

"What backup plan?"

Gregory whimpered for another few seconds before answering in multiple breaths. "In case those rubes had gotten second thoughts about letting us bury them under the floor—if they had gotten second thoughts about *any* of this—we were going to force them into the Command Wing and blow the tunnel. Keep them sealed in there and out of our hair until we were done!"

Sean eased up. He leaned in close to Gregory, eyes ablaze. "But they *did* go under the floor, asshole."

"Yeah," answered Gregory, glaring back at Sean. "But *you* didn't. Kishiyama must have figured that you and your buddy would find a way back in. He's one crafty son of a bitch. But he doesn't know dick about explosives, so he would have had Mitchell set them up, probably by putting a gun to his head or threatening to do something to his friends in the pit. They're fish in a barrel down there."

"How would Mitchell have had enough time to do that? Kishiyama hasn't been back inside that long."

"It would have only taken Mitchell a few minutes," said Gregory, his eyes closed as he took in a deep breath. "Destroying something's a hell of a lot easier than an excavation. That's where things get difficult.

Once your friend entered the Command Wing, all Kishiyama would have had to do is push a button. Kaboom."

Sean recalled the retractable antenna he'd seen on one of the detonators. Gregory's story was likely true. Sean gazed at the ground, his eyes sinking in despair. When he lifted his head back up to Gregory, he found the sly grin back on Gregory's face.

"So I'd say your friend is fucked," said Gregory.

Sean moved his hand from Gregory's thigh to his neck, digging his fingers into his throat. "You'd better pray he's okay, jackoff."

Gregory's eyes bulged, his face turning apple red as his body twisted under his binds.

"Where's Kishiyama now?" Sean yelled, finally pulling his hand away.

Gregory let out a series of sick coughs. "Where . . . Where do you think he is? Sure as hell not in the Command Wing. I'd say he's going for the diamonds."

"But he's already used the explosives."

Gregory took in some deep breaths. "He wouldn't have used them all."

Sean nodded. "Got it. Thanks for the information." He then drew back his right arm and sent a wicked right cross into Gregory's head, spinning it to the side. Gregory's body went limp.

Sean shook his aching hand. His chest heaved in and out as his eyes wandered along the driveway. His mind raced to figure out another way inside. He knew he couldn't squeeze his body through the twisted corner of the blast door. There just wasn't enough room, not without widening the gap. And with the bus's engine dead, he couldn't ram it a third time.

He thought for a moment about strapping the handle of the main door to Mahan's pickup, but without Oldhorse around to hotwire the vehicle, the plan was a non-starter. Besides, the move would have likely torn off the handle while leaving the door in place.

He circled around to the other side of the bus, past Gregory.

That's when he spotted Hammer Jack leaning up against the retaining wall. Despite taking a good hit from the bus, it was still mostly in one piece. Its remote control lay beside it on the pavement just a few feet away. Sean's eyes lifted to the corner of the blast door again, shifting from the bent metal to the cement wall at its edge.

Chapter 37

The lightbulb on the ceiling above flickered on and off before finally stabilizing. Oldhorse's ears rung as his clenched teeth took up most of his dust-filled face. He tugged on his bloody right thigh with both hands, ignoring his body's excruciatingly painful warnings not to.

If he'd been moving slower through the tunnel, he would have been buried under a couple tons of concrete, but the sound of the detonator trigger had sent him into a full sprint. He hadn't gotten away unscathed, however. Large chunks of rubble—mostly cement—had fallen across his legs, pinning him to the floor. As fine particles of concrete floated in the air above him like chalk blown from a classroom eraser, he did his best to assess his injuries. Sharp pain shot up his shin when he bent his right knee, and he knew at that moment that there was at least one break in the bone. Still, sensing some give, he continued to pull his leg from the scree, crawling along the floor on his back while using his elbow like a pickaxe. He grunted and scraped until he was free.

Cringing and swearing under his breath, he grabbed his pistol from the floor with his trembling hand and reached up to a short railing beside some steps to his right. He gruelingly pulled himself to his feet, putting nearly all of his weight on his left leg. He then wiped his face with his sleeve and glared at the collapsed tunnel. It was a garbled mess of cement, metal, and other material. Grit still filled the air, making it difficult for Oldhorse to tell if there was any space above to provide a means of escape. He'd have to let things settle.

His head spun when he heard a baby's cry. The noise continued as he hobbled and hopped his way down the steps and around a corner. He entered a small linoleum landing, his eyes adjusting to the site of a mangled vault door to his left and another hallway straight ahead.

"Shhh," he heard coming from a lit doorway to his right.

With his gun pointed forward, he grabbed the side of the doorframe and swung himself inside. At the opposite end of the room was a woman, lying on the floor with a blanket covering her body. A baby rested in her arms.

"It happened," she said softly, her pale face pointed toward the ceiling. "God, it really happened . . . Nibiru." Her hair was soaked with sweat.

Her arms shook, and when Oldhorse saw them begin to slide off her chest, he stuck his gun behind his belt and quickly hopped over to her, lowering himself to his good knee before dropping down to his butt. Wincing from the pain, he took the baby from her arms.

"No," she moaned, turning her head and taking notice of him for the first time. "That's my . . . baby." She was barely conscious.

"I'm helping you," he said, grabbing the sleeping bag beside him and bunching it up into a large pillow. His eyes widened at a large hole in the floor beside her.

He propped up the baby on top of the sleeping bag, elevating its head. The little girl watched Oldhorse with curious eyes, no longer making a sound other than a few raspberries from between her lips.

"Who . . . who are you?" the woman asked, her eyes confused.

"I'm with Sean," he answered. "Let me see your wound." He moved in behind her head.

"Sean? Where is he?"

He tilted her body to the side and examined her back, noticing a blood-stained black t-shirt on the floor beneath her. "Outside," he answered.

"Oh God."

"He's okay. The world's still here."

"It . . . What? That terrible sound . . . The shaking . . ."

"Your leader blew up the tunnel." Oldhorse eased Heather back down, then put two fingers to her throat, checking her pulse.

"If . . . if I don't make it out of this . . ."

"You will," said Oldhorse. "Stay calm. Don't move. You've lost blood but you're no longer bleeding. You don't want to stir up the bullet inside you and change things."

She nodded.

"Is anyone else on this side of the building?" he asked, reaching over her and grabbing one of the other sleeping bags. He began bunching it up as well.

She shook her head. "No. Kishiyama, he . . . he took Mitchell. They left through . . . through the tunnel."

He carefully lifted her legs and placed the sleeping bag under her feet. "Is there another way out of here?"

"No."

Oldhorse grunted and sat up. His gaze slid to the baby, who was still watching him. "I'll find a way out," he said, turning back to Heather. "Then we'll get you to a . . ."

Before he could finish his thought, he noticed that Heather's eyes had rolled up into her head. Her body began to seize.

Chapter 38

Hammer Jack's reverse beeper pulsed as the machine backed up again. Sean stepped in front of it, swatting at the cloud of concrete dust that also covered his clothes. It had taken him a while to figure out how to use the contraption, but he'd gotten the hang of it. He dropped to his knees at the corner of the blast door, setting the remote control aside before using his hands to move fresh rubble out of the way. It was the third time he'd gone through the process over the past fifteen minutes.

He had known he couldn't bend the metal door any further to squeeze his way through the crevice, but breaking apart the wall it bordered was achieving the same directive. Sean's lacerated arms ached as he pulled out a good-sized slab of concrete. He then crawled to his stomach and began twisting his body through the opening. The cement scraped against his back as he slid along the wall. Gritting his teeth and squeezing his arms together as tightly as he could, he finally managed to fit his shoulders all the way in. His eyes widened as he pushed the rest of his body inside using his legs. He used the side of his foot to drag in the rail he'd torn off of the school bus.

He grabbed the rail as he climbed to his feet, taking in a deep breath as he grasped it in both hands as if he were holding a baseball bat. He ingested his surroundings, gazing at the thin layer of dust across the bay floor—likely a result of the tunnel explosion. There were two sets of footprints that crossed the dust, overlapping with seemingly erratic changes in direction. They had to belong to Kishiyama and Mitchell, suggesting a momentary struggle between the two. The footprints led toward the lower-level room where the diamonds were buried.

When Sean heard a tapping from across the bay, his head shot forward.

"Hello!" came a suppressed voice followed by an echo. Other voices joined in, shouting Kishiyama's name in unison. They sounded like ghosts, calling out the betrayer from beyond the grave. It was the rest of the group from down in the exhaust pit.

"We heard the drill!" one of them shouted. "What's happening?"

They were trying to make sense of the sounds they were picking up from under the floor. Sean wasn't going to try to talk to them, nor try to free them. Not for the time being anyway. They didn't trust him, and he wasn't going to waste the time it would take to try and clue them in. For now, they were safe and out of the way. Oldhorse and Heather were of more importance, but even with their condition unknown, Sean knew he had to address Kishiyama first. If the leader wasn't neutralized, any effort to help the others would be subject to his interference.

It worried Sean that the group under the floor had heard him using Hammer Jack to drill his way inside. That meant Kishiyama could easily have heard him as well. Yet the leader wasn't standing there, waiting for him with a drawn gun. With any luck, he'd been too busy with Mitchell and the explosives on the lower level to focus on much else. With better luck, Kishiyama believed that Sean had come in with Oldhorse and had been killed or trapped by the tunnel explosion.

Sean slid along the wall to his left. Large maps and posters beside him fluttered from the outside breeze entering through the crevice at the blast door. He poked his head around the corner, gazing across a row of old copy machines and some shelving at a tightly grated metal wall about twelve feet wide. Embedded in the right side of the wall was an open door made of the same material. Beyond it was a metal staircase, flush with the wall below it, that led down to the lower level.

Shadows danced off the tall, metal-ribbed ceiling of the room below, partially visible through the mesh of the wall. Fresh voices carried up into the air as Sean snuck over to the copiers. The louder, sharper voice belonged to Kishiyama. He was angrily barking orders, though Sean couldn't make out exactly what he was saying.

Lowering his body, Sean made his way along the copiers, ready to take cover behind one if needed. When he heard brisk, echoing footsteps ascending the staircase, he dropped to his knee and switched the rail to one hand.

"How far back do we need to be?" Kishiyama said, voice coming nearer. He was out of breath.

"The bay wall!" Mitchell shouted.

Sean raised his head up from behind the dusty copier and watched through the grate as Kishiyama emerged. His face was a bloody mess. He held a red-soaked rag up against the side of it while his other hand gripped his pistol. His head was twisted back toward Mitchell who followed him up the stairs, shirtless. Sean clenched his body, and the moment Kishiyama turned and lowered his gun to pass through the doorway, he lunged to his feet and charged toward the leader.

Kishiyama's eyes bulged when he caught view of Sean. His arm lifted to fire his pistol but Sean brought the rail down across his wrist like a lumberjack splitting wood. Kishiyama cried in pain, the rag falling from his face and the gun skipping along the floor and down the stairs past Mitchell. Kishiyama spun and slammed the door shut between him and Mitchell, just before Sean grabbed him by the collar. Sean yanked Kishiyama away from the wall and swung his arm with a grunt, sending the leader toppling into the row of copiers. He crashed face-first into one before collapsing to the floor.

Sean raced in as Kishiyama scrambled to his feet. The moment

Kishiyama turned toward Sean, he was greeted with a metal rail, swung like a bat, into the center of his stomach. His body doubled over hard, air spewing from his lungs. He fell to his butt and then to his side, clenching his stomach. Sean reached down to grab him by the collar when he heard Mitchell scream in panic.

"Help! God! Help!"

Sean turned to see Mitchell savagely yanking at the closed door, his fingers gripping through the mesh as his bare chest pressed against the grating.

"It's about to blow!" yelled Mitchell, his eyes the size of eggs.

The explosives.

Sean ran to the door, remembering even before he reached it that it locked automatically when closed. He twisted and pulled on the handle but got nothing.

"Where are the keys?" Sean yelled. Just as he was about to move back in on Kishiyama and rifle through the leader's pockets, Mitchell responded.

"Wait!" he said, jamming his hands into his own.

When he brought them out, a ring of keys dropped through his fingers, landing a couple of steps down on the staircase beside him. Mitchell desperately leapt down to retrieve them. Not waiting for him, Sean took a step back and launched forward, sending the sole of his boot into the door, just beside the lock. The framing was solid, and there was no give. He snarled and tried it again, getting the same result. Out of the corner of his eye, he could see Kishiyama clumsily crawling to his feet.

With the keyhole on the opposite side, Mitchell's shaking hands tried to shove the key through one of the diamond-shaped holes in the grate, but the ring and other keys made it impossible.

"Oh God," whimpered Mitchell. "Leave me."

"No!" Sean yelled. "Take it off the ring!"

Mitchell nodded, his face wrenched with nerves as he pried at the ring with his fingernails, twisting the key along it.

"How much time?" Sean yelled. He flipped his head to Kishiyama, who was stumbling his way toward the bay, seeking cover.

"Seconds," Mitchell gasped, his hair wet with sweat.

Mitchell finally freed the key and breathlessly slid it through the wall. Sean grabbed it and immediately shoved it into the keyhole. A high-pitched beeping noise emitted from somewhere below.

"No time!" Mitchell screamed.

Chapter 39

Oldhorse had nearly reached the end of the main tunnel when a loud blast shook the ground, throwing him off balance. He fell to the walkway, twisting his body at the last moment to cushion the landing of Heather and her baby whom he held in his arms.

He grunted from the agonizing pain that shot up his broken leg, now splinted straight with a steel rod he'd found in the control room. He'd cut strips of nylon from one of the sleeping bags to keep the rod in place. They held firm, even after the fall.

With glazed eyes, Heather twisted her colorless face up from Oldhorse's chest. "What happened?" she asked, her arms still wrapped around her baby.

"I don't know," he said, looking down at the baby.

The child, frightened from the landing, was holding her breath. Her mouth hung open at the center of her reddened face. Oldhorse leaned forward and blew on her face to get her to cry and take in air. A second later, she wailed loudly.

It had been a painstaking journey to get as far as the three had. Once the dust had cleared in the north tunnel, Oldhorse had discovered a narrow gap between the rubble and what was left of the top of the ceiling. If Kishiyama's demolition man were as good as he was supposed to be, the collapse would have been complete. He wondered if the damage had been limited on purpose.

Regardless, the tunnel was in ruins and far from stable. Oldhorse had to crawl back and forth across it twice—once with Heather and again with her baby, his heart nearly stopping each time he'd feel a tremble or movement in the foundation.

His initial instincts had told him that Heather shouldn't be moved, but after the seizure, he feared she would die without medical attention. He'd deemed the trip through the tunnel worth the risk. Heather protested throughout, insisting that something called "Nibiru" was on its way, and that they mustn't go outside.

The word meant nothing to Oldhorse, but he'd gathered from the interrogation of Gregory that she and the others were of an end-of-the-world mindset that Kishiyama had taken advantage of. He'd ignored her objections and fought through the pain of what felt like a hot spear being twisted in his leg.

From his side, Oldhorse carefully lowered Heather to the floor, sitting her up against the tunnel wall. When he pulled himself to his feet, he saw that Kishiyama had left his keys in the inside lock—something he wasn't expecting to find. If he had known about the keys, he would have let Sean inside before making his way toward the Command Wing.

Oldhorse hobbled over to the door, removed his pistol from the back of his jeans, and twisted the key. He felt the door give and he quickly swung it open, guiding his pistol through the doorway.

"Sean?" he said, raising his voice over the baby's cries. He saw and heard no one.

He returned his gun to his waistline and hobbled back into the tunnel just far enough to help Heather upright, and then back into his arms.

"No," she muttered, cradling her baby. "Please."

Discounting her pleas, he made his way with the two to the driveway, checking his surroundings again. As he moved closer to the pickup truck, he saw the ramp and Gregory's body still strapped to the bus. Gregory wasn't moving.

He slid a hand to the handle of the truck's driver-side door, opening it and plopping Heather down across the bench seat. She cried out from the movement, her voice rising above her baby's for a moment. He crawled in next to the two, moving them across to the passenger side. He lowered his head and began tugging at the steering column.

"Hmm," he mumbled, his face stiffening when he felt an object taped to the underside of the column.

Oldhorse pried at it until the tape tore and he held a black pistol in his hand. A Smith & Wesson 9-millimeter. It had likely been put there earlier by either Kishiyama or Gregory, perhaps to assist with their getaway. Oldhorse placed it on the seat beside him and went back to work.

"Where's Sean?" Heather groggily asked, her baby's cries beginning to lessen.

"I don't know," he said. "Maybe he found a way inside."

Heather nodded. "Then he'll be safe . . . when the time comes."

"Time's not coming," Oldhorse said matter-of-factly. He pulled some multi-colored wires out from under the column, peeling away their insulation with his fingers. "And he's not safe. Not until your leader is dealt with."

Heather glared at him for a moment before responding. "Then why . . . why aren't . . . you helping him?"

Oldhorse began twisting stripped wires together. "Because I think you're dying. And you were Sean's first concern."

He watched her face tighten out of the corner of his eye. She shifted in her seat a bit, her baby grumbling from the movement as Oldhorse tapped an exposed wire up against another. The truck's starter cranked but the engine didn't ignite.

"Help him," Heather said.

Oldhorse continued on, his focus still on his work.

"Help him!" she wailed, drawing Oldhorse's eyes. She was holding the black Smith & Wesson in her trembling hand, pointing it at Oldhorse.

Oldhorse let go of the wires and sat back in his seat, staring at her.

"If we're right, I'm dead anyway," gasped Heather. "If you're right, Morgan and the other man died for nothing." Her chest moved in and out. "I can't live with another man dying. Not because of us."

Oldhorse nodded. In a flash, his hand jolted forward. He grabbed the pistol from Heather's hands in one fluent move. Her eyes left wide and confused, she sank into the door panel behind her, her empty hand moving back to her baby.

"I'm sorry," she whispered.

Oldhorse quickly checked the pistol's action. He then switched the gun to his other hand and reached behind his back, pulling out his revolver. With the flick of a wrist, he held the revolver by its barrel and offered it to Heather. Her colorless face riddled with suspicion, she took it.

"Stay low. Stay put," he said.

Oldhorse exited the truck, carefully closing the door behind him. Flashing Heather one last glance, he hobbled over to the blast door. The second blast had come from the Launch Wing. Sliding back through the opening Sean had made with the bus, instead of doubling back through the tunnel, would put him there in seconds.

Cringing with each step, he skirted the front of the bus. His eyes widened when he saw dust hovering in the hole. The cement beside the door had been chipped away by the demolition machine beside him, affirming Oldhorse's belief that Sean had re-entered the silo. He went horizontal and squirmed through the opening.

Inside, the bay was a cloud of airborne grain and grit. The ceiling lights above were faint, hazy glows towering above a sharp, musty odor. What looked like white soot covered everything from the floor to the pictures on the walls. A pile of concrete and metal debris, which hadn't been there the first time Oldhorse had entered the building, crept its way around the east wall.

He pulled himself to his feet along the wall and began making his way toward the rubble. He suppressed a cough as he rounded the corner, holding his gun in front of him. His breath left him as he gazed across the destruction. The platform ahead was a menagerie of broken cement, twisted metal fencing, and ravaged equipment and furniture. Behind it, fluttering shadows from what looked like a small fire cast across the ceiling.

A few yards away, a chunk of concrete rolled off a collapsed metal barrier and crashed to the floor. Oldhorse raised his gun in its direction, saying nothing as he slowly approached it. He glanced over his shoulder, checking for anyone behind him, before homing back in on the barrier. Stepping in between the rubble as best he could to cloak his presence, Oldhorse watched a section of the grated metal rise up a few inches, knocking more debris to the floor.

"Fuck," he heard from underneath it.

"Sean," said Oldhorse.

Oldhorse hopped over, stuck his pistol in the front of his jeans, and leaned forward to grab onto the edge of the grated barrier. Putting all of his weight on his left leg, he lifted the metal up a few inches. He soon noticed that he was being helped by a large pair of dirty, bloody hands pressed against the underside of the barrier. Sean turned his body, loosening more rubble as he worked his way to his hands and knees. With his body covered with powder and blood across the right side of his face, he pressed his back into the metal. Both men grunted with effort until the angle was sharp enough that the remaining debris began to slide and roll onto the floor.

"Mitchell?" Sean asked, his voice coarse. "You still with me?" He coughed.

A few seconds floated by before a muffled response came from somewhere close by. "Uh huh."

Oldhorse's eyes shifted to some movement beside Sean. What he had originally mistaken for the top of a mop or broom was a man's head and hair, blanketed with the same dust that covered Sean.

Sean wiped powder from his face with his arm, his eyes blinking as he gazed across the room. "Jesus Christ," he said, surveying the damage. He twisted his head toward Mitchell. "What the fuck did you do?"

Mitchell coughed and then cleared his throat. "He wanted me to blast . . . I blasted."

"*Nuked* is more like it," said Sean.

"You were right, Sean," said Mitchell, swallowing and rolling to his side. Blood streamed from his nose and open gashes were visible on his chest. "Wasn't about Nibiru for him. He wanted somethin' in the cement. Wanted me to get it out for him. Wanted it so badly that nothing else mattered. Not our lives. Not your life. Had a gun on me, so I did the only thing I could to stop it."

"You blew it all to hell," said Sean, his lips curling.

Mitchell nodded, his chalky hair dangling in his face. "Used three times the explosives. He didn't have a clue."

"I can't hold this all day," said Oldhorse, his eyes shifting back and forth between the two men. "Crawl out."

Sean nodded. He arched his back, better bracing his shoulders under the metal as he reached for Mitchell's arm.

Oldhorse suddenly heard movement from behind him. He spun his head to see a short figure with his hand pressed to the side of his face slogging his way across the bay toward the blast door.

"Kishiyama!" Sean yelled in rage.

Oldhorse felt his pistol pulled from the waistline of his jeans. A second later, it was in Sean's hand and being fired repeatedly from around his hip. The blasts tore through the bay, peppering the wall that led to the driveway just as Kishiyama lunged behind it.

Chapter 40

A series of blasts roused her to consciousness. They sounded like gunfire. She instinctively felt for her baby and calmed when she found Diana still lying on her stomach, asleep. Heather lay on the floorboard of the truck, weak and barely able to move. The back of her head was propped up against the passenger-side door just below the armrest. She had heeded Oldhorse's warning to stay low.

When a shadow cast itself along the truck's driver-side window, moving toward the back of the vehicle, her heart froze. A dog began barking sharply, somewhere in the distance. It grew closer in seconds.

"Shit!" she heard a man yell. He sounded just a few feet away.

The truck door flew open and a dark figure entered, dark hair plastered to the side of his bloody face. Out of breath and covered with grit, he slammed the door shut. He peered out his window, wheezing as a large white dog leapt up against the glass, baring teeth. It jumped up and down, snarling as the man she now recognized as Kishiyama jammed his hand into his jingling pants pocket.

"Fuck you!" he screamed at the dog. "Fuck! Fuck! Fuck!" He pounded his free fist on the steering wheel.

Heather covered Diana's ears with her left hand, her right slipping to the floor and tracing their way along the floor mat. She held her breath.

Kishiyama whipped a ring of keys from his pocket and shoved one into the truck's ignition. He then reached under the steering column with his other hand. Heather watched his eyes widen, then lower to the where her shoes were directly in his line of sight. He slowly twisted his head toward Heather, finding a shivering revolver pointed at his chest. His mouth gaped open.

"What I do . . ." Heather said, her voice waning. "I do . . . for humanity."

"No!" screamed Kishiyama, his hands flailing.

Heather pulled the trigger. The sound of the blast bounced off the walls of the cab. Kishiyama glared at Heather in shock, his eyes blinking. Diana woke with a startled cry and kept crying as the dog outside continued to bark, its head bouncing up and down outside the window.

Kishiyama raised his hand to his heart, where blood pumped through his shirt and between his fingers. Unintelligible words streamed from his mouth as his body slowly began to fall to the side. His eyes remained on Heather's, and hers on his, as his shoulder fell against the steering wheel, depressing the truck's horn. The horn blasted as Heather continued to scowl at the man she had put unforgivable faith in.

Only when his eyes finally went dead did Heather lower her arm, dropping the gun to the floor. She lifted her eyes upward, her baby's tears drawing her own.

"I'm sorry, Morgan."

Chapter 41

The morning sun baked Sean's broad shoulders as he sat on the weathered pavement just a few yards out from the blast door. With his forearm resting on his knee and Avalanche at his side, his eyes—surrounded by mostly dry blood—remained fixed on the lifeless body of the cult-leader con man that lay just feet away.

Mahan's truck was now gone, Oldhorse having raced off with Heather and her baby to the hospital in Greeley. He hoped she would be all right. Enough time had passed that Oldhorse had probably already called Lumbergh and the local police and slipped off of hospital grounds undetected. The authorities would have endless questions once they arrived, and Sean would have to answer them all, even though all he wanted to do at that moment was get drunk and sleep for a year. Still, the irony wasn't lost on him that for the first time in months, he'd managed to go over twenty-four hours without a drink. It wasn't by choice, but he had survived. And like his father had once told him, "Every summit begins with a good foothold."

Sean's head lifted to the back of the nearby school bus where Gregory began to stir. He mumbled to himself for a bit before going silent and motionless again.

A chirping noise soon emitted from Kishiyama's body, raising Avalanche's ears to full mast. Sean crawled over to Kishiyama, leaning forward and unfastening the leader's watch from his wrist, letting his arm fall back to the pavement afterwards. He wiped blood from its display to see the time: 7:43 a.m. It blinked on and off. He nodded his head.

Sean climbed to his feet, wincing as he did, and made his way to the opening in the corner of the blast door. He shouted Mitchell's name through it and chucked the watch inside where he heard it bounce along the floor.

When Sean re-entered the bay area, Avalanche following closely behind, he found Mitchell sitting on the floor with his back against the wall, glaring at the watch through sagging eyes. His body was marred with open lacerations from his waist to his forehead. Its alarm continued to chirp. He moved his hand to his face and began sobbing. His body trembled as he threw the watch across the room, his crooked teeth clenched.

"Bullshit. It was all bullshit!" he cried out, his voice returning off the walls.

"Look on the bright side," said Sean. "It's not the end of the world."

Avalanche trotted over to Mitchell and began licking his face. Mitchell initially resisted the intrusion but soon succumbed and found his fingers tenderly rubbing the dog's jowls.

A minute later, Sean was working a ratchet attached to a large chain above the exhaust pit. His teeth grinded as he flexed his arm. "Show them your face right away," he told Mitchell. "I don't need them shooting me on sight and asking questions later."

When the steel sheet closest to the wall lifted a few inches, Mitchell helped guide it forward to the top of the one next to it. Seconds later, Mitchell slid his head over the opening where several flashlight beams lit up his face. He opened his mouth to explain the situation, but nothing came out. Instead he began sobbing again.

"C-c-come on out," he finally sputtered. "Come meet our friend, Sean."

One individual after another rose up out of the pit, their faces expressionless as the sounds of police sirens funneled in from outside.

Mitchell had called on his group to leave their firearms down below, despite their will to carry them having already left. Several of them wore their own watches and already understood that the time had come and gone. They congregated in the bay among the debris from the explosion, glaring despondently at each other.

Tammy swallowed and approached Sean. "I'm sorry," she said.

Sean returned her gaze but said nothing.

She glanced around the bay before turning back to him. "Where's Heather and Diana?" she asked, her eyes sober. "Are they okay?"

"They're in good hands," he said.

Mitchell stared at the two for a moment. He then cleared his throat and raised his voice, addressing the group.

"No words . . . No words are gonna change how we're all feelin' right now." The others slowly turned their heads toward him, some expressing surprise that the normally quiet man had chosen to speak up. "I don't know what we're gonna to do from here, or what all is gonna happen to us. But it probably ain't good." His voice cracked. "So we've got to rely on each other as best we can now, okay? Just like before."

He had the room's full attention as shadows and the sounds of police radios and rapid footsteps poured in under the blast door.

"We're family," Mitchell said. "We're at our strongest when we stick together—when we rely on each other. And we'll use that strength to get past this, no matter how bad things get. This doesn't have to be the end."

Sean watched the others. Some nodded. Others just met Mitchell's gaze. Their respect for what he had said was apparent.

As brisk footsteps made their way along the adjoining work room, Sean instructed everyone to lower themselves to their knees and place their hands behind their heads. He followed suit, intent on making the job of the first responders as easy and as free of confusion as possible.

Within fifteen minutes, Sean's credentials as the site's security guard were verified and he was released from custody. He confirmed to the authorities that the man they'd found outside, strapped to the ramp of a school bus, was one of the perpetrators, as was the dead man. He also told them where Mahan and Morgan were buried. He then watched as the others were escorted back through the workroom in handcuffs and around to the east tunnel. Some of them, including Mitchell, offered Sean a parting glance. He nodded in return.

Sean took a breath and turned, gazing at the devastation behind him. He knew that there was plenty more to be seen on the other side of the compound. It was clear that the site, as a county facility, would be shut down indefinitely while investigators poured over what had happened and contractors decided if the building was worth salvaging.

"Looks like we're going to need a new home, boy," Sean said to Avalanche. "Or maybe an old one." The dog stood up, tail wagging.

Sean cracked a grin and shook his head. He let his eyes wash over the site one last time. He skimmed the bay area and the missile cradle above him, taking in their history as he'd done many times over the months. When he turned back to the rubble between him and the lower-level room Mitchell had destroyed, his grin dissipated and his eyes narrowed. Lying above broken concrete near the copy machines was an old metal box, similar in size and shape to a tackle box. It was rusty and well dented up, but otherwise appeared intact.

He probably wouldn't have noticed it at all had it not been for the glare of the ceiling light directly above, and a stenciled name painted in black across its side.

Verifying that no one else was in the room with a few glances over his shoulders, he focused on the box and read the name it bore.
R. Collins.

"Collins's ghost," Sean muttered. He lowered his eyes to the floor as he retrieved the box, thinking about his future.

About the Author

A lifelong Coloradoan, John A. Daly graduated from the University of Northern Colorado with a business degree in computer information systems. He spent the next sixteen years developing accounting software and internet-based solutions. With a thirst for creative expression that went beyond the logic and absolutes of computer programming, John developed an interest in writing. He currently writes political, cultural, and media-analysis columns for multiple news publications when he's not working on the next Sean Coleman Thriller.

Other Books in the Sean Coleman Thriller Series

by John A. Daly

There are times when the truth invites evil, and there are times when the truth can get you killed. Few residents in the secluded mountain-town of Winston, Colorado, have kind words to say about local troublemaker Sean Coleman. He's a bully, a drunk, and a crime-show addicted armchair detective with an overactive imagination. After a night of poor judgment, Sean finds himself the sole witness to the 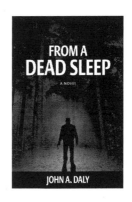 unusual suicide of a mysterious stranger. With the body whisked away in the chilling rapids of a raging river, no one believes Sean's account. When his claim is met with doubt and mockery from the people of Winston, Sean embarks on a far-reaching crusade that takes him across the country in search of the dead man's identity and personal vindication. He hopes to find redemption and the truth— but sometimes the truth is better left unknown.

Sean Coleman is back in the latest thriller from John A. Daly, set in the mountains of Winston, Colorado. Six months after the murder of his uncle, Sean is trying to get his life together. He's stopped drinking, he's taking better care of himself, and he's working hard to keep a fledgling security business afloat. At a blood plasma bank Sean frequents to earn extra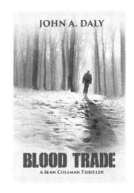

income, he meets the distraught relative of Andrew Carson, a man who went missing weeks earlier on the other side of the state, with a pool of blood in the snowy driveway of his home as the only clue to the man's fate. Sean decides to help in the search for Carson and quickly finds himself immersed in a world of deception, desperation, and danger—a world in which nothing is what it seems, and few can get out of with their lives.

———————

Thirty years ago, Sean Coleman's father abandoned his family in the Colorado mountain town of Winston, and was never heard from again. The reason for his disappearance was always a mystery, but a lifetime of blaming himself put Sean on a rough, dark path that took him years to return from. Now content in his life, Sean receives unexpected word that his father has finally reemerged, on the other 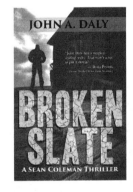 side of the country in Pawleys Island, South Caroline . . . as a murder victim. At the wishes of his sister, Sean flies out to retrieve the body, and hopefully find answers to why his father left, and the life he went on to lead. What Sean discovers is a second family, a web of deception, and a brutal killer who's still on the loose . . . and isn't finished killing.